Aldémah

The Queens

Elizabeth, Queen of England and Mary, Queen of Scotland

Aldémah

The Queens
Elizabeth, Queen of England and Mary, Queen of Scotland

ISBN/EAN: 9783337328580

Printed in Europe, USA, Canada, Australia, Japan

Cover: Foto ©Raphael Reischuk / pixelio.de

More available books at **www.hansebooks.com**

꒐꒐꒐꒐꒐ ꒐꒐꒐꒐꒐

(THE FIRST PROOFS.)

THE QUEENS:

BEING PASSAGES FROM THE LIVES OF

ELIZABETH, QUEEN OF ENGLAND,

AND

MARY, QUEEN OF SCOTLAND.

By ALDÉMAH.

Printed for the Brothers by
F. J. SCHULTE & COMPANY, PUBLISHERS,
CHICAGO, 1892.

INTRODUCTION.

It may be stated as a general truth, that all intelligent conceptions of the human mind are based upon fact. Regarding thought as but the reflection of an impression received by the inner consciousness, though often imperfectly translated by the external perceptive faculties, we may state that whatever is impressed upon the mind, or inner consciousness, with sufficient vividness to enable the mind to express the conception in intelligent thought, may be understood. It is a maxim of civil law that "ignorance does not excuse." Applying this wise axiom to the domain of human intelligence, are we justified in absolutely denying, as erroneous or false, a conception of the mind which we do not fully comprehend, or accepting, without careful analysis, a reflection that may be but imperfectly translated by the external faculties?

To arrive at a positive and reliable understanding of a mental conception we must supplant the testimony of the external evidences by an appeal to the inner consciousness. Reason, which formulates conclusions based upon the evidence of the senses alone, cannot be relied upon to positively answer the questionings of the soul. It is only when the soul of man divests itself of the bewildering evidences received by the external senses, and communes with the intuitive conception, which alone has access to the fountain of all truth, that he is able to intelligently comprehend and understand his own being and his relation to God and his fellow sojourners.

That there are many occurrences which baffle the keenest observation, and escape the sharpest attempts at analysis, may be admitted. This admission necessarily implies that the explanation has escaped simply because of ignorance. Remembering the maxim of law, are we satisfied that perpetual ignorance is the heritage of man? We leave the arguing of this question to those who contend that ignorance may excuse, and who are willing thereby to remain groping in the fog of bigotry, and astray within the swamps of superstition.

To those who wait reverently for more light, and who accept gladly and thankfully every grain of truth, every step of advancement, every proffered help that may be offered with the honest intention of increasing the store of human knowledge, and advancing all to a higher plane of intellectual liberty, and especially to a greater spiritual freedom; to these,—and they are brave souls who have come up from out the valleys of doubt, and stand now on the highest peaks of trusting expectancy, with their faces turned to the light, their minds free from the bondage of superstition, and from the chains of creed,—to these inquiring ones, to these earnest searchers for light, we offer the following work.

It is commonly held, although rarely expressed in writing, that the one cardinal deficiency in the world's accepted religions is the absence of a demonstrable proof of the existence of the human soul after it has passed through the portals of what we call death. Immortality is generally accepted more as a hope than a certainty. Within every thinking soul is the earnest hope that immortality is true. This hope is the corner-stone upon which rests every form of religious belief, and yet the world has accepted the thought, as has been stated, solely and entirely because immortality is so desirable, and because it is the one thing for which the soul hungers and thirsts. There was a time in the history of the human race when this belief in immortality was universally accepted, because the then purity of the mind gave it access to the source of knowledge, and this knowledge had among its cardinal principles the truth of immortality.

Through strange perverseness and willful blindness the world drew away from its knowledge, until that which had been actual at last became but a hope. But the truth was not wholly lost. A few souls remained faithful; a few souls closed not their eyes to the light; a few souls forgot not that purity, that innocence, that simplicity that is the endowment of perfect understanding. They preserved the truth, and the knowledge of it gave them understanding. Now, after long years of lamenting over the world's aimless wanderings — after watching with sorrow the useless beating of the air of those who vainly struggle for light, but still turn their faces to darkness — we, who possess the knowledge, who retain the proof absolute of immortality, have, from observation of the signs and careful study of the heart-throbs of hoping humanity, judged that the time is ripe for the attempt to give again to the world its old knowledge of the truth for which it hopes and longs.

In this age of material advancement and spiritual activity, many wonderful occurrences are startling the attentive world. And while, to the outer senses, mankind at large seems to be given wholly to material advancement, and the preferment of physical attainments, there is evident to the careful observer a quiet, deep, steady undertow of searching, penetrating, inquiring spiritual thought. And while materialists may not know it, and in their busy strife and labored anxiety they may not realize it, still this resistless undertow of deep spiritual thought is gradu-ally, but absolutely, drifting the whole world out into the bound-less ocean of spiritual truth. Having waited for years for this opportune hour, we gladly take advantage of the general drift toward higher spiritual thought to so show our light that it may throw its beams far out onto the troubled waters of the world, so that the honest, earnest, trusting mariners of thought may guide their ships in from the sea of doubt to the harbor of cer-tainty.

Generally stated, then, the object of this work is to offer the first of a series of proofs that shall satisfy inquiring minds of the truth of immortality. When this statement is first read it may appear startling, and require deep thought to determine the connection between the presentation of a work of this char-acter and the proposed establishment of the truth of immortality. The inquiry here awakened is natural, and to answer it will the better assist us in unfolding this our introduction.

To establish a proposition it is necessary that some known and recognized fact should be used as a basis upon which the whole fabric may be built.

So, in order to establish the truth of immortality, it is neces-sary to select some object the existence of which is beyond con-troversy. This leads us to the threshold of our statement.

That such a person as William Shakspeare was born and wrote most marvelously, and that the years of his life were among the most fruitful in intellectual advancement of those of any age, needs no proof; a simple reference to the fact is all that is necessary. The genius of Shakspeare has challenged, and will continue to challenge, the admiration of the world for ages. The grandeur of his thought, the breadth and depth of his inspiration have rarely been equaled and never surpassed. In all ages of the world's history an intellectual giant, he stands clear, distinct, and needing but the reference to his name to recall his sublime and immortal works.

The acknowledged grandeur and the universally conceded beauty and sweetness of this man's intellect would most naturally mark him as being the one most likely to be first selected, were it within the power of the world's united effort to recall into renewed activity that which, in the past, has been such a source of intellectual gratification, the reflection of which, in the present, brings such enjoyment. It was for this purpose that we selected this author, this universally known and universally accepted genius. And here we may retrace our thought a moment, in order that we may note the fact that the surest and safest method of reaching the thinking world is by directing its attention into paths the traveling of which has hitherto afforded unalloyed satisfaction.

The grandeur and beauty of the productions of this poet need no applause from us. Their admitted excellence and universally accepted worth may not be contemplated without the heartfelt desire that the world may again be blessed by a similar mind.

This admitted excellence necessarily implies the general wish for its continuance. That which has such wide and deep influence for good must be a necessity. Admitting this, it is most desirable that an influence so beneficent, so far-reaching in its good effects, should continue; and the natural conclusion in the minds of those who accept the recurrence of good as the result of law, is, that whatever has benefitted and worked good to the world, cannot be lost. And thus we are led to our first positive statement.

The mind of William Shakspeare, once having been called

into existence, can never be extinguished, for the procession and progression of mind is endless. Once having, by Divine law, received its individual identity, it may not surrender that identity, but, ever passing on and on, through countless stages of existence, it must retain its individuality unimpaired through each successive stage.

We, recognizing this fact, hereby seek to establish the general acceptance of the continued existence of the soul as a fundamental truth; for this is the true idea of the immortality of the soul and mind of man.

There are many noted minds that have labored to enrich the archives of the world's knowledge, but we have chosen that of Shakspeare, because of the breadth and depth of his intellect, which affords the most congenial field for the elucidation of the truth we seek to present.

We have waited with untiring patience for this intellect to come again within the range of our influence, that we might draw aside the veil which the world has voluntarily hung before its eyes, and display to the waiting ones the first evidence of the truth. This, then, more correctly stated, is simply the doctrine of reincarnation, or the progression of the soul through numberless life existences. We hold, and we submit the statement without argument, that that which has once existed, and has proved a source of benefit, must always continue to exist.

It is this fact from which the world has drifted away. So general has the belief become that individual genius and individual intellect cease when the possessor of these attributes passes from this short life existence, that when these master minds are again re-incarnated they find themselves ushered into a world which so strongly and positively regards them as dead — lost — that, notwithstanding their power, they find it utterly impossible to exhibit again those masterly traits which the world has repeatedly and positively declared to be lost. Consequently their marked peculiarities and their towering genius have been gradually and finally completely obscured, so that they pass through the new existence unrecognized by the world, unknown even to themselves.

This condition arises from error in belief, or, rather, from the absence of a positive belief. In the place of positive knowledge the world has formulated creeds, faiths, dogmas and systems, which all rest on the one great "HOPE" of immortality. Feeling that this mighty corner-stone of Truth, this everlasting fact, should no longer be regarded as a supposition, based upon *hope* alone, but that it should be as absolutely accepted as it is devoutly wished for, we seek to give knowledge for ignorance, certainty for hope, and light for darkness. Too long has the world accepted the shadow when the substance was within reach. Bathed in an ocean of positive knowledge, the world still continues to grow faint with imbibing an ignorance that only exists because of error.

Believing that our statements have been sufficiently plain to prepare the reader, we will make again the original proposition, which is, to establish the truth of the hope that the existence of the soul and mind is endless. To do this we propose to exhibit to the world a series of writings that are the productions of the same mind, the same genius as that possessed by the immortal Shakspeare, whose works, written over three hundred years ago, are to-day regarded with universal admiration. The first of these works here presented has been written within the present year (1891), and is to be followed by others, and in such variety as to exhibit fully the wonderful gifts of this wonderful man. If the writings brought forth by the present mind shall equal the productions of its previous existence, we shall have not only conferred a priceless literary favor upon the world by influencing this master mind to again display itself, but shall have made a mighty step in establishing the Truth of Immortality.

And here we would state that it is not our purpose at any time to engage in discussion or to assist in argument. In the natural world, the changes of seasons, the movements of the planets, and other known and accepted facts do not need argument to establish the truth of their different phases. If this be so of the natural world, it should be so of the spiritual, and will be when the world gives up its self-imposed blindness.

We hold, as a part of the truth of immortality, that the mind, including the intellect and genius of Shakspeare, having once existed, still exists, although the world at large holds to the general supposition that, when, on that April morning, he lay down and ceased to exist as the mortal man William Shakspeare, the play-writer, then and forever that brilliant light went out, and that the world from that day and forever must be satisfied with the reflections only that have been transmitted through the records of that brief existence.

We hold, and shall endeavor to prove, that the mind and soul of Shakspeare still exists, and is as capable of unfolding its masterly self as it was during that previous life which a blind world believes to have terminated.

We have, therefore, in obedience to known and natural laws, ascertained the re-birth of this wonderful genius, and after removing almost countless obstacles, and striving for years to bring about harmonious conditions, at last succeeded in freeing this mind, that it may again exhibit itself, and thereby lend its powerful aid to us in re-establishing the acceptance of the truth of immortality. Were we to make this claim unsupported, we should, of course, be obliged to sustain the statement with labored arguments and exhaustive propositions. We have, therefore, deemed it better to adopt that which seems to us the most natural course, namely, to allow this mind to again exhibit itself, for in this way we prove our trust and confidence in our belief, and display our honesty of purpose. Therefore we submit the following:

Having recognized that the world is again in possession of its honored and revered poet, we have simply brought him under the influence of well-known laws, and allowed him the same natural freedom that he enjoyed while in a previous existence. The liberated mind at once, and gladly, took advantage of the happy conditions that permitted it to enter its loved fields, and the result is before you.

We claim, therefore, that the production herein entitled " The Queens," etc., is the literary work of the same mind, the same genius, that formerly composed and wrote the immortal works now known as those of William Shakspeare. We submit this statement without a desire to enter into controversy, and with no intention to take part in any argument. We state that which we know; namely, that the genius of Shakspeare, after passing through an earth existence ordinarily measured by fifty-two years, died, in the sense in which the world at large regards death, and having, in obedience to a Divine and eternal law, passed through a state or condition involving nearly three-hundred years, has again, also in obedience to a Divine and eternal law, resumed an earth existence.

In proof of this plain statement we offer the drama here presented, relying upon the support vouchsafed by the internal evidence of the work itself to sustain our statement.

A word of explanation in reference to the play itself. It covers a period from the departure of Mary, Queen of Scots, from the Court of France, to the day following her execution at Fotheringay Castle, a period of a little more than twenty-six years. As was necessary, in preparing a work of this kind, many details have been omitted, and in arranging the acts and scenes more attention has been paid to the production of a connected story than to the exact date of the events portrayed.

The affixing of dates is not deemed necessary in a work of this character; however, in behalf of its accuracy, we would state that in no case has the author represented an action so out of harmony, with reference to time, as to be historically inaccurate, with the single exception of the introduction of the parliamentary committee that visited Queen Elizabeth and urged upon her the propriety of her marriage. This event actually took place about two years previous to the time at which the rest of the scene occurred. The author's object in introducing it was, first, to exhibit one of the marked peculiarities of Elizabeth, and, second, to give needed variety. Also, in order to maintain a connected story, it was necessary to condense events and actions that occupied days, into a single scene. This is notable in the trial scene. This memorable trial occupied four days, but the author has condensed it into a single scene, and in this scene the action portrayed is selected from that of the whole trial. It may be noted here also as a fact, that the author himself was an interested spectator of most of this celebrated trial, having, with the enthusiasm of youth, gained entrance to the great hall, where he, by his sympathy with the royal defendant, became deeply impressed with all that took place. The acuteness of his observations, as portrayed in this scene, may be verified by reference to history. Many noted events are necessarily omitted, and only such striking points touched upon as present the most marked characteristics of the two central figures. The historical accuracy of the prominent part taken by the Earl of Leicester, assisted by Sir Nicholas Throgmorton, in involving the Duke of Norfolk, and finally Queen Mary herself, in a net from which neither could escape, will not be questioned by careful students of English history.

The subject of the drama is of the author's own selection. And this brings us to the manner in which the work has been written. Having satisfied ourselves that the author could produce a work of literary merit equal to that of any previously put forth while in a former life existence, we brought him, after months of training, into that condition which, for the want of a better term, we designate "Individual Recognition," and then arranged for the author to proceed with the work as here presented.

To explain the method in which the work was received, we will state that, some months previous to beginning the present writing, the author was by us, in conformity with known laws, removed from the influence of his present surroundings, and permitted to assume the conditions most natural, which were those which dominated his previous existence. When under the influence of these conditions, he dictated to friends who are associated with him the work as herein presented. Scene after scene and act after act were rapidly dictated and transcribed. In order that there might be other witnesses than those who assisted him, it was directed that certain persons be invited to meet the author, to observe the method followed, and to listen to the dictation. These directions were carefully obeyed. Several well-known and locally prominent persons were invited to attend, and did so. The author, in a normal condition, dictated as long as the persons who were invited as witnesses remained present. This method was repeated as often as was thought necessary. At other times he dictated for hours without apparent effort, giving, correctly, date of years and days of the month to important events described in the drama. This was done entirely without any previous preparation, without consulting at any time any work relating to the history of the times in which the drama moves.

In regard to the literary character of the work, we would say, in behalf of the author, that, dealing with facts as he does, and relating incidents and conversations that are parts of recorded history, he was, necessarily, confined to plain and actual dialogue, this leaving little room for the operation of imagination and the display of sentiment. This will explain the absence, in the present work, of those grand flights of imagination, and beautiful outbursts of sublime sentiment, which graced many of the author's previous works. That this omission may be supplied, we will state that the author will produce, at an early day, another work of an entirely different character, which will afford him every opportunity to exhibit all the delicacy and expressive depth of sentiment, and sublime imagination, that has marked him among the most gifted of the world's geniuses.

Most of the events portrayed took place during his lifetime. Of some of the incidents he was an eye-witness. Others he drew from such friends and acquaintances as were conversant with the facts.

As has been stated, the arrangement of the scenes and acts is nearly chronologically correct, and the reader's mind will be satisfied in regard to the historical accuracy of the work if he but recollect that no note is taken of the interval of time which actually elapsed between the several scenes and acts, and that the whole drama is arranged in its present connected shape in order to afford a continuous story.

With these explanations we unhesitatingly send forth this work, taking this opportunity only to announce that other and more startling writings are to follow; and, as each will have its proper introduction, it is only necessary to ask that all be given that respectful hearing to which our sincerity, and the desire we have to benefit the world at large, entitles them.

In answer to the natural inquiry that may arise in the minds of the readers of this work in regard to the *personnel* of the

" BROTHERS," we would only say at present that our Brotherhood is composed of a number of learned persons who have devoted their lives to the study of all Truths, and to ascertaining
and formulating the best methods of presenting these truths to
the world.

As a distinct and organized Brotherhood, we have had an
actual existence for over eight hundred years. Through all
these years the members, during their life-connection with the
organization, have devoted their whole time to earnest study
and searching investigation.

We have in our possession many ancient manuscripts, scrolls,
tablets, transcripts from ancient monuments, tombs and obelisks,
some of which record events many years prior to accepted written history. The larger part of these writings are unknown to
the rest of the world.

From the earliest times our Brotherhood has collected every
attainable scrap of history, recorded traditions and writings of
every character pertaining to the most remote history of the
world, until we now possess an immense and invaluable collec-
tion of ancient histories, traditions, historical hymns, songs of
the people, and other writings pertaining to periods far antedat-
ing any other records known to be in possession of man. These
have been carefully preserved, diligently studied and handed
down from Brother to Brother.

In addition to all this, our Brotherhood retains oral instructions, traditions and written explanations of natural and spiritual laws which were the heritage of the founders of our Order.

In regard to ourselves, it need only be said that we are the
inheritors of this vast mine of knowledge, and also that we,
from long and earnest devotion to the highest promptings of our
spiritual natures, and earnest and attentive listening to the pro-
foundest communications received by intuition, and by commun-
ion with the highest source of knowledge, have fitted ourselves for
spiritual research and intellectual understanding. Our attainments are ours only because of years of study, and long and
earnest attempts to perfect our understanding of the laws gov-
erning mankind, and our relation to the One Source of Life.

Now, therefore, in obedience to our vows, and in compliance

with our inclinations, we attempt, in the presentation of the following work, to carry out the objects for which our Order was
instituted.

The present work is but one of a class, and is to be followed
by others, which we hope will do much in forwarding the principles which actuate us in our labors. We do not deem it
necessary, at present, to make further explanation, adding only
that our object and aim is to establish, firmly, the Truth of the
Fatherhood of GOD, the Brotherhood of Man, and the Immortality of the Soul.

For truth and light,

"THE BROTHERS."

[*Translated.*]

TO THE READER.

In compliance with the suggestion of the Brothers, I have written the following personal note. I have no explanation to add to that given in the "Introduction," and most positively no excuse to make for the following pages.

A few months ago, the remarkable statements made by the Brothers in their "Introduction," and the almost marvelous claims therein put forward, would have astonished me as much as they will the most incredulous reader of this book. When the impressions first came to me I could not, and did not, fully realize what a strange, wonderful experience was before me, nor could I accept the startling statements made by the Brothers in regard to my most remarkable reincarnation. After some months of mental struggle I at last was compelled not only to have my impressions transcribed, but also to fully accept the statements as made in the "Introduction." Then, with the assistance of friends selected by the Brothers, I commenced work by dictating a number of hours each day. The result is before you.

I have no comment to make upon the literary part of the work, and can only say that it is a truthful and exact transcript of the vivid and life-like impressions that came to me. The book has not in any sense been edited, and now appears just as it was dictated; no one has added to or taken from the work as originally given.

With the exception of an indescribable feeling of buoyancy and an excessive acuteness to sound and all outward impressions, I may truthfully state that I regarded my condition while dictating as in every way perfectly normal. There was certainly no trance, nor did I repeat the words of another, borne to me by what is known as "thought transference." There was at no time any condition or influence that could possibly be designated as " spiritualistic." To myself I appeared to be an actual spectator of the acts portrayed; that is, I described the several scenes just as if they had occurred in my presence but a few hours before I dictated them as they now appear. So life-like and real did the more exciting parts seem to me that I felt as if I could have gone on for hours describing the moving scenes that so strongly impressed me.

With the exception of consulting, *after the book was written,* a work of reference to obtain the correct spelling of the names of the persons represented in the drama, I did not, either before or during the writing, refer to any historical or other book treating on English history; nor did I read or have read to me any of the plays of Shakspeare. I do not desire nor intend to supplement the marvelous statements and claims of the Brothers by any words of my own. I seem now only called upon to write as I am impressed. This I shall continue to do as I have done, trusting, with confidence, not only in the merit of the writings, but in the noble, high and pure aims of the Brothers, as expressed in the " Introduction," that I may not only help to substantiate the claims made by them, but gain for my efforts a respectful hearing.

THE AUTHOR.

THE QUEENS.

ELIZABETH, Queen of England.
COUNTESS OF NOTTINGHAM,
LADY DOUGLAS SHEFFIELD, } Ladies in waiting to Elizabeth.
LADY FRANCES HOWARD,
LADY SCROPE, wife of Lord Scrope.
LADY KNOLLYS, wife of Sir Francis Knollys.
COUNTESS OF SHREWSBURY, wife of the Earl of Shrewsbury.
EARL OF LEICESTER,
SIR WILLIAM CECIL (afterwards Lord Burghley), Members of
SIR CHRISTOPHER HATTON,   the privy
LORD WALSINGHAM,   council of
SIR THOMAS SMITH,   Elizabeth.
LORD BROMLEY,
EARL OF ARUNDEL, friend of Leicester.
LORD SCROPE, first keeper of Queen Mary.
EARL OF PEMBROKE, friend of the Duke of Norfolk.
SIR FRANCIS KNOLLYS, officer of the court of Elizabeth.
LORD LUMLEY, friend of the Earl of Leicester
DUKE OF NORFOLK, suitor for the hand of Queen Mary.
SIR NICHOLAS THROGMORTON, Elizabeth's ambassador to Mary;
    afterwards recalled by Sir William's advice.
EARL OF SHREWSBURY, one of Queen Mary's keepers.
SIR RALPH SADDLER, one of Queen Mary's keepers.
EARL OF SUSSEX, friend of the Duke of Norfolk.
EARL OF MURRAY, brother of Queen Mary.
DR. DEE, a magician consulted by Queen Elizabeth.
WORCESTER, a book-binder and confidant of Queen Elizabeth,
    called by her " BOOK."

FELANGO, an Italian agent of the Earl of Leicester.

DAVISON, secretary to Lord Burghley.

BARNEY, servant to the Earl of Leicester.

SANDY, a servant of Queen Elizabeth.

SNOWDON, chairman of the parliamental committee.

MARY, Queen of Scotland.

MARY LIVINGSTON,
MARY SEATON,   } Ladies in waiting to Mary, Queen of
MARY BEATON,   Scotland.
MARY FLEMING,

D'OYSELL, ambassador of Queen Mary.

DUKE OF GUISE, uncle of Queen Mary.

BISHOP OF ROSS, adviser and agent of Queen Mary.

STEPHENS, agent of Queen Mary.

Lords, ladies, commissioners, sheriff, watchmen, members of
Queen Elizabeth's parliament, servants and other attendants.

THE PROLOGUE.

WITH no intent to foster feud, or wake
The burning smart of memories long asleep;
Nor so to praise or frown with favors lean
That my lines may seem other than exact;
I would yet make of truth such good display,
That, hearing, you might choose the better part
From out the deeds of those who, good or ill,
In life work'd out their ways; and in the choice
Make small the loss of that which weakest is.
Thus may you, in the grander, nobler traits,
Know, then judge that which better was, and is.

  Of two brave hearts my story chiefly treats,
Pray give to both your charity's sweetest wish.

  For her who, craving deep the warmth of love,
And feeling sore the loss she could not hide,
Made pretense stand for that her heart was not,
While her poor hungry soul made cry within,
I ask but such forbearance as the weight
Of her yet better deeds so well may claim.

  Think, I pray you, on both the state and times,
And then so measure your conclusions fair,
That the good may, by contrast with the wrong,
Be still the larger of the deeds she wrought.

  So for her who, by force of hapless birth,
Urged rule of realm with more of trust in men
Than comprehension of the ends they sought;
And who too soon made care the shift of joy,
And thus robb'd the sad, darksome years that came
Of wisdom's weight, by over-stress in youth,
I would crave such rate as sweet compassion
Shall urge is just to clew the ends of right.
But with full sense of both the loss and gain,

Fitting decision well to circumstance,
Ask that justice may be so measured
That none a touch of quittance shall regret,
Remembering that often lesser sins
Are not of choice, but chance, and that sometimes
One is not the knave he would be, for lack
Of wit doth clothe him with garments so pure
· That he may strut in an innocence that
Hath not a place within his washy soul.

I would not have you make a prize of wrong,
And so cheat the right, that that which is hurt
Might, by strength of force, o'ercome the better;
But giving greater weight to ends than means;
And, mindful that the corn of good intent
Is oft o'errun by weeds of accident,
Learn that the good that men would gladly do
May be lost in the maze of plot and parle.
For, oh! man's will is oft so soft a thing,
That it may, perchance, do a monstrous wrong,
Hoping that good as recompense may come.

But on your hearts I've play'd enough, so now,
Lest I be thought to impeach your judgment,
I'll urge no longer this my poor prologue;
But, turning back the years, before you bring
Those who strove and won, those who strove and lost,
Leaving the verdict of their acts with you,
Feeling that, whatever it is, 'tis true.

THE QUEENS.

ACT I.

SCENE I.—*Room in the Palace of St. Germain, France.*

Enter MARY, QUEEN OF SCOTLAND, MARY LIVINGSTON, MARY
   FLEMING, MARY BEATON, MARY SEATON *and* MONSIEUR
   D'OYSELL.

Q. Mary.   I do now repent me that I did ask
Of my cousin this poor favor, for what
Need have I, full as much a queen as she,
To crave as favor that which is my right?
Has now this Queen of England grown so great
That she doth claim the right to rule the sea?
But tell me, friend, how made the queen answer?

D'Oysell.   I pray, your Majesty, that you do only
Ask of me such a report as the words
Of it would not profane your ears to hear;
For if I do drag before you fully
The speech which the English queen did assay,
I have good need to be unmindful of
Your Majesty's presence, and so loud-mouth'd be
As would shame yourself and gentle ladies.

Q. Mary.   Have no fear, good friend, for I hold you
So fair ambassadeur, so tall a man,
That rough, unseemly words, though from a boor,
Would, when filtered through your honest lips,
Make no offense to gentlest, máid or queen.
Say on please.   *Solus!*   [*Exeunt attendants.*

D'Oysell.   I will keep in bond
The harsher words, or make of them good props

To stay my zeal for truth, that they may urge,
By remembrance of the wrong to thee,
A yet fairer report of royal spite.
I now repeat that which ros'd my cheek
With shame to hear at large from queenly lips,
And alas! wrung such dolor from my soul
That I could no fitting answer make.

 Q. Mary. You did honor your sense in matching not,
To grievous hurt of self, the queen's hot words.
But sure the waters between have so cool'd
Your choler that thou mayest now repeat
With no harm, her baneful spleen, word for word,
Withholding only such poor slurs as shame,
By their intent and port, our intellect.

 D'Oysell. When I had come, by her most gracious leave
Into the presence of the queen and court,
I made to deliver privately
Your Majesty's most reasonable wish.
But scarce had I disclosed my office quite,
When lo, at sight of your royal seal,
The queen did such hot salutation make,
That I lost by surprise a fuller sense
Of her brunt.

 Q. Mary. Why! did sparks so quickly blaze
At this poor show that reason was consum'd?

 D'Oysell. It does not become me to judge her words,
Except to point their force and full intent.
With such words as I had fully shap'd,
And with much of care to escape offense
I did address the queen as was fitting.
But methinks it was not the words nor form,
But rather the favor which I did ask,
That did so much anger the English queen.
Pray judge you now how you would have made cess.
I do use again the self-same words, for
So oft had I school'd myself for this
That I had writ it down on memory's page,
So that for your sake I might make no slip.

Then in this wise did I deliver myself.

Q. Mary.   Did not the queen my cousin make a sign
That would have given you private hearing?

D'Oysell.   Nay, rather so loudly did she herald,
That not a few came in from outer rooms,
As boys do mob after drollery shows,
And they, wide-mouth'd, did chuckle at the rout.

Q. Mary.   A shameless show of spleen.

D'Oysell.   I thought it so,
But for your sake I helped it not o'er much,
Thinking the exhibit should English be.
So, when the clamor of her tongue did offer,
I said I fain would plead your royal cause.
Then, following your own sweet words exact,
I said: Being widow'd now, you had mind
To return to Scotland and your people,
And you craved but that fair consideration
In your passage as friend would give to friend.
I said that you would not lay money tax
On her friendship, but, in just, full, fair coin,
Make recompense as right for meat and drink,
Nor tarry longer than would meet your need.
Then, to soften even this fair request,
I did display your loving, queenly trust
In her gracious remembrance of your strait.
And when, by force of plea, I had tapped
The founts of other eyes, I bolder grew,
And would have yet further softness spoken,
But the queen, with a face as hard as flint,
Bade me stop, and, turning her sharp about,
She said: " The Queen of Scots may sail to hell "
(*Sit venia verbo,* — I do speak exact.) —
" My kingdom is no inn for such as she.
Let her first keep her honest bond with me,
And sign the fair covenant made and seal'd.
I would, indeed, make small use of my hand
To sign for her safe conduct, that she may
The nearer be to plot and plan and scheme.

If your mistress had more of years and sense,
Or could she barter face for craft of state,
She might have spared you all this useless bruit.
Od's hate to her and all her tricky tribe.
Not a grain of my realm shall feel her foot
Till she shall fully mend her broken word.
Tell her that the Scots need a firmer hand,
And yet more a head than a pretty face.
Let her stay, the plaything of your gay court,
Such as she is fitter to dance than rule.
Yet she is not so young that she hath not
Learned to quibble and play the hypocrite.
Look! her fair paper, with its seal and crest,
I thus do spit upon.   To the devil
With it and her, till she do rightly sign
The compact whereof she hath so agreed."
Then, with far more of strut than royal grace,
She stump'd with noisy fling and lofty swag
Out of the room, leaving me amaz'd and sham'd.

   Q. Mary.   Oh that I did so belittle myself
As to ask, from so hard a heart, that which
I had no need to crave, nor wish for now.
Good friend, I pray you, if I have not lost,
Through this lame affair, your sweet respect,
That you do spare me further, and, perchance,
Yet baser report of this wanton hurt.
I'm sick at heart to think how woman's wrong'd
By such a vixen as this proud antique.
But did not her courtiers seek to becalm
Her hot and riotous blood?

   D'Oysell.   Did man e'er still
So sharp a tongue? I think an earl or such
Did assay to cool her fiery ranting,
But if could be got more of lip than I.   •
Why, she doth rule so much with fist and foot
That I fear her court hath yet more of thumps
Than thanks.

Q. Mary.   Indeed, can this be so of truth ?

D'Oysell.   That it is so doth save me from contempt,
Elsewise I should merit your displeasure
By fouling the atmosphere about you
With a rehearsal that's so distasteful.

Q. Mary.   Make no apology, I pray you sir,
For your part in this most distressing jaw.
You have so acquitted yourself for me
That I do put myself in pawn to you
To hold until redeem'd by like return ;
But I trust you ne'er shall have need to sue
Again a court so hard for case so poor.
But tell me, pray, how spoke her ministers —
Softly, as becomes gentlemen ? or did
They fear her ruffs, or yet perhaps her cuffs ?

D'Oysell.   When I had taken mind of mine affront,
I made quick demand for my official pass,
And, speaking to Earl of Leicester, said :
" Sir, should I have cause to visit again
Your court, or, perchance, interview your queen,
I'll be prudent enough to wear my sconce,
That I may save my head from royal bolt."
So much to taste and style have these things grown,
That they did make them merry o'er my plight,
And, laughing at what they dubb'd " English grit,"
Tried not to soften the unseemly twist.
But, mindful of your royal dignity,
I shook their hateful dust from off my feet,
Feeling the rough sea better bred than they.
But I would mention that the queen did send,
By ship that brought me back, her minister,
Who will fully acquaint your Majesty
With such reasons as policy affirms
Is just and right, from their scope and warrant.

Q. Mary.   Yes, true it hath been so proclaimed to me,
And I have set to-day to hear him out.

D'Oysell.   There be such need for this as but becomes

Your royal birth and most gracious pleasure.
These Englishmen do shut the door themselves
By consenting to thus import to you
Their churlish refusal, so shamelessly put.

Q. Mary. I shall hear this, her agent, unburden,
And then so reply that, haply, I may
Extract from his mind something of the shame
Of my poor, weakly play at state-craft's game.
But I shall make the entertainment so
That he and I alone shall see and know
How much the blood of England's queen and mine
Doth foam and fume alike when equal heat
Stirs up the natures of our human hearts.

Enter Page.

Page. His Grace the Duke of Guise.

Enter DUKE OF GUISE.

Duke of G. I salute you all.
From eye and face I judge some work of weight
Doth deep concern you. Pray do I intrude ?

Q. Mary. I did but hark to mine ambassadeur,
Who hath just return'd from the English court,
Where both he and I have been so befoul'd
That I now feel that only long penance
And much of pax will, alas! make us clean.

Duke of G. Not you two so much as the English court
Do need the holy office of the church.
I have heard how reformation would treat
A christian and a prince, who only ask'd
Such common favor as the granting would
But prove one's relation to God and man.
If this be the fruits of their prated creed,
I fear their hot reform doth spring from hate,
And hath in it more of devil than God.
O that some good, brave, christian prince would wrench
This red-hair'd bastard from her stolen throne.
I have mind to counsel that France demand,
By threat or force, such apology

For this hurt to the relic of our king
As will make them mindful of right and wrong.
My indignation hath hid the reason
Of my coming. Plum'd and booted, without
Doth wait the representative of spite,
Who, with oily tongue and cant and lies,
Would bolster up his pagan court and state,
By plea as excuse for this heartless front,
" The necessities of the public weal."
Will your Majesty see this man?
   Q. Mary.   Of choice,
I would hear him not. But the good tenets
Of our better faith do plead kinder thought.
I pray you, good friends, let this interview
Be between this diplomat and myself.
I would curtain all anger and hot speech,
And so keep in the bounds of good intent
That I stand by contrast not the less right.
What blow or sting hath come to me may not
Lighter be, or less hard, if I do send
A like hurt back to her who coldly struck.
Let me, then, be alone.
   Duke of G.   If you so mind.
[*To Page*], You will say to Monsieur l'Ambassadeur,
Her majesty doth await his presence.   [*Exit Page.*
   Q. Mary.   Monsieur d'Oysell, I pray that you wait near.
Should I call thus [*blows whistle*], you will attend me.
   Duke of G.   I, too, will remain within summons' reach. [*Exit.*
   D'Oysell.   I shall await your Majesty's command.   [*Exit.*
                     Enter Page.
   Page.   Monsieur l'Ambassadeur.   [*Exit.*
   Throg.   Your Majesty,
By command royal, and choice, I salute you.   [*Kneels.*
   Q. Mary.   If your good smiles do prove your mission fair,
I bid you rise, and pray accept
The offer of my frendship in good heart.
   Throg.   I have my duty to my queen to say.
If it hath not in it words oversoft,

That, if there be but a small spark of love
Between the queen your mistress and myself,
It be fann'd into a better blaze,
To the end, that we may yet be as doth
Become two queens akin.

  Throg.   I am not here
Of my own choice, but rather to appeal
In affairs of state to one who is wise,
But whose wisdom doth need a broader scope.

  Q. Mary. Such wit as I have, be it small or great,
I have no desire to measure it now
In a field not of mine own selecting.

  Throg. But, madam, the treaty is sure your own,
Inasmuch as the king ——

  Q. Mary.   Enough, I pray.
Alas, though a skillful player, you do
Harp upon a single string far too much.

  Throg. If there be those whose souls are not attun'd,
Except ——

  Q. Mary. It is not the player so much
As the air he doth assay to play
That sore offends.

  Throg.   If I offend, I pray
That I may withdraw.

  Q. Mary.   It were better so.
But, in going, I pray you to take
With you sweet remembrance of the good
I meant to say, forgetting not, alas,
My lack of that wisdom which doth so grace
The queen your mistress, and doth leave me now
So poor when weigh'd with her.

  Throg.   I have only
Your refuse to say to the queen my mistress.
Is this " a thin glaze of bland, wee confect
That policy doth append?" You do seem
Better arm'd than I; or, from practice, do
Keep your most deadly shafts to close the bout.
In affairs like this 'tis not meet to sue

Pray lament the necessity.

Q. Mary.   I do,
And in so lamenting I grieve me most
That the queen your mistress hath so much lost
Of her good amity toward myself,
That I feel aggriev'd.

Throg.   You can have no more,
I trow, than hath the queen my mistress,
Of grievous pain.

Q. Mary.   You bring your queen's reply?

Throg. Such is'my mission. I pray that you
So weigh my words that they have such force
As the gravity of my charge doth bring.

Q. Mary. As doth become me, I will hear you, sir.

Throg. It was your good pleasure to lately send
To her majesty, the queen, my mistress,
Monsieur d'Oysell, your good ambassadeur,
To pray of her majesty safe conduct,
First, for your free passage, by land or sea,
Into your realm, and also therewith
To be accommodated with favors
Such as upon events you might have need.
The queen my mistress hath not thought it good
To let Monsieur d'Oysell pass to Scotland,
Nor to satisfy your further desires.
The queen my mistress hath deemed herself
Right fully justified in refusing
Your supplications, inasmuch as you
Have not kept good, as yet, your honorable bond
With the queen my mistress, as you agreed;
But I am commanded to assure you
That, if you will be yet better advis'd,
And think with more reason and sweeter will,
And agree to the ratification,
The queen my mistress will not only see
You within her realm, but grant you freely
Such accommodations as you may need;
And make for you your voyage to your country

Safe and pleasant. For the queen my mistress
Doth desire that between you should still be
That amity that becomes you two akin.

   Q. Mary. I pray you, Monsieur l'Ambassadeur,
Be seated. I see you note the absence
Of my friends and attendants. I know not
O'er well mine own poor infirmities, nor
How far I may by them be transported.
I like not to have so many hearers
Of such weakness as I may, perchance, speak,
As did the queen your mistress, when she talk'd
With Monsieur d'Oysell.

   Throg.   I pray you think
On the time and place when he did assay
To approach the queen my mistress.

   Q. Mary.   I do,
Good Monsieur l'Ambassadeur, and yet
The thinking doth not mend the case a whit.
A queen may always be a queen, I trow,
Nor place nor time urge loss of dignity.
How far the queen's your mistress' deportment
Doth with the fashion of your country run,
I know not, for I do lack in wit of courts.
I am, as she said, not old, and lacking
Her experience, I have requested
That I be permitted to exhibit
My loss of sweeter mind and lack of craft
To you alone.

   Throg.   Not of reason need you
So appoint.

   Q. Mary. I know your ready hand,
Good Monsieur l'Ambassadeur, and how
The queen your mistress would hear of my slips,
Either in speech or manner.

   Throg.   Is this kind?
Your words do make a most unfair accuse,
Or by ambuling, force my gallantry
To claim that you do wound another, absent,

By prick of words to me.

   Q. Mary.   Who makes report
Shall, of truth, repeat what a queen should say,
If they put down aright my simple speech.
My dearth of words doth cut me short, I fear,
Of the flood wherewith your mistress the queen
Did make her answer to my poor request.
If to you I do lack in this respect,
Recollect that I have not the schooling
Which so goodly a court as yours affords.
You do make, good Monsieur l'Ambassadeur,
Too much force of this your point of signing
What the queen your mistress names a treaty.
Pray, have I not already made to the queen
Your mistress a full, fair answer on this point?
When this you are pleased to call a treaty
Was writ and signed, I had such lack, as too,
Alas! also had the king, my late lord
And husband, of the yet deeper meanings
Of this binding bond you do now urge me
To sign, that neither he nor I then thought
How far these smoothly-running words would reach.
I feel I am not, either in justice
Or honor, bound or held by decisions
That were made and consented to while
I was yet under advisement, being
Still young, of my uncles, his holiness
The Cardinal, and his grace, Duke of Guise.
And more yet, good Monsieur l'Ambassadeur;
At the time when I did seem to consent
To the signing of this treaty, mine affairs
And interests, and, alas! all my poor heart,
Were bound up in this realm of France. But now
That I am widow'd, my further interests
Turn, as is most natural, to the country
Whereof I am rightly queen. And feeling
That now this matter doth deeply concern
My lords and estates, I do see that I

Need their judgment, which is far wiser
Than mine, in this most important business.
I had mind to return soon to Scotland,
That I might counsel with those whose interests
Are akin to mine own. When I had spoken
Mine intent to the queen your mistress,
She not only refused the asking, but
I am told by mine agents in the north,
That your queen hath lurking ships that will strive
To lay themselves across my path, that they
May impeach my return to mine own realm.
I pray you, good Monsieur l'Ambassadeur,
That if you have in store yet other words
Which shall more fully acquaint my poor mind
Of the queen's your mistress' full reason for
This sore displeasure which she doth feel for me,
That you will advise me of their import,
So, that if haply I do discover my faults,
I may yet the more quickly remove them.

    Throg. There is naught of displeasure that the queen
My mistress doth hold toward you, save that
You do continue to avoid that which you
Should of right make good at once by signing.
And further : Pray do you think it is meet
That you do now emblazon, even blend,
The arms of England with your own on this
Your shield ? By this am I to judge of the full
Degree of your amity toward the queen
My mistress ?

    Q. Mary. Is this, then, so great a thing ?
Have these harmless, outlined marks here engrav'd
Upon this field, now, so much weight and force,
That the queen your mistress would make estrange
Two hearts that should loving be ?

    Throg.   But, madam ——

    Q. Mary. I pray you, good Monsieur l'Ambassadeur,
Do hear me out on this matter touching
This crest and arms. ' Tis true I bear it not

    3

Of mine own will, but, making friendly the guide
Of those wiser in the affairs of state,
I did consent to this harmless blending.
But since the death of the late king, my lord,
I have made no use of this as a sign,
And only now, by most unhappy chance,
Had I this poor, useless toy about me.
But see, I lay it down, nor wear it more.
This I do as a token of friendship.
I fear me, good Monsieur l'Ambassadeur,
That the queen your mistress hath time that doth
Hang idly on her hands, if she would make
So great a rift for a thing so smally.
But that I may do yet more than my half,
To show that my feelings are of better growth,
I will say to you that I will wear it no more,
Nor use this that hath so much of fright
Upon its face.   In laying it aside
I do sue the better thought of your heart,
That you may say to the queen your mistress,
How glad I am for peace.

   Throg.   You say good plea,
But the words you speak make so thick a cloud
Of dull, foggy seeming, that I do miss
Your plain answer to the queen's plain request.

   Q. Mary.   Had I not vow'd to myself and to God
To hold in leash the sterner, biting words
My lips would speak, I might here make sharp tort ;
For my soul doth rail at this your fell stir.
But no.   We may not meet the ends of right
By this our poor, vain pitting wrong to wrong.
Have I not, Monsieur l'Ambassadeur, shown
The full reason for withholding my sign ?
Is, indeed, your message so poor and short
That you do need to stick on this one point ?
I do have it in mine heart to spare you
A further tilt with your own better thought ;
For I know full well that you but sneap me

With words which you brought with you ready-made.

Throg. I have not, madam, from my very youth
Been so far lost for speech that I had need
To blab another's, and palm it for my own.
I am commissioned by the queen my mistress
To insist on this most rightful signing;
The goal of it is whereof I am sent.
The words I do use, madam, are my own.
That I have made choice of softness thus far,
Doth right well show that I would gently lead,
While straight law would surely force a quarrel.

Q. Mary. If, Monsieur l'Ambassadeur, it be true
That, indeed, you conned not these your words,
I might have kept mine innocent excuse
For your sharp speech, and sent my thought of grace
To the queen your mistress as was better.
If she be earnest to potch that you do name
As quarrel, she herself must drag before
The eyes of the world the poor, weakly hitch
She doth now halt at, and show how she bid
You swim a sea, that she might thus herald
How small a point a queen may stick upon.
I well know that both the queen your mistress
And yourself, think that because there are some
In mine own kingdom who are discontent,
And use mine absence as signal for broil,
That perchance if she but use me hurtfully,
Others of my land may turn against me.
You must know, as does the queen your mistress,
That I have still many friends and allies,
Who do not only speak good word for me,
And the righteousness of my cause, but stand
Ready, with stronger force than words, to help.

Throg. I have no need to remind you, madam,
That you have good cause to seek the friendship
Of the queen my mistress; for you must know
That in your own realm there be very many
Who, discontented, plot your overthrow.

The queen my mistress seeing this full well,
Hath deem'd it yet more prudent for your good
To have and hold her friendship, as you may
In affliction have need of her support.

    Q. Mary.   I ask nothing but mine own rights of her.
I do not trouble her state or subjects.
And yet I know that there be not a few
Among her people who have not the mind
She hath, in religion or other things;
Yet I have no will to fret her subjects.
The queen says I am young. True, I am not
As old as she, but I am old enough
To use myself toward my kin and friends
Uprightly and as becomes a christian ;
And I trust my youth will not lead me
To so heat my passion that I shall use
Other language than doth become a queen.

    Throg. Madam, you do so beat about with words,
That you do hide the point as yet unmet.
I pray you let us have no more stilting.
If you have it not in your heart to now
Redeem your rightful pledge, pray make to me
As you may, your pleasure as to signing.
That whereof your lords and self have agreed,
While yet the king, your late lord and husband,
Was alive, and did right fully assent.

    Q. Mary. You do, indeed, so shake my good intent
With the smart of your purpose to offend,
That I am near constrain'd to ask a truce,
Lest I be plung'd into a foreign sin,
And be yet weaker by imitation
Than I ought to be, who am so nearly
Akin to so grand a model.

    Throg.   By my faith,
I do not know which to lament me most—
This stiffness in one that's so young and fair,
Or this unwillingness to meet aright
The wise course the queen my mistress doth show.

Q. Mary. Wise! How so? Is it good wisdom to throw
Myself into an unknown sea of trust,
Where I must needs look alone for mine help
To those who would but gladly see me sink?
Monsieur l'Ambassadeur, you have my say,
Nor will I my rashness now further tempt.

   Throg. This then's final?

   Q. Mary.   Reason doth so affirm.

   Throg. Make not reason parent so wrong a thing;
But pray send to me a yet fairer word,
That doth the more befit your royal grace.
I have good mind to lag me yet awhile,
Or until a sweeter lull doth follow
This resentful storm, which hath only cast
These words of broken drift upon the shore
Of your troubled sea, which must calmer be
When self and soul shall take account alone.

   Q. Mary. I see the queen your mistress hath, forsooth,
Well equipp'd her ambassadeur.

   Throg.   How so?
Can I fail to see that which is not hid?
For, with all your queenly seeming,
You do but play the sterner parts, though well,
Yet still, beneath the biting frost I see
A warmer self.

   Q. Mary.   If I do play, and gain,
In the playing, your gracious meed, I do
Yet feel the want of care, lest your sweet praise
Lead me to so mistake the false for true
That I may miss my wit, and fail to see
That this shallow glaze of bland, wee confect,
Is but an after-touch of lush softness
That policy doth append.

   Throg.   You wrong both
The good queen her majesty and myself.

   Q. Mary. If I do wrong, pray forgive. I only
Make such a defense as my case demands.
I pray you that you so use your office

As rustic lovers do, by gush of parle,
Nor even trust a kiss to mend a breach,
Nor yet the damper office of a tear
To patch a broken pledge.

    Q. Mary. [*Blows whistle. Enter* D'OYSELL.] I have fin-
    'ished.

[*To* D'OYSELL.] I pray you, hand Monsieur l'Ambassadeur
That whereon we have so agreed.   In this,
My seal, you will discover our answer.
There are no tears, nor yet a queenly kiss,
Only an equal's most needful render.

    Throg. If this your written word doth but contain
The fore-fix'd speech you have just made to me,
There be small need to bear it hence.

    Q. Mary.   I ask,
Good Monsieur l'Ambassadeur, that you use
Your noble office as doth fit a man
Whose aim it should be to foster rather
Sweet amity than strife.   Your loyalty
I praise, though its use be askew a wee ;
Yet I gladly bear witness to your zeal,
And, as an earnest of mine esteem, pray
Accept the better wishes of mine heart.   [*Gives him her hand.*

    Throg. The pleading of your eyes shall more affect
The good tenor of my report, than shall
The wisdom of your queenly words.

    Q. Mary   Of truth ?
Then let mine eyes speak what my lips have miss'd.
If you do see that which doth better seem
Than that which you have heard, pray so report.

       Enter DUKE OF GUISE *and the* four Marys.

    Throg. I see the private interview is o'er.

    Q. Mary. These who now attend do but witness bear
That we part as friends.

    Throg.   'Tis true, as friends.

    Q. Mary. Then with these sweeter words, more to mine heart,
I wish you safe return, and God's dear care.
May the sea be calm and the winds blow fair.   [*Exeunt omnes.*

SCENE II. *Room in Westminster Palace, London.*

Enter SANDY *and* BARNEY.

Sandy. Aye, guid Barney, thir be sturtsome times. What wi'
the lairds an' gentles yeding wi' ae' anither, an' the awsome
dunt the queen gie ye master yestreen; an' I say thee nae as ae'
what hae it hack, for be the bars me mither wore, I saw it; an'
wi' sic smart skill did the queen pit the lounder, that his lairdship was glad to skyt out o' reach frae her nive, an' hald his
wud for some lesser chucky.

Barney. Sure, mon, ye prate o'er much for a thing so small.
Sure that's no clout the quane did fling. 'Pon me saul it was
but a pat.

Sandy. I dinna ken what ye ca' a pat, but na sma' blaw canna
mak' sic a knoost as ye master did dree. Why, mon, na runyon
wad gie a war' ae', an' wi' the nevel gade sic wyte, that ye master norsed his haffet in lown, as was halesome; tho' I ken his
lairdship wad gie a wee to hae mends o' a lesser, or yet a sma'
tooly wi' underling.

Barney. Sure, mon, nither pat or speech would harm the earl.
Sure lovers oft spit like that, then when alone the goose will sue
for peace, and the silly gander, with the promise of a buss, will
forget the dig.

Sandy. As ye will, guid Barney, as ye will; but I ween ye master wad lure tak' the buss than the flewitt, seeing he's her jo na
lang, an' anither may be nist owk. But muckle mair be in the
mirk, Barney, muckle mair, nor ony sturt or snib o' queen or
blether o' earl. Why, I was tauld yestreen that our Scottie
queen hae skt her ain hame an' raught Ingliss cosie in sic sorry
brats that hersell maun thig len o' busk an' sark to pit her
brands in.

They gossie she doth orp muckle an' claver o' church, an'
quoth, "she do dree a' for religion." Ah, me, what unco
haviour fowk will hae, an' say it's a' for God. Why, here's
Inglan's sain'd queen, God bless her saul, she doth gar the popish knaves to grace fou mony a woody; an' she's lifting mon's
taps frae aff their backs, then in her haly prayers she doth quoth,
"For thy sake, O Jesu, I do it a'." Then here's this forfairn

queen, wi' mair looe's an' prets than siller or wat, an' I fear
less o' virtue than has ye mither, an' mair youdith than
harns, spanging o'er eard an' sea, wi' na time to greet o'er her
blowed up guid mon's mools; gowling in the gurly wind wi' odd
ho's an' half ungeared, till she fain wad drain her eens to speel
to her fawn throne again.   An' then, forletting her own wangrace, she quoths, " For haly church an' sweet religion I gie
up a'.". Ah me, guid Barney, wha's got religion an' what be it?

Barney.   Religion, fool! why, your wit must have a ban on it.
Know ye not what religion is? Why mon, he's most of religion
who's most atop.   In our good, fair England her majesty hath
the true religion, for she doth ride the heap.   But if the Span-
ish Philip came and blocked her head, and put the Scot in her
robes, why she would hoist her religion in, and then that would
be the true just the same.   So, my lad, religion, as played by
kings and quanes, is but a see-saw mock.   The common folk with
small pretense, have most of honest faith.   But list, Sandy, for
such as we should not bother our pates with matters that plum
not our puddings.   Have you a mind to tell me how the earl got
that pat.   I wouldn't mind a pint of scuds to have it straight from
you who saw it sure.   Some day when master's in his stroot I'll give
him how much I know, and so making shame a leash keep self
and barns in pence.

Sandy.   Gin it be ye fother to trade on the haps o' court
I'll na' sta'k your sta'; for how ken I you'll na' twig me wi' the
ding, that a dog'll fetch a ban will na' be hooly to sneak twa
away.

Barney.   O make not of yourself boast of that ye got not.   If
you keep a secret it's your forebears hanging.   Sure I've no
need to ear o'er much to con all in your pate.   But come, let us
as of yore, go snacks on what we know.

Sandy.   What we ken? Gin ye spelder what wee you ken,
he'ven len' ye the glare o' sin to mak' a halsome show o' what's
left.   Why, Barney, ye canna forleet muckle mae an' miss the
dolt catcher.

Barney.   Stilly mon, stilly.   Is this wit, or something you've
heard, and in the hearing lost its comprahension?

Sandy.   Pray lud, ye mauna stent at sic lang words, ye might

split a gut, or swelt yoursell.   Nay, Barney, hald ye rift to cool
ye het speech.   Nay, sic ye gie sic ye get.

Barney.   O, let us be friends, and save our sharp tongues for
those who would shame us if they could.

Sandy.   Ri't, Barney, ri't.   Tak an affer an' 'gree, the low's
costly.

Barney.   Say, overheard you the tilt when it laid on ?   Or
saw you but the smite ?   How first it ?   Did the earl make some
slip, such as praise a comely maid ?   Or did he trip and stir up
yellowness by bilking to some new jade in sight of queen ?

Sure, he has need of care, for when he's long away from court
he picks up so much unfit for gentle ears, that I wonder he
hath not more of the queen's resent.   Sure, you folk at court,
who make no long stay in outish lands, can keep your manners
elegant.   But say, Sandy, give us the bout, for I know I'll get
it fine of you; and being so near the throne your say of currents will lack the tint of brag, but have the glare of truth.

Sandy.   Weel, gin ye maun, this is how it came aff.   Ye
master speer the queen for sunkets at court for a friend, or sib,
an' to beit the case he pu'ed the billy's braw sister in, an'
mowsing o' her bonny face an' tydie body, as mon are wont to
do, grew knacky o'er muckle while he prated o' her eens and
lips, and e'en spoke o' ither charms.

Now the queen, an' I'se hald ye leal that ye keep it whisht,
a'ways forleets her havins when mon at court do praise a face,
save it be her ain.   Sae when they speak o' charms, whilk she
but kens frae sic she sees on ithers, she looses quite her hald o'
tongue, an' in the quiet o' speech gains pith o' spaul.   An' sae
it was when ye master strove to 'sist a friend, an' as a prop o'
er-mou'd the sister's canty sell, the queen, mair mindful o' her
ain loss than o' her laits, did fling the earl sic a flewitt that I
amist feared he'd smite her back.   But the blaw she pit was
frae her right, an' when he saw her left on guard he hid his
dirle, an' petted the stang in quiet.

Barney.   Is this the first, or has his lordship had other favors
such ?

Sandy.   First ! why ye fozy, toom pate must be stuck wi'
fause eens gin ye see na ony the wow haviour about the court.

The earl's had feil sic taikens aff by tensomes. Why, nane amang the court, save ablins, Sir William, hath escaped, an' e'en he dinna sit wi' dull een to queen. Of truth, mon, gin ye ken it, ye'll find at court a swatch that takens them a'. The lasses hae lugs pu'ed out, while the gentles be garnished wi' clours an swells. Ay me, ay me, how wee the world kens how sma' a queen may be.   [*Sings.*

The brawl and groff that fishwi's make,
Whilk proves them wanton dowdies bauld,
Doth, when glibly sung as royal prate,
Twist sic clatter to queenly scold.

Ken ye not, I be singer to the queen?

Barney. Singer! God save the quane. Of truth, the Scots be the ban of England's sovereign.   [*Bell heard without.*

Sandy. By me saul that bell doth ding the meeting o' the council. I maun to me duty, as the guid wife quoth when she whisked her spouse out o' bed. This meeting to-day hae muckle nuts to crack, sae I maun make ready for the wordy council.

Barney. What say you of the stiff business the council will mull o'er

Sandy. I canna afford ye baith tale and lugs. Sic as ye, guid Barney, mauna ken a' the council wage.

Barney. Council! Sure and what do council mean? The great bugs plot and plan, then the small ones must pay the pence. To the devil, say I, with all this rule and sputter. You and I must eat our porridge just as thin, and cut our kilts just as scant. Sure we inside folk know how it's done, and the measure we make of the lords and ladies, would illy fit the think of the outer world. But mind your bell, mind your bell; as the priest said to the nun: There's two roads lead out — one to heaven, one to hell. So there be! so there be! Well, as saints do get askew and miss the road, I'll trust me own wit and make me own choice. Mind your bell, mind your bell.   [*Exit.*

Sandy. He's a hempy; he'll ne'er blin' his buff till the chattow do steek his mou'. He gesse to culzie me wi' his slidry gab, but I ken him as weel as gin I had gan thro' him wi' a lighted candle. Weel, he'll mend when he grows better, lik' sour ale in summer. He has some wit, but a dolt hath the guiding o't.

[*Exit.*

Enter EARL OF LEICESTER, DUKE OF NORFOLK, EARL OF SUSSEX *and* EARL OF PEMBROKE.

Lei. True, my lord, true, this new turn doth bring with it a sorry gambit. Enough, already, had her majesty of trouble with the Scots when they kept their queen at home; but now the waif doth seek a shelter within her majesty's realm, the case has a most darksome look.

Duke of N. Has her majesty been informed of this new turn?

Lei. A messenger did bring her the Scot's letter from Workington yesternight?

Earl of S. Workington! Was it at that slip she did land? What retainers did she bring?

Lei. With little thought of queenly dignity, and less of womanly comfort, her passage over was in old Degg's fishing boat.

Duke of N. Of truth this is a most sorry plight. How little we know what a day may bring. It seems only a season ago, so swift is time, that this young queen sailed away to the gay French court. Well do I remember how our late king made vain reach to stay her passage thither, even as the queen her majesty strove to check her coming back. And now, another turn of fortune's wheel, and lo, she sues at England's doors for favors. I do believe that fate has sadly mixed her fortunes up.

Lei. Your Grace, you do exhibit more pity for her who hath ugly threat against the realm and our queen than caution to protect your sovereign.

Duke of N. Aye, my lord, but must one lose all sense of pity, and be dead to touch of heart, before he may have wisdom fit to give advice? Pray, do I slip my better thought of queen or realm when I do pity the distress of one misled?

Lei. Take my advice, your Grace, and keep leagues between you and this fair lassie queen. For a heart so over soft, may melt at the light of those bright eyes, which they say the Scot doth flash.

Duke of N. Caution, my lord, comes well from you in affairs of the heart. But pray, if you have so much to give, would not prudence suggest that you keep a grain for use at court?

Earl of S. Tut, tut, gentlemen. Let us rather think of how we shall spread this delicate matter before her majesty. There be good need that we do use such care as shall stay undue haste.

Duke of N. This unwelcome visitor hath, in her hasty flight, not left behind her queenly rights, and her very stress doth the more proclaim that we should make of this affair an opportunity to teach, as would right gladly please the queen her majesty, that subjects must respect their princes.

Lei. How think you, your Grace, would you counsel such a reception to this broken queen as would offend the lords and estates of Scotland?

Duke of N. I would house and feed, as doth become a Christian, any soul that doth crave so small a gift. But saw you the letter the Scot did send? What was its import? Was it as one who demands? or did she humbly crave? Is she broken in spirit, or still rides she her pride?

Lei. I myself read to the queen her majesty that wherewith the Scottish queen did announce her coming. I make no fault with the letter, but I do lament me sore the need of the sending. She doth use a flood of words, plastered with high-sounding speeches. She doth rehearse the hot revolt and sudden turning in her fortunes and realm. She prates of one Knox, and says he hath stirred up sedition; and then says her brother, the Earl of Murray, hath turned against her and the state. She doth give as a reason for her hasty flight, that she was deprived of the advice of her loyal council, and she also laments in tears, that she was forced from her lord and husband. O, heaven! how low one may drag her sense of right to so far forget thy law, that she will seek to bolster the results of sin by pleading religion's need as excuse for wrong.

Earl of S. She preach of husband! The brazen wench! So little regard hath she for that good name, that she doth plot and plan to send her lawful lord and husband out of the world in dust and smoke, and then make quick haste to bed with his murderer. Had she more show of virtue, I should have more pity for one so young, but she hath banished the sweeter thought of charity by her low traffic on her charms.

Duke of N. I have no thought to even condemn the faults of which you speak, my lord. We men are oft too prone to preach and slur, and take to ourselves a virtue not our own. Those who soil themselves by our help are full as pure as we who join in the soiling. We hold ourselves in proud disdain, and oft avert our faces at woman's plight; and yet the best of us but need the dark to smutch not alone ourselves, but those we sham to blame, and so become by our weak mockery weaker still than those we so falsely condemn. There never yet fell a throne of womanly virtue that went not down either to love or siege. In passion's sin two must trade, and if two sin, wist you which is the greater sinner, the one who sells or the one who buys?

Lei. Your Grace, your pious words would fit our bishop. But are we here rather to preach than to plan? I feel it meet that we proceed with the business which to my mind is more of policy than morals.

Earl of S. Gentlemen, as neither of you have the queen's let to preach, but rather her full desire to mind this affair, I pray you that we do so attend.

Lei. Such is my choice.

Duke of N. For that end came I here by royal command. But we have no need, gentlemen, in our coming, to forget the good graces of our common blood.

Lei. I have no desire, your Grace, to forget, but rather to learn. But this affair doth so disturb me that I do use the tools first at hand, that I may the better unwind this ugly snarl, to meet the wishes of the queen her majesty.

Duke of N. We must so shape advice that naught shall be hastily done, and so counsel action that there shall be no need to make a move but once. No *faux pas*.

Earl of S. From the tenor of the letter judge you that there was yet much in blindness, or did the Scot speak openly and frank?

Lei. I have made some study of the letter, and I disguise it not from you, gentlemen, that it doth become us to look most carefully to our every move, and not alone to our own actions, but also to the Scot's and her friends.

Duke of N. When is this matter to be brought before the queer ?

Lei. This hour, in council, and I am informed that you, your Grace, have been invited to consult with her majesty and her council.

Duke of N. I have been so summoned.

Lei. It is her majesty's good pleasure that this affair shall be as quickly arranged as may be. For she doth rightly feel that, in dealing with one who makes so many speedy changes, there be most earnest need for decision while the Scot doth remain within decision's reach.

Earl of S. Where lodges the Scottish queen? and who has she in her train ?

Lei. At Workington, in Cumberland, at the inn of " Horse and Boots." But, as that hostry be not to her liking, she may make short tarry at so dull a place. Above sixty tailed after their flecked queen.

Duke of N. My Lord Scrope be not afar from that place, at his manor, Carlisle castle. He hath ever been mindful of her majesty's best interests, I trow. He would make good host for this most unwelcome, though needy guest.

Earl of S. He has a most watchful eye, and there would be little hatching that would miss his ken.

Lei. [*Rings bell. Enter* Page.] Say to the keeper of the council chamber, that he shall acquaint her majesty that the council awaits her pleasure.   [*Exit Page.*

Enter SIR WILLIAM CECIL, SIR CHRISTOPHER HATTON, SIR THOMAS SMITH.

Earl of S. Gentlemen, we do now attend her majesty the queen.

Cecil. Such is our intent.

Lei. May our prayers keep step with our resolves.

Duke of N. Let us go to the council, gentlemen, understanding one another. I am here by royal command. I do but advise in the matter of the Scot. This is so new a turn, so rare

a hap, that we have good need for care, that we may draw not
the eyes of those who would float their arms to answer affront
to this unhappy queen, if unhappily affront should follow our
action. This queen may have lost her throne, 'tis true, but
methinks there be those even in her topple who would burn not
a little battle to help so fair a beggar.

Enter Page.

Page. My lords and gentlemen, the queen, her majesty,
doth await your presence.   [*Exit.*

Cecil. Gentlemen, we will to the council.

Lei. Your Grace, I pray you, as you love a calm yet more
than a blow, look to it that you praise not overmuch this
northern dilling, nor speak of her graces to the exclusion of her
faults. Between ourselves we may smack of charms, and even
long a wee, but before her majesty, the queen, it doth become
us, as we prize our skins, to be rather advisers, however thin,
than playing gallants.

Hat. Good Earl, your caution is finely shown, and you who
have had so many marks of royal jests, do right well know the
value of caution.

Duke of N. I trust that if I pity, as any Christian may, I am
not the less fit to advise with her majesty, the queen If the
good earl hath need to restrain his overheat for bonny faces, I
see not the force of his urging like bit on those who make no
show of fire. They who cry in the market places, with much
noise, their stock of virtue, are sometimes found poorly off in the
light of inquiry.

Earl of S. I fear, your Grace, that you slept not over well
last night.

Duke of N. The sleep was good, my Lord, but it is this rude
awakening that doth disturb. But pray forgive this poor resent.
I have but added another's stress to my own, and, by weak
defense of self, made thin my attempted shielding of the needy.

Lei. I did but speak advisingly, your Grace, yet meant not
all I prated.

Duke of N. I like not a glib, oily tongue, that doth bluster
that whereof it has no purpose save sound.   [*Exeunt.*

SCENE III.   *Council Chamber, Westminster.*

QUEEN ELIZABETH *and* Council *discovered.*

Q. Eliz. My Lords and Gentlemen: I desire that you list to the important matter that shall now be brought before you.   I have thought it wise and proper that we proceed in this affair as doth become us as Christians who have been appealed to by one who is most grievously and sore oppressed.   You have heard the letter read wherewith we were acquainted with the arrival of the heir of James V. of Scotland within our realm. A portion of this strange letter relates to matters that properly come before you, my Lords and Gentlemen, for consideration. In adjusting this unhappy business I ask you to measure well the distress and full circumstances of the sender of this unusual message.

Lei. May it please your Majesty, I did, with my Lords and Gentlemen, in a slight manner, discuss this affair, breaking to them such of the contents of the ——

Q. Eliz. That you have done this doth show that you have not as yet outgrown your guardage.   That I did so far forget myself as to make you privy to this delicate deal, doth but remind me that I have afore had occasion to remark on your looseness.

Lei. I pray your Majesty that you do but consider to whom I did reveal——

Q. Eliz. What matter, I pray you, doth it signify to whom or when one doth blab the affairs of court?   Had I meant to make public proclamation of this most skittish thing I should have announced it, and so have saved you the post of herald.

Cecil. May it please your Majesty, as this matter has not as yet gained public ear, I pray you overlook this slight slip the Earl of Leicester has most unwittingly made.

Q. Eliz. So oft have I to overlook these slips and haps the earl doth make, that I have good need to search for taller man, and so save you, gentlemen, and myself this oft reprove.

Lei. May it please your gracious Majesty, I did but speak of this while yet we were waiting in the outer room, seeking thereby to so acquaint his grace the duke, that when we had met we might proceed with that understanding that the gravity of the case did demand.

Q. Eliz. How so? This, then, is another slip. You sought to so cut and dry, and make of this matter a pattern fitting your own sweet will, that the weight of my counsel would be but as seeming. Your explanations do but thicken your exposure. For yourself it would have been better had you but played the double with more of hush and less of blab.

Lei Your Majesty, I am done.

Q. Eliz. It were well that you were done before you began.

Cecil. I pray your Majesty that we do proceed, for even now while we make play of words, she, for whom we would counsel, doth tarry not to her liking, and may change her decision, and so rob your Majesty of the opportunity that providence seems to have vouchsafed to place within your hands, one who, for the good of our kingdom and the peace and quiet of your Majesty, doth, indeed, need safe disposal, and such wisdom in the counsel of her affairs as shall prevent the spread of sedition and the uprising of foes.

Q. Eliz. It is my purpose, my Lords and Gentlemen, that we proceed with this matter at once. Why, if we are to judge by the volume of this strange letter, we have good need to be solemn in our actions.

Duke of N. May it please your Majesty, it doth seem that that which first demands attention is this show of real want which the Scottish queen has, with sad tale, made known. It doth not look that there be now so much need of deep and searching counsel, as there is want of new gowns for her, who in her wow flight hath dropped among us illy clothed.

Q. Eliz. Pray your Grace, let not your kind reach for the proper false poverty of this motley-minded breed-bate make thin your better judgment. I trust that you will credit me with at least having mind for the comfort of the body of this mountebank, that doth ask so impertinently for alms.

Duke of N. It was my purpose, your Majesty, in alluding to this, to but display your goodness of heart, by directing atten-

tion to the fact that you had already met the full wants of her
who did impetrate you so strangely.

Q. Eliz. Have I so poor a reputation for gifts, and thoughts
of others, that I do need, in my own council chamber, to be
rudely heralded to the end that my subjects may be informed
that I have not forgotten a sister in distress?

Duke of N. It was my good purpose, your Majesty, not so
much to note the need, as to infuse the spirit that prompted the
relief into the discussion of this most important matter.

Cecil. May it please your Majesty, it seems that that which
first demands promptness in our action is, that this Scottish
queen, and such as are with her, shall be more properly, if not
more safely, housed. That she be in Cumberland, doth make it
yet the easier for your Majesty to afford her such entertainment
as doth not only befit her rank, but shall the better provide
means for obtaining full knowledge of the movements of such as
may attempt to hold counsel with her, who should be most carefully watched.

Q. Eliz. Where do she and her retainers lodge? Are we
so informed?

Lei. At Workington, where she did land, at the inn of " Horse
and Boots."

Q. Eliz. Ah me, how hath royalty fallen! From the French
gay court to Scotland's throne, then slip to way-side bush.
True, she hath need of counsel as well as prayers.

Earl of S. May it please your Majesty, it is not unknown that
in that part of your Majesty's realm where the Scot doth rest,
my Lord Scrope doth reside, and Carlisle castle is a strong and
goodly place, where one even with a greater disposition to break
might yet be held fast.

Q. Eliz. There is wisdom in your words, my Lord, and as
wisdom has been so scant a thing, I pray you gentlemen lose
not time in acting on this, that you may prove that you know
what wisdom is.

Cecil. Shall then an order be made, your Majesty, that the
Scottish queen and her attendants be conveyed and made the
good care of my Lord and Lady Scrope?

Q. Eliz. In her flight how many did brave her sinking fortunes, and trust their luck with hers?

Cecil. By courier we are informed that all told there are sixty odd, who, with more a show of faithfulness than judgment, leeched themselves to their fallen queen.

Q. Eliz. Sixty! and I trow sixty as hungry Scotchmen as ever munched oats. So great a swarm of hungry mouths must not be thrown upon my Lord Scrope at once. In this matter I think there's wisdom in division. I pray you, then, that such among them as are without mark be hurried back, but such as are of some estate be quartered where the ear of this, their fallen mistress, be not yet within too easy reach, for it be wise if we be solicited to guide her fortunes while she doth tarry within our realm, that there be not over many to thwart our plans.

Lei. May it please your Majesty, there be among this company, which doth attend the Scottish queen, those whose youth and tenderness would suggest the propriety of affording them the protection of those who are sedate and discreet.

Q. Eliz. This class among the Scots, then, have good need to feel affright did they know that you, my lord, had a voice in their protection. I trust, for their sweet sakes, that you may not feel that urgency of business would call your lordship into that part of the country where they now are.

Duke of N. The Scottish queen herself, may it please your Majesty, hath not yet so far succumbed to years that she hath lost that comeliness that would make a bounty in the eyes of evil; and so if she be bereft of protection while she doth dwell among folk not acquaint, she will need, to save her from uneasiness, your Majesty's order concerning her personal safety.

Q. Eliz. Fig on her comeliness! Have I need to ask that my parliament pass some stiff act that shall throw about this falsing face a protection that my own ladies stand not in need of? I pray you good Duke, if this be the humor that doth run with your blood, that you do give more time to poesy than to affairs of state. But, I thank you that in this softness of speech, you have set me good warning that not such as you should take into Cumberland whatever message we have to send.

Duke of N. I have but closely followed, may it please your Majesty, what I have learned of your sweeter will. If I have made poor slip, by shifting from your lips to mine a thought that did you honor, I pray your Majesty that you blame rather my lack of words than my perception of your royal goodness of heart.

Q. Eliz. Your Grace, you have, indeed, missed your calling. One who can so clearly read that which has not been expressed should lose no time in providing himself with an owl, a black cat, an empty skull, dress in green, cross himself, then cast the future for trusting fools.

Duke of N. So wide a field, your Majesty, doth your great learning cover, that your deep allusions are quite beyond my reach, and because you have such knowledge so well in grasp doth near urge me back to bench and birch.

Lei. It is understood, then, your Majesty, that the Scottish queen shall be housed in Carlisle castle?

Q. Eliz. Such is my pleasure. But it were better had you not known the lodging, nor yet the country.

Lei. I do know the country, may it please your Majesty, and there be few hills and valleys o'er which I have not followed my hounds in many a hot and galloping chase.

Q. Eliz. See to it, my Lord, that both you and your hounds shall hunt no more in that fair land, at least until such game as you do mostly chase be safely housed.

Earl of S. May it please your Majesty, would it not become your thought to make such provision as would meet the necessities which this queen in her letter doth so urgently disclose?

Q. Eliz. This matter, my Lord, hath already been fully attended to. [*To Cecil.*] Make in your instructions that earnestness for her comfort that shall betray to Lady Scrope my desire that there be not over much time pass when she cannot, with good readiness, bring within her sight this flitting outcast.

Cecil. It shall be as you desire, your Majesty. When I have the order prepared it shall be submitted for your approval.

Q. Eliz. I pray you, go not out of the way to net for over soft words. There be such need for firmness in this matter that not one line should be writ down that the twisting of it would mean

aught than what we say; for so slippery a matter is this that if
we nurse this stranger overmuch we may plant within our sides
an ugly thorn.

Duke of N. The kinder will that has so far made sweet and
good your gracious reign, has not yet so far spent itself, that
from very poverty, there needs be shut from this your order,
your Majesty, some word of Christian tenor, that shall stand in
sweet contrast, in your reception, to the barbarous coldness and
heartless fury that has compelled this young queen to flight.

Q. Eliz. Is there need for longer that you, your Grace, should
prate and slabber such weak drivel, and thus display your
chicken-heart? If you have so much milk in your blood, I pray
you seek a nursery, and there with sucklings creep and bilk,
and lament the crushing of a fly. There is so much softness in
your play at counsel, that, indeed, your words do sound like
children at close of shuttle-cock. If you have so much heart for
this fouty fallen drab, seek her out, and on bended knee make
full display of your tender passion. Perchance this loose flirt-gill
may turn to you, and with eyes swimming with tears, give, as a
recompense for your girlish interest, a smile, or perhaps a chuck.

But I have done. I pray you, Mister Secretary, make to me
a fair copy of this order; and it is my pleasure that Sir Francis
Knollys shall be the messenger who shall bear these instructions. And further, this is my pleasure: Say to this Scottish
outcast, that my ears are offended with the report that reaches
me of her conduct, and the dark suspicions that do attach
themselves to her in the manner of the taking off of her late
lord and husband. Likewise, I am shocked at the unholy speed
with which she did wed with the Earl of Bothwell. Say to her,
when she has cleared herself of these and other dark and foul
suspicions, of which the air is full, that I will treat with her for
that protection which her case shall warrant.

It is my pleasure that this message be despatched at once.
Make no delay because of night. Furnish horsemen and such
escort as shall safely determine the delivery of this most important matter. And it is my express command that I shall be
kept fully and completely informed, not only of every act of you,

gentlemen, in this affair, but all rumors that the people do mouth.

I shall summon presently such of you, my lords and gentlemen, as I have need, and I therefore ask that you tarry with that end in view. I have finished.

Enter Keeper of the Council Chamber.

Keeper. Your Majesty, I crave to announce that there be without a committee from your honorable parliament, and they pray that your Majesty do grant them a hearing.

Q. Eliz. Admit them. My lords and gentlemen, remain that we may hear this committee.

Enter Committee.

Q. Eliz. Gentlemen, make known your message.

Chairman. Most gracious Majesty, by vote of parliament assembled, and by its further direction, we do appear before you and most humbly crave your most gracious indulgence.

Q. Eliz. Gentlemen, say on. Let this that you have to make to me be quickly said.

Chairman. Your Majesty, that there shall be nothing undersaid, and that we may make no loss of time by oversaying, we have thought it proper to set down in writing that which is the wish of your parliament. And that we may the better enforce the full meaning of the sentiment that hath invoked our presence, we would crave permission to read to your Majesty the resolve passed.

Q. Eliz. Gentlemen, let not this interview be overlong. If the weight of your communication be right and agreeable, it will gain nothing by overmuch speaking; if it contains that which hath in it matters not pertinent, it were better that you left it unsaid, and that your assembly use their time in marking the boundaries to Hick's field, rather than importuning your sovereign.

Chairman. We have, your Majesty, but our duty to perform, be it ill or pleasant, it is not of our choosing.

Q. Eliz. You have my permission to read

Chairman. [*Reads.*] May it please your most gracious Majesty. Your parliament in assembly, with most anxious hearts, and full

sense of your good, have thought it fit and proper to express to
your Majesty their wish and most earnest desire; that happily
you may find it in your mind to accord with them, to the end
that there be yet more quiet in your realm by reason of the
peacefulness of your reign, and the hope that it may be continued by yourself, and in the end be further continued by your
most blessed and devoutly desired rightful heir.   To this end
your parliament would most earnestly pray that you do, of your
own free will and choice, select from among those of loyal blood
and goodly line, a lord and husband.

Q. Eliz.   So my parliament would force me to marry?   I sup-
pose before your reading is finished it will appear that your most
audacious assembly has instructed you to season your bold,
brazen address with a dash of threat.   I pray you, gentlemen,
twist your courage, and out with it, that I may the better make
answer to the whole of your fat address rather than a part of it.

Chairman.   For this, your parliament would pray and beseech,
with no thought save your own happiness, and safety of the
realm.   And your parliament would further pray that you do
take this matter under advisement right speedily, to the end
that you make choice of a lord and husband, loyal and true, so
that by the blessing of Almighty God you may present your
loyal and happy subjects with a rightful heir.

Q. Eliz.   I would not interrupt, save that I might remark,
that your importune for my marriage doth bear with it yet a
still further bit, that I shall become a mother.   Think you not,
gentlemen, that this is a matter not within the province of your
great body to settle?   I have no experience in these affairs, yet
I would be greatly astonished to be informed, even by your
august fellows, that conception may take place by act of
parliament.   I know, gentlemen, that your house be almighty
pert and gush, but I fear you have taken unto yourselves far too
high a degree of importance.   If I mistake not, the matter you
do so glibly spread doth the better rest, as heretofore, in the
hands of God.

Chairman.   If it shall please your Majesty to signify your
compliance in this most righteous wish of your people, it has
been voted that your parliament do grant to your Majesty the

full amount asked for in your royal demands. If, after due reflection, your Majesty shall not find pleasure in a compliance with the expressed wish of your parliament and people, it has been voted that the allowance asked for shall be withheld, in part, at least.

Q. Eliz. So! so! my sense did not play me false. I did, then, sniff this, your trick. So you would force your sovereign. Gentlemen, return to your house. Say to parliament that, as they have retained a part of their senses, and did not seek to force upon me, their rightful queen, a husband by name, nor yet so far forget themselves as to fix a date which, in their great minds, should be the limit of my singleness, I do answer to their broad address, that I will take the matter, of which you speak so freely, into my mind for reflection, and, if I can be made to feel the need of this which you have pregaged to deliver to me, I will inform your honorable body. Say to parliament that I am not pleased that they have thought it fit and proper to attempt to force me, their rightful sovereign. You do make your base threat of withholding the just and righteous demands of the throne a lyam, that you may therewith drag or drive me, your queen, to meet your sturt orison.

Return to your house, gentlemen, and say to my parliament that I am no stupe, that I do need advice on the matter that they have so much ranted over. If my parliament has no better use for their time, they might, with good grace, rap their office for more deedful labor, and so save themselves this over-straining. Gentlemen, you have discharged your supposed duty, and as there remains nothing further for you to communicate, you may retire.

Chairman. Doth your Majesty, then, consent to the withholding of the allowance?

Q. Eliz. I consent to nothing. When I have had further conference with my council, I will send for you. In the meantime, pray betake yourselves to your duties. You may retire.

[Exeunt Com.

My lords and gentlemen, we may not prolong this sitting. I will confer with you after this matter has by myself been considered.

Force me! This is indeed strutting highness! This is puffed littleness grown big by feeding on its own tough conceit. To the devil with parliament, and their milky threats! When I need the ornamental consort of a man I'll have one made, and so meet my fancy's desire. Men nowadays are so loosely flung in nature's mold, and grow so twisted by unsafe lunes, that a woman, who bargains for the loan of their company through life, must needs have more stiffness than doth stay a queen to rule a kingdom.   [*Exit Queen. Exeunt Council.*

SCENE IV. *A Street in London. Earl of Leicester's house right.*

Enter BARNEY.

Barney. Whoop! Stiddy top, stiddy. Sure you're tripping me pins. Swaddle, daddle, walk straight or straddle. Belly-ful, woful. A lout holds so much, a lord can hold no more, and both are twin fools when noggy full. Sure I've good, fine company to-night. I'm full, but the high old moon's fuller yet.

Sure I must keep both eye and lugs well out for the watch. Devil take the watch! Was ever a land like this? Here's a gentleman who, as is his good right, hath made merry with his sweet friends, and now, forsooth, when he would to bed, and doth by grace have the company of the parish lantern, he must needs sneak and spy like a river thief, and all because he hath sung a stirrup-verse over longy to toy his cheery mates. To the devil with the watch, say I; to the devil with the watch. Whoop.

Who watches the watchman? Who oaths whether he be noggy or neat? Sure where he's wanted most be never is, and when its better grace that he stay away, he's thicker than bees. This be a strange slip of right. Here these bashy hangbys, in their fine becomes, click their gilt for padding, while I, every whit as much a man as they, if I be caught out over late, must needs be stocked for doing what they make their betters fee them for.

Wide and long, deep and high; tide comes in and tide goes out; bloaters float, but the slim must swim. Big fish eat the little fish, and the devil gets the fat.

O moon, moon, moon!   What makes you so sheen?   The
scullion that shines your jowl has a jovy high job.

Softly, here's master's house.   Jumbals to nuts he's as full as
I.   Sure here's another slip of right.   When he's full he's laid
atuck, while I must go to bed end-for-end, head down, feet up.
Heads is it?   Sure his head'll be as puggy as me own next
sun-up.

Enter Watchman.

Watch.   Stand!

Barney.   Stand is it?   Let them stand what can, I can't.
Falls down.

Watch.   By my word, good man, had you as much strength
in your legs as you have in your breath, you had need never to
fall.

Barney.   Breath is it?   Why man, my belly is no proof to my
standing.   Howbeit, in thy country do leeks make a man?

Watch.   No, not leeks, nor yet leeks when well mixed with
that which hath taken away thy sense, doth make a man.

Barney.   Praith thee!   Where did'st thou learn what makes
a man?   Is that a part of thy calling?   Sure, if that be, then
indade thou art fitter to be her majesty's chief justice.

[*Watchman blows a whistle.*

Enter Second Watchman.

Second Watch.   What have we here?

First Watch.   That which when the rightful be in, is a man,
but now at this unhappy hour, he hath made change, and in the
making hath so lost his self that he indeed doth but wear the
clothes that would become a man.

Second Watch.   Come fellow, come, who are you?

Barney.   Praith thee what's o'clock?

Second Watch.   Never you mind the hour.

Barney.   O, time's no matter to me, but when my royal
pompous here did ask, as any honest man might, who I was, I
would truly, as doth become a Christian, tell him who I am; and
as what I am is but the larger growth of what I was, so
between what I am and what I was doth such fatness lie that I
have good need to know the hour——

First Watch. Come, my fellow, come, you talk over-much. If you could walk with your mouth, you'd have been well home now, even had you lived in Shore Ditch.

Second Watch. If you have no better account to give of yourself than this gust of balder words, there be nothing for us to do but walk you in.

Barney. Walk is it! Sure, have you with you an two pair of legs? I have so little hope in these dabby ones of mine, that I think 'em more for show than use. Sure! and it do become me that I am proud of their good mold, but, by me faith, I would have yet more pride in them, if I could break them of this habit they have of losing their straight-up and strength when I do most need them.

First Watch. I think I know this man. He belongs to the household of the Earl of Leicester.

Barney. How know you us folk at court? Sure, I thought that eye of yours had got its pop from peeping, and that red head would indade give you favor, were it not that with the quane, red is dowdy.

Second Watch. No slurs, my man, no slurs to her majesty. If you do belong to the household of the earl, your slandered legs have far more wit than your noddle, for they have wallowed you to your master's door, and that you have so good a master, we'll save him the disgrace of 'porting you muzzy.

Barney. Sure, you've had a dab of court holy-water, and it hath balmed thee; gunpowder with thy beer would stand thee better.

First Watch. Let us arm him, and so round to the servants' door and then knock up the butler.   [*They take Barney up.*

Barney. Sure the rich may ride, but it takes a cob to stride the quane's watch. Gentlemen, will your stent end when you've put me a bed, as they do the earl when he's naught? I wish thee good night, bright moon, good night. [*Sings.*] Fing, ding, to the moon I sing. Good night, all night, full moon.   [*Exeunt.*

Enter FELANGO, *cautiously.*

Fel. So long has that drunken brawler blocked the way that it's now past the hour when I did appoint to meet the earl. I trust that sleep hath not so dulled his ears that the signal will not assail them.   [*Strikes three times on the ground.*

Enter Leicester.

Lei. *Piano!* This brawl and tumult will so keep the neigh-bors' ears alert that we have need of caution.

This wherewith I now acquaint you needs your utmost wari-ness, and that there be no slip, I pray you give good ear to my instructions. First, it is my desire that you ride to Workington, in Cumberland, to-night. To do this you have been named as one of the guards that shall accompany Sir Francis Knollys.

Fel. Maëstro, this be bat-fowling, of truth! I had but just the matter well in hand that did concern Lady Alice, and by your blind order, sent her good, slack lord into Durham, and so made clear the field for your lordship.

Lei. I! that be but weeds beside the corn I would now garner. This easy game will do for leisure times; but look you, here's no lesser fruit than queenly plum, which by rudely winds has been detached from its supporting limb, and dropped, plump and fresh, at our very feet; and we have but to stoop to pick it up.

Fel. Be there reason, Maëstro, for my starting at once?

Lei. Yes, Felango, at once. And of reasons make no fear; I will supply them. Look you! At council to-day his grace, the Duke of Norfolk, was over soft toward this young snipped queen who has dropped among us so strangely. If I be good at guessing, the duke has more water in his mouth than grace in his heart for this vender of charms. His warm pleading did book for me the cue I needed. What he doth chatter at I'll gamble for. And as he is one of the slower sort, and will wait him for light-o'-day before he moves, I, who have learned pru-dence in my Cupid's wars, will plan by day and fight by night. And now, as I must needs keep eye on matters here, I bid you fly to where the Scottish queen doth rest, and then fully acquaint me with every move she, and those who are with her do make.

Fel. Is it your purpose, Maëstro, to give me full measure of the ends in view? Is this an " *in* " or an " *out* "?

Lei. Neither yet an "*in*" nor an "*out*"; but I would so hedge my knowledge with understanding that I may with fore-warning act.

Fel. Shall I go armed, Maëstro, as one who would remove such bars as may hap?

Lei. How much of arms you prepare is a matter for your own decision, but, as you are a Christian, there should be no striking in this affair, except to preserve self, and do my bidding faith-fully. This, then, is your mission: Learn who goes to the Scot, as well as the full import of their business. Let nothing come from her, either to her own people, or to the queen our mistress, that you do not know the full measure of. I have little need to tell you how to gain the ear and lip of the under help; one so skilled in sucking and bolting has little need to list to instructions from me in this.

Fel. How Maëstro, is this information, when obtained, to reach your Lordship? The comes and goes would make the betweens so long that I would do little else than ride.

Lei. I will send with you my man Bowe. Make careful seal of that you would return, and so disguise the pack that it shall not awake suspicion. But in all these matters your full ac-quaintance with the needs will make to you good suggestion for their fulfillment. It may please the queen our mistress to change her royal guest from where she now is to yet another lodgment. If this be so, her change is yours. Should I need you here in town, I will so inform you, when you are to return at once.

Fel. [*Taking out a purse.*] Maëstro, the slimness of this good friend doth suggest massing——

Lei. Had I more leisure I would give to your accounts that scanning which they seem to demand. When we have this peat well in hand they shall receive my attention. Add this to your skimmings [*Gives him money*], and heaven help me if I get not back richer returns than the last allotment.

Fel. Mayhap, Maëstro, you may find an agent that would have the will to do your bidding, and still have such honesty in pence that your questioning would be yet less than your directions.

Lei. O, prate not of your morals now. Such as you have in

store you better need than I. Pray hoop your conceit, and lend your spirit more to this affair, and less to bolstering up your virtues.

Fel. This be a poor hour, Maëstro, to enter just with me. If this matter which you now do entrust me with merits a fair settlement, there be little righteousness in asking your steward to pay for wines he may never taste. I do but make a trade of my small part, and if I do ask such render as you would but give any faithful scrub, I have not stepped beyond the bounds of yet good ask or fair plenish.

Lci. There, there; the hour be late, and already the clatter of hoof doth warn us that the troop would start. Make quick change and be off. Master Gray will mount you, and as he has been instructed, will make small interference with your movements. See to it that you ride not near the link-men, this business needs not over much of glare on it. Now, go. Keep fear a stranger and caution a bed-fellow. If you must spit, spit with the wind. Eat light, drink lighter, sleep lighter still. Let your ears stand sentry over your mouth, and your eyes guard over all. Be a gib by night and a man by day. If you know any charm that's good as wit, take it with you, but still let wit be master, and jingle your charm for grace. Do you know a prayer? Say it while you ride; for when you come to business you will not find it of a prayerful kind. Now, go, and make such hush of your going that you shall lose your very shadow — *Basta.*

[Exit Felango.

Now, my fine lady, it is my turn. You thought it as adding to your dignity to spurn my offer. Now the asker shall turn, and, spurning thee, make thy plight his opportunity. Gay and handsome, I? Men dance to you, they say. Well, let us see who will do the dancing now. You will have good need, O uncrowned queen, to make your prayers to heaven more from heart and soul than from gilded portace, for I, who have been a cully in days agone, am now in form to make my gifts worth the asking, and woe to you who have incivil been.   [*Exit Leicester.*

ACT II.

Scene 1. *Room in Carlisle Castle.*

Mary Queen of Scotland *and* Maid *discovered.*

Enter Lady Scrope.

Lady S. I trust, your Majesty, that you will find good ease, and so nurse the present comfort, that it will stay a fresh remembrance of your trials.

Q. Mary. I have, forsooth, good need to hold an' keep a leash upon the awsome past, and so muster my better thoughts that they may dwell on the present alone; an' so soothe memory that its stalking ghosts may hie away to Lethe, an' let me palm this new sweet rest upon mine aching soul.

Lady S. Will your Majesty make further suggestion for quiet and ease?

Q. Mary. Almost this good comfort doth surfeit me, in that I have this unremembrance o' my leal friends; and do now bask in a warmth that doth shame by thought o' their impending wants.

Lady S. Your Majesty need not so sore lament your good friends, they have, by the queen's command, been both carefully housed and comforted.

Q. Mary. I most lament me that I do loll in this soft ease with no mind for others. Had they as unmindful been o' me, I would have so far missed this sweet fare, that in its stead I should now have been in bonds. This dulcet feast would gall my graceless lips, had I not your ladyship's good assurance they felt no need.

Lady S. This tender thought doth well become your Majesty; but I pray you, slur not the present comfort by overweight of wistfulness for friends. Their needs have met full satisfaction;

and you do make most of comfort for them by surrendering your-self to your present rest.

Enter Page.

Page. Please yer la'yship, me lud say me ter say ye wi' his hereabouts, an' ter say that he hae in his presence an afficer frae the court o' her majesty, the queen. An' me lud bid me furthersum ter say when yer la'yship wud make ter him yer say for his speech wi' yersel.

Lady S. I am instructed, your Majesty, that my lord and husband, together with Sir Francis Knollys, who, by the queen, her majesty, hath been sent, do await your most gracious pleasure.

Q. Mary. So sore hath my heart grown that I do shrink at this weighty message. O, that I could barter all this queenly care for some day-maid's ease. Throne, crown, scepter, robes, alas! how vain are these! In the last great sweeping up such poor toys shall mingle with the vulgar dust o' earth's forgotten joys, an' I shall have only left at last my small acts an' deeds to buy or lose heaven's eternal bliss. But pardon me, my lady, I will hear these gentlemen at their good pleasure.

Lady S. Announce the gentlemen.   [*Exit Page.*

Q. Mary. Whatever fate hath in store for me, whether o' good or ill, I shrink no more. If there be in this a hope for bet-ter days, I do already too long delay. I have so oft eagerly waited for the unfolding o' a hope only to see it fade, that I do need the strength o' trust to stay me now.

O God, take from mine heart this vain struggle; too long have I sought to master fate. Give, O give in exchange for my feeble strife, that sweet trust in Thy dear love and care that doth satisfy and fill.

Enter Page.

Page. Sir Francis Knollys an' me Lud Scrope.   [*Exit Page.*

Enter SIR FRANCIS KNOLLYS *and* LORD SCROPE.

Lord S. May it please your Majesty. I am commanded of the queen, my mistress, to present to you this gentleman, who doth bear from the queen, her majesty, a commission, addressed by name to this gentleman, Sir Francis Knollys, and myself. Of the full import of this commission Sir Francis will acquaint your Majesty.

Q. Mary. As one who needeth sore the sweet proffer o' a friend, I welcome this gentleman, and yourself, my Lord, with the hope that you do bring me balm.

Sir F. I am directed by her majesty the queen to convey to you her tender wish for your welfare, and to make known to you the full expression of her pleasure, touching the letter you did send her majesty. That I may not forestall your judgment, or bolster your expect by seeming promises that our mission and message are twins of sweetness alone, I would declare, flatly, that whatever words I may say must have in them but the deep concern that the queen, our mistress, doth feel in this affair, that doth so greatly affect, not only the realm, but foreign states and princes as well. For there be those who have no mind to regard, save with misunderstanding, her majesty, the queen, our mistress, in all that she doth attempt for the good of her people and realm; and in her strivings for sweeter concord with neighboring princes, but would missay quickly any move touching your affairs that had not their full approval.

Q. Mary. I bespeak you, sir, that I have not taken unto myself, nor am I likely to take, more o' a hope for gladness than would meet the need o' one who doth faint for friendly counsel. Alas, sir, so few the joys that come to me, that I should, indeed, be poor at schooling did I look for sweetness in affairs of this nature, when so few pleasures come even from more hopeful sources. So long have clouds o'erhung my sky, that I have grown a stranger to the sun of peace, an' now amid the fogs o' doubts an' fears, I blindly grope for a hand I may not touch. If this, sir, which you bring me doth have in it a still darker weight than that which has so far ridden my grief-shot heart, I pray you exhibit it, for so tired have I grown, an' grief hath so worked me frail, that even if you do bring but a slighter weight of disheart, I fear the fount may break, an' in the breaking set free a spirit that hath known no freedom, save in its trust in God.

Sir F. It is not my purpose, madam, to so conduct this interview that it shall be one of reminiscences. But the past has so

over-lapped the present, that there be not a few matters that
prudence can but suggest a better understanding of. Your letter to the queen our mistress was first read privately then
before her honorable council.

Q. Mary.   Had I known that my poor missive would have assumed the dignity o' a paper o' state, I would have made yet
more careful selection o' the words wherewith I did betray my
stress, for such haste did oppress me, that my letter was far
more a cry, than an orderly recital o' the announcement o' one
queen arriving in the realm o' another.

Sir F.   Such as your letter was, madam, it conveyed to the
queen our mistress a full understanding of your present situation.   Your private history had, alas, become so public a plaything, that you had no need to write down more of the causes
that did haste your flight.

Q. Mary.   I withdraw all parley, an' will give you, gentlemen,
such attention as your message shall meed, an' my welfare
demand.

Sir F.   That we may the better understand one another, and
avoid the employment of words, that from their very number
may miss the meaning we would convey, I will shoot the tide by
launching out, and so reach the very heart of the matter.

Q. Mary.   Alas, sir, I trust that you do not make play o'
words, an' so fling the phrase, heart, as to mean for me further
hurt.

Sir F.   I fear, madam, that I am poor at poesy speech, and
lest my attempt to be plain and fair be further turned, and make
a prick of that which I would have soft and tender, I'll speak
outright.

Q. Mary.   I am listening, sir.

Sir F.   The queen our mistress hath deemed it right and
prudent that, before she doth offer you further assistance, or
stand as sponsor for your cause, you do submit to her full answer
to the charges wherewith the world at large hath made tax on
your name.

Q. Mary.   Charges, sir!   I did not know, until informed by
yourself, that I was charged by the world at large with aught
that taxed my good name.   What, sir, is this that you do so darkly

hint at? If answer be required to clear murkness from my reputation, I would right quickly make it.

Sir F. If, madam, your answers be as earnest as your efforts to dibble, you might, of truth, satisfy the queen our mistress by a straight denial at once. As you do ask plainly as to the charges, I will answer plainly. First, then: As to the manner of the death of your late lord and husband, Lord Darnley. Rumor doth say, with how much truth I leave to your own soul and your God, that you were privy to his untimely death; and that those who did stain their hands and souls by the unholy deed were known to you, and that the act was approved by you.

Q. Mary. Sir, if this be the thickness o' the queen my cousin's reception, I pray you let me depart at once; for I would by grace have better fate to trust myself in the hands o' my friends, even in my distracted realm, than to place myself in the power o' one who hath harbored this foul suspicion against her sister an' next o' kin. If this blot be laying, in all its ugliness, athwart my soul, it were a most unholy show indeed, that I should raise my then unshameful face an' crave e'en the pity due a dog.

Lord S. That there be need for a full and free answer, your Majesty, to these most darkly charges, must to you seem fully warranted. If you are innocent in your soul, as you say, and as your lips so quickly proclaim, you need have small fear; for if these foul rumors be but the sting of weak scandal, or the sleet of foes, you need no great denials to hush them. We read that the well need not a physician, but they that are sick. If the ugly fame that doth so affect you be but of such substance as doth make the weight of troubled dreams, you may hear and make good answer, and give full satisfaction to the queen, our mistress.

Q. Mary. It doth grieve me most that this hearsay should so have found lodgment in the mind o' the queen my cousin, that I have need to macerate mine heart to prove this awsome murkness is foreign to my soul.

Sir F. The queen our mistress hath reserved, as is her right, her judgment as to the sleet and slime that have come to her on the wings of vulgar report. It is but meet that, having been pained by the recital of the rumors touching yourself, she should now ask for such assuage as the proofs you say you can adduce may afford her.

Q. Mary.   Sir, it doth not please me that the queen my cousin doth réquire that before she may house me, or afford me needed protection, I do drag the sorrows o' the past before the whole world. That persecution hath ridden hard along my track doth not license any, queen or common, to foul their thought o' me by harboring a belief in deeds so black as is this monstrous slander.

Say to the queen my cousin that I came not here for trial, an' if I had, the common laws o' justice would withhold judgment until after pleading. I ask naught o' her save that entertainment that one may find at better inns. If she hath not the grace to grant me this, I will seek in less coldy lands that welcome due a Christian in distress.

Lord S.   Your Majesty, you have forgotten that it be not becoming to the queen our mistress to treat upon this matter, which doth not only closely concern our realm, but also foreign states and princes, until she hath a full and satisfactory answer, upon which she may base her actions in this your case.

Q. Mary.   Treat? Pardon me, your Lordship, have I made such careless use o' my tongue, or hand, as to give you gentlemen, or the queen my cousin to understand that I desire to treat with you, or her, as ambassadors do? You mistake, your Lordship, I do not ask your queen to interest herself in mine affairs. I have simply been thrown upon your coast, an' am like a ship-wrecked mariner, an' only ask that kindly assistance that your honest shore-men would give to any storm-tossed soul. Is there need in giving so small a gift as a cup o' cold water to one that asketh, that it doth require a formal treaty? Is there need, gentlemen, that before your queen my cousin can offer to exhibit her Christian charity, she doth require of me a rehearsal o' my purely domestic affairs? I pray you, gentlemen, return to the queen your mistress an' say to her, that I will not vex herself, or her council, with my temporary distress. I think there be those in my company who are able to

5

make the ordinary returns for such entertainment as we have
had, or may need, for the few days we shall remain in your
realm; an', when I have counseled with my friends, if they
should not deem it expedient for me to return to mine own
country, I will make good their better directions, an' seek quiet
and rest at a more friendly court, where there be less o' officious-
ness an' more Christian grace.

Sir F. Coming as you did, madam, and acquainting the
queen, our mistress, with your arrival in her realm, has, both by
common law and the laws of states, invested her with full and
complete authority to proceed in this matter with that gravity
that the situation demands. We have not been delegated, nor
is it our wish, to force you to comply with the queen our
mistress' simple suggestions.

Q. Mary. Force? This I did submit to when my very weakness did both prevent me from resisting, an' gave the cowardly
opportunity. I had thought that this very weakness would save
me from further show o' force here.

Sir F. The queen our mistress hath heard, and the same
hath been reported to her officially, that after your late lord and
husband's death, you did submit to the embraces of the Earl of
Bothwell, and this, too, before that season which law and common decency do prescribe as fit and legal. The worth and
weight of this foul slander, if such it be, you wot better than
any. Marriage is honorable, this we all——

Q. Mary. Sir! This is most unnatural, o' truth. I have so
far kept in check an indignation that you seem to have done
your best to loose. How far I may be able to control myself I
know not. The queen my cousin, if she be deeply concerned
in matters o' embraces, hath small need to go beyond her own
court to satisfy her curiosity. I do fear me that she doth make
this keek inquiry more to gain variety than to accomplish that
which you seem to suggest.

Sir F. Madam, the subjects of the queen our mistress do
not incline, nor dare they, brawl such speeches as you have just
committed yourself of. What her own subjects are by law and
decency restrained from doing, an uncrowned, loosely heralded
foreign stranger should not dare to utter.

Q. Mary.   The recital o' my misfortunes should, to gentlemen
o' blood, afford me that protection that I do seem sadly to have
missed here.

Lord S.   Madam, we have our duty to perform, and as I have
afore said, if these unpleasant rumors be not true, there be no
harm likely to follow, if you do consent to permit the queen our
mistress to act as your arbitrator.   As you are a person of
quality, you should judge that other lands and other peoples
will think themselves of this matter.

The strangely unsettled affairs in the kingdom of Scotland
seem not over likely to become peaceful in a day; and as you
have yet deep interests in that kingdom, your standing before
the world should be made in as good a light as may be.

That the queen our mistress hath ears is not in our land
counted a sin, but if she have ears, and give no attention to the
intrigues of neighboring princes, and yet more especially such
as are her next neighbors and near of kin, she doth sadly miss
that wisdom which is so becoming a mighty prince, such as
she is.

Q. Mary.   Gentlemen, if this matter be stripped o' the words
an' usages o' courts, an' stated as man to man, plainly, what
then be this that the queen my cousin doth require?

Sir F.   Madam, it be required, as is right and proper, that
you do permit the queen our mistress to make full inquiry into
the truth or falsity of the serious charges against you laid.

Q. Mary.   Already, sir, in the very beginning you are too
broad.   If it must needs be that the queen my cousin would
perform my laundry maid's work, I do much prefer that she
shall cleanse my linen singly, piece by piece, an' not by one
quick plunge attempt to do that which from her very misunderstanding she may misdo.

Sir F.   Madam, you have asked that in discussing this, your
sad case, we refrain from the use of court language and etiquette.
In granting this, are we to descend to vulgar drabbish babbling
in arranging this affair?

Q. Mary.   Pardon me, gentlemen, if this, my allusion, was
unsavory.   I did but try to match the requirements.

Sir F. I fear, madam, that to prolong this interview would deprive us of the presence of a lady, and submit us to the pain of treating with a vulgar.

Q. Mary. That there be two o' you doth give you an advantage which, added to the heartlessness o' your instructions, forces me to display weakness, I admit.

Sir F. Already too long have we ridden over barren fields to chase game not to our liking. If you have no mind, madam, to hear us fairly, and answer the queen our mistress graciously, there be but one course open to us as commissioners; that is, to proclaim you and your blind followers as lawless invaders, landing upon her majesty's domain without her let. And, if it doth please your temper to slight her courtesy and refuse her most righteous inquiries, we are instructed to impeach your further movements, and restrain your correspondence.

Q. Mary. I did more than half guess me that with her usual *pseudo* generosity, the queen your mistress would offer me succor, an' then, as a return, force me to meet her hard demands. Under the thin guise o' friendship an' charity, she now offers to shelter me, on conditions that I do place myself in her power. As you count it sedition for me to speak my mind freely in this matter, I can only say, that were the queen my cousin in my place an' I in hers, I would not make for her so hard a task for so small a favor.

Sir F. Madam, will you make to us, direct, such an answer as we can make to the queen our mistress direct?

Q. Mary. I will, sir, when you have as directly acquainted me whereof I am to make answer.

Sir F. That you may not have even this poor excuse, madam, I will repeat. First: You are charged with a foreknowledge of the murder of your lord and husband, Lord Darnley; and second, that you did, with unholy haste, wed with the Earl of Bothwell, knowing him to be the cruel instigator of the murder of your lord and husband. Also——

Q. Mary. Gentlemen! Enough! Enough! Spare me, I pray! If I be guilty o' but one o' these crimes, I am no longer worthy o' the consideration o' even the most heartless. If these liggs have gained such currency as to so affect my good name, as to thus compel the queen my cousin to these hard measures, I am, gentlemen, ready to wash the stain out, if happily I may, by mine own denial an' the proofs o' my friends.

Lord S.   At last your Majesty has struck the better thought that did urge the queen our mistress to make this wish.

Q. Mary.   Then I pray you, gentlemen, let us to business.

Sir F.   [*Writing at table.*]   Do you, madam, make formal denial of the charges mentioned?

Q. Mary.   My God! My God! I do! I do!   [*Crosses herself.*] I pray you, gentlemen, make no stop; let this unhappy business be quickly despatched.   But see to it that you do inject nothing more hurtful than your commission doth call for.

Sir F.   And you do, of your own free will, consent and ask that the queen, our mistress, shall make full inquiry, by her proper officers, into the charges and unpleasant rumors that are mentioned in these instructions?

Q. Mary.   I do consent; but, sir, write it not down that I do consent o' mine own free will.   If there be need o' this most cold business, I pray you, as we are Christians, let us write down no liggs.

Sir F.   You do, then, consent?

Q. Mary.   That I do consent doth not carry with it that I do consent o' mine own free will.

Lord S.   Your Majesty, this strange hesitancy would not plead over well for your innocency.

Q. Mary.   My Lord, I pray you to consider I am alone.   There be with me no friend or adviser to whom I can turn and say: " How shall I make answer?"   Alone! Alone! My God, alone! and so sorely pressed.   How know I that in my consenting to make the queen, your mistress, mine arbitrator, I make her not my gaoler, an' mayhap my executor?   If I do hesitate, think, O, my Lord, think of my utter loneliness.

Lord. S.   Your Majesty, the queen our mistress doth bethink herself of your comfort and safety ——

Q. Mary.   Safety! My Lord, safety? If she hath in her heart a single thought o' my safety, she hath, alas, made a most unhappy showing of its good proffer.

Sir F.   I have, madam, written that you deny the charges

heretofore mentioned; and that you do ask the queen our mistress that she shall appoint and convene a commission, which shall make a full inquiry, to the end that you may, as you claim you can, satisfy the world of your innocency. And that you do hold yourself in readiness to answer to the queen our mistress at such time and place as her good pleasure and the ends of justice shall determine.

Q. Mary. O, gentlemen! Mine heart doth ache to cast among your hard legal words some speech o' woman's tenderness; but as such poor weakness doth not become so stiff a paper, I pray you remember something o' the stress in which you find me, an' make o' the best I may have said, something that shall display a sweeter ending o' this cold reading.

Sir F. It doth require, madam, that you affix here your legal sign.

Q. Mary. Do I, sir, sign this which be not yet mine own words?

Sir F. I did acquaint you with the full import of the writing, and did but set down your own asking.

Q. Mary. It do matter little. If this be my *quietus*, it may be a happy despatch. So sorely am I pressed that if this do express the knowledge o' mine end, it shall be a relief to know even this o' a surety.   [*Signs.*

Sir F. Madam, there be no further need vexing yourself. My Lord and Lady Scrope will, by the queen our mistress' command, afford you every entertainment. Your people have been housed, and you have yourself but to rest content until this your case can be adjusted. My Lady Scrope will shield you from every intrusion, and so minister to your comfort that you shall not regret that providence hath given you so sweet a hostess.

Q. Mary. [*To Lady Scrope.*] O, I pray you, give me but the touch o' thine hand, that it prove to me the coming o' a little rest. Speak some word that may happily be the key that shall unlock the store-house of my tears. O, if mine eyes would only swim, mine heart might sail into a quieter sea.

I pray you, my lady, touch me as you would your own child;

say to me some sweet word that shall quiet this sad tumult o'
my poor soul.

Lady S. It is over now, your Majesty. [*Bowing to Sir
Francis and Lord Scrope, who retire.*] Here by ourselves we
may find sweet release from the burdensome cares that oppress
you. Forget now, your Majesty, this cruel necessity. Rest
here, and I will make to you such play of good words, that you
will but hear, as in the dim distance, the mutterings of this
harsh affair.

Q. Mary. It doth grieve me, your Ladyship, that I have thus
made you partner o' my woe. O, that I might have strength to
bear this mine affliction alone. O God, if I do shrink, an' almost
rebel at this bitter cup, I pray Thee remember mine humanity.
O Blessed Saviour, grant me the sweet uplifting o' thy love.
O tender Virgin, give me the fullness o' thy petition.

I am better now. Let me seek the quiet o' the apartment
you, my Lady, have assigned me; and there let me with my
God alone work out this mine hour o' trial.   [*Exeunt.*

SCENE II. *Room in Westminster Palace.*

Enter COUNTESS OF NOTTINGHAM.

Countess of N. How much of life, how much of joy has this
poor driven queen now made loss. In my memory I do picture
the shatter of her days. Of royal blood, and so kindly touched
by gift of God, that form and face do right well merit love's
kindest office. Yet here she is an outcast; broken by those who
should mend, rent by those who should cheer; without a land,
without a throne, without a home. Ah me! Ah me! How sad a
plight is this; wrung by despair, haunted by fear, pursued by
guilt. How far, alas, hast thou, O Queen, missed the sweet of
thy woman's part. A wife, and yet unwed, a mother, yet un-
loved. The saddest thing that hath yet befallen thy poor
woman's heart, is thy great loss of mother-love. O God, make
for this poor soul thy light of peace to good that whereby she
hath lost.

Enter Maid.

Maid. May it please your ladyship, her majesty doth
approach.

Enter QUEEN ELIZABETH.

Q. Eliz. What hour is it? I am so worn and so grieved at heart, that I do find yet more comfort in this, my awake, than I found in my useless wooing of sleep. Ah, me! Amid this pomp and all this power, how tied and useless are my hands.

I saw Hester's nurse to-night kiss and lay baby Beatrice down, and then the mother came, and with that sweet softness, which is more a badge of woman's love than is yet this mighty scepter that I sway, she caught and transferred to her loving heart the baby's tender form. I turned me away, sick at soul, for in that smile I saw and felt my loss. The saddest chamber within my heart must remain unfilled. How much I have missed, and turned aside by my own selfish pride! But there be yet left me this sad comfort of review: what I have missed must be measured by what I have gained. For thee, O England, I hush the yearnings of my heart, and so, hiding beneath a smile I do but assume, I make a color of that which to me is white as death.

[*To Countess of Nottingham.*] Countess, why did you not signal your presence? It is, indeed, well that I have made but trial of my scholarship, in rendering into English that which I had read in outish tongue.

Countess of N. I pray, your Majesty, that you do acquit me of the sin that your words do imply. I but saw your Majesty, and in the onset, made notice that you did not address your words to me, and so closed the avenues to my senses.

Q. Eliz. I pray you let not this affair rest as a burden. That which I did rehearse was some nightmare, written by some early Latin, love-sick poet; and so poor a sleek have I made of it that I fear the silly dolt would not know his dull lines from my poor rendering.

Countess of N. What is your Majesty's good pleasure? The fatigues of the day do so haunt you that you have, indeed, good need of rest. Let me, I pray you, bring you some softer gown, and then with suggestion of a happier thought, perchance, launch your troubled heart out into the peaceful sea of sleep.

Q. Eliz. How know you I am troubled? In my face do there grow lines that mark the tramp of care?

Countess of N. Nay, your Majesty, I have oft heard it re-marked, and by older heads than mine, that there n'er yet was seen a face that so well bore the trials of a crown as doth the kindly face of England's queen.

Q. Eliz. Heard you this? or is it some sycophantcy that, ready made, you keep to serve as wit shall prompt?

Countess of N. Of truth, your Majesty, not once but oft, have I heard foreign ministers, and even princes, remark how well you stood the cares of realm.

Q. Eliz. [*Aside.*] Alas, prince nor minister hath seen, nor known, my aching heart. Well, be this as it may, I make no complaint. If the years do sap my youth, they shall fill the store-house of my age, and that which I give up of face or form shall come to me again in the thought that I have tried to do my duty, and this shall be a recompense for seeming loss.

Pray observe if his grace the Duke of Norfolk hath yet left the palace.

Countess of N. I will, your Majesty.

Q. Eliz. Out of the North, out of the East, come thou who doth bring in thine embrace destruction. O, turn from me this awful hurt that doth haunt me like a ghost. [*Takes paper from her bosom.*] These are the directions. [*Reads.*

At two burn the yellow, at three burn the green, at four burn the purple.

O, if this last fail me, then I have, indeed, need to make good search for other shifts. [*Burns the yellow paper in the light.*

Turn and twist, tremble and writhe. Yellow burn! burn! burn!

[*Takes burnt paper and throws it from her.*

Into the South I cast thee, return no more!

> *I've burned thy color in fire,*
> *I've scattered thy ash in air,*
> *Help me now, O fates,*
> *And save me from despair!*

O, if this bring me not that peace which I do so sorely need, I fear good Doctor Dee hath missed the charm wherein he had so fine a promise. I make no complaint. God grant me that I do so sorely need.

Enter COUNTESS OF NOTTINGHAM.

Countess of N. May it please your Majesty, his grace the duke of Norfolk doth yet attend, as by your royal word, and he doth await such commands as shall please your Majesty.

Q. Eliz. Say to his grace that I await him here. I do but require that you direct him.   [*Exit Countess of N.*

Now must I make such a use of words that this over-tender duke may turn his softness into such channels as will save his judgment for my strength. I think me that he hath good honesty in his heart, and if I can but bend the tenor of his ways so that he shall feel the common need rather than the stress of one who has not the good of the realm at heart, I shall have done that whereof I do feel the weight of state doth demand. Why should he pant to succor this outcast, who with plaintive wail doth thrust the asking palm? I shall strive to save his loyalty from too great a strain. O, that I had eyes that now I could scan the leagues between this doxy queen and me. They say she hath a lovely face, and a form that doth fire even foes. Ah me! ah me! God help the English fogs that they do spatter that fair skin until it shall breed on its luscious whiteness a score of ugly warts, and fade her soft, pink blush to a pale, dingy gray.

I have need to work a change in the mind of this tender duke. Why, he doth even babble in praise of this flirt-gill at my very face.

Enter DUKE OF NORFOLK.

Welcome, your Grace. Pray be seated. I will detain you but a few moments, happy if in those few moments I may make such choice of words as will fully acquaint you with the gravity of the charge I would now make to your Grace, and whereof I have felt compelled to require your presence.

Duke of N. I await your Majesty's pleasure, and I do bring with me a heart singularly tuned for your Majesty's sweet comfort and peace.

Q. Eliz. If fairness of speech, your Grace, proved your loyalty, traitors would drop dead at the sight of your shoes, and your morion would turn an army.

Duke of N. I am pleased that your Majesty doth rate my loyalty from my feet up, for now that I have removed my head-piece, I stand with loyalty on my feet, and might in my hands, and trust that I may make so good a sign with my lips that your Majesty need not miss the fullness of my heart in its devotion to your royal person and your cause.

Q. Eliz. If I credit but half your words, your Grace, I have no need to feel dread that I may over-tax either your friendship or your loyalty.

Duke of N. Your Majesty doth confer in your good opinion praise beyond my desert.

Q. Eliz. I have sent for your Grace in that I do most fully trust the wisdom of your acuteness. It is my desire that you, with my Lord Chief Justice, fully acquaint yourselves with the laws of states touching this affair of the Scottish queen, now abiding within our borders. Leave no point undiscovered; and see to it, as doth become loyal subjects, that every turn be carefully guarded; for this matter is one of such delicacy that combined wisdom is right fully needed to avoid unseemly slip. When you have well mastered the points in this business, I pray you confer with me again, for this deal will not brook delay. On the return of Sir Francis Knollys, we must be fully prepared to act at once upon any condition of affairs that he shall report to us.

Duke of N. It shall be as your Majesty doth command. I will make sleep a stranger to mine eyes until I have fathomed the rule touching this matter. That I may the more lawfully act, your Majesty, and in acting exhibit my authority, should not the right, as attested by your royal seal, be mine for favor? And further, should not your honorable council be informed of my hand in the adjustment of this most taint affair?

Q. Eliz. Your suggestion, your Grace, has already been acted upon, and my secretary has prepared an order which only needs the royal seal to become a command. This, when pro-claimed, shall give you full authority in relation to this whereof I have summoned your Grace.

Duke of N. Pray, your Majesty, no longer so divide the hours of night that you do rob yourself of rightful sleep. This affair is so well in hand that you may retire now, feeling that those who love thee will watch your interests, even while your tired heart is lulled by the consciousness of your well acquitted duty.

Q. Eliz. Thanks, your Grace. Do you, too, seek that rest which you yourself must need after the fatigues of the day. Peace go with you. *Au revoir.*   [*Exit Queen Elizabeth.*

Duke of N. Sleep dear Queen, and may sweet angels bring thee light to see thy duty, and strength to do it. God send thee quiet of soul, and rest of heart, and wisdom to know the better part.   [*Exit.*

SCENE III. *Council Chamber, Westminster Palace, London.*
Council *discovered.*

Cecil. My lords and gentlemen, we may not proceed further in this matter without the presence of her majesty, the queen.

Smith. May not we now acquaint her majesty of our presence?

Cecil. [*To Page.*] Say to the keeper of the queen's chamber that he may announce to her majesty that the council awaits her pleasure.   [*Exit Page.*

Lei. My lords and gentlemen, may we not now speak with such earnestness as shall exhibit to her majesty, the queen, our deep concern touching the great need of moving at once in the case of the Scottish queen, and the matter of the hearing?

Smith. If to move quickly is to move unlawfully, I pray you, my lords and gentlemen, that we make a virtue of slowness. We may have less display in caution than in precipitance, but caution doth better become statists, while haste may curtain wisdom and shift justice.

Lei. Far be it from my intent to counsel an act unlawful. I did but imply that we make such haste as would assure us a defendant when we had named a day for the hearing. I have, I trust, not missaid in my effort to advise.

Smith. Not missaid, my Lord, but from your dilogy speech I did not catch your full meaning.   [*Enter Page.*

Page. Her Majesty, the Queen. Gentlemen, the Queen.

Enter QUEEN ELIZABETH.

Cecil. Your Majesty, we do await your gracious pleasure.

Q. Eliz. Pleasure! my lords and gentlemen; my soul doth make the hope that you have brought this rare commodity with you, or happily you may make discovery of it mid my over-looking.

Cecil. Your Majesty hath indeed sweetest pleasure, and doth liberally bestow it by the permitting of this audience.

Lei. Heaven in its shower of blessing hath indeed been most liberal to your Majesty, and so graced your royal person with its tokens that the silent sense of your presence doth crown the now as king of pleasure.

Q Eliz. Had I my back turned to you, my Lord, and were your voice less familiar, I might have thought I heard the truth, for so cunning do you gild your flattery that it were almost a joy to be the target of its shafts. You, and such as you, have so soft a speech in seeming, that your very falsity doth assume the form of luxury; yet your words, to those who understand, are but the shadow of the sweet they sound; still so weak are human hearts that they do prize the deception, knowing that they are being fed with weakest pap.

Lei. Your Majesty, if happily in my strivings I have so far answered my desires as to even seem that for which I so eagerly contend, I am the better encouraged to so shape my acts that my seeming may grow to such a degree of reality that your Majesty shall finally credit me with honest endeavors to serve.

Q. Eliz. If I did not know that your time, when out of eye, was mostly spent in ends not fully public, but yet not unknown where least suspected, I should ween that you made such store of honeyed words as would make you good game for bees.

Lei. Not alone, your Majesty, have you stored the stock of bees in honeyed words, but you have borrowed not a few of their stings.

Q. Eliz. If these stings were indeed my only weapons they would leave me quite defenceless, for your armor of flattery would turn even sharper halberds than stings.

Cecil. May it please your Majesty, I have brought with me the papers relating to the Scottish queen.

Q. Eliz. Gentlemen, please be seated. What new turn has

this affair taken? The assent of the Scottish heir to the hearing in her behalf has not been advantaged as yet.

Cecil. Your Majesty, the assent hath been so far amended that it doth now assume the form of a request for a redraw of the agreement.

Q. Eliz. How so? I did fear this. Does my cousin repent her that she did entrust this matter to our hands?

Cecil. I fear, your Majesty, that the Scottish queen has been so wrought upon by those whose interests are not akin to your own, that she doth repent her aforetime decision, not so much from her own thought as from the urging of others.

Q. Eliz. My poor cousin be, indeed, sorely pressed. I pray you, my lords and gentlemen, in considering this lame affair, that you be not unmindful of the loneliness of her who seeks of us advice and guidance. Think you well first, on the frailty of humanity, and then the weakness of this storm-tossed soul. As far as her acts do effect the realm we may judge them by the laws provided for such cases, but there is a court, my lords and gentlemen, that shall even with greater justice measure her deeds, and not hers alone, but ours also.

It is my pleasure that this hearing be kept from every semblance of oppression, and that we do so proffer fairness that judgment shall not miss approval. I would have you find in this case an opportunity for the full breadth of your Christian virtues. I know no better rule in the judging than to so show your justice, that were you the judged you might well approve the fairness, if not the verdict, of the judges.

Cecil. Your Majesty, the propriety and sweetness of your counsel doth well admonish us to use fairness, and urge us to charity. In the contemplation of this matter, and assaying a better understanding, it doth become us to no longer avoid meeting a necessity. If the Scottish queen be, as she claims, innocent of the charges against her, she has small need to fear; but we would give to her, by your Majesty's command, the noble gift of a full vindication, if her innocency shall merit it.

Q. Eliz. How think you, my lords and gentlemen, shall this matter be the better righted?

Smith. As you have, your Majesty, so far tempered your

counsel with sweet compassion, and folded your directions in
tender charity, it doth the more fitting seem that your Majesty
shall order and convene a commission empowered to hear, not
alone the accused, but the accusers.

Q. Eliz. I, myself, have had this thought, and to this end I
would hear suggestions.

Cecil. Your Majesty, in matters of this nature it has been
deemed proper that there be suitable bounds set to the answer
of the accused to the charges. To excuse the act of a day, one
need not be called upon to explain the folly of a life-time.
These charges are so properly headed, that to meet them would
be, when fairly answered, good basis for verdict.

Q. Eliz. Such details as do involve legal procedure I leave
to the proper officers to insert, who are better advised, withholding alone my sanction to over harshness.

Lei. I have matured a suggestion, may it please your Majesty,
that I crave the honor of advancing.

Q. Eliz. Say on, my Lord, remembering that this affair is to
be heard in the halls of justice, and not in the courts of Venus.

Lei. Your great learning, your Majesty, doth equip your wit.
My suggestion doth embrace the convening of a commission
which shall be fully authorized to command the presence of the
Scottish queen, and request the attendance of her accusers. As
the matter under consideration relates entirely to a question of
personal rectitude of the accused, but still has such far reaching
effects as to involve political ends, it would be meet that the inquiry extend not only to the charge already made and prepared,
but with the addition of a clause looking to the attitude of the
Scottish queen as to her supposed rights of succession.

Q. Eliz. I pray you, Mister Secretary, that you draw up, as
is becoming a paper of this character, a statement which shall
include my pleasure as to the convening of this commission.
When this shall have been finished, I will name the gentlemen
who are to compose the assembly. It is my pleasure that this
commission shall have its duties so defined that they may escape in their actions an over show of hardness.

Smith. That it doth please your Majesty to so soften these
most important directions, that they shall attain the desired

end with as little hurt as is possible, doth, indeed, credit well
your heart, and add to your wisdom. But, if I be not
over forward, I would proffer the introduction of clauses looking
to caution, for it be well known that this person who has voluntarily requested your Majesty's action as her fautor, doth lack
that steadfastness that would rightfully assist in the just ends
you have in view for her own betterment, and the safety and
peace of your realm. It be necessary, therefore, that the decision of this hour shall be so carefully framed that it may not be
set aside, either by the craftiness or willfulness of the faultful
and designing Scot.

Q. Eliz. Better justice would demand that this hearing
should, as far as possible, lose its appearance of a trial, and but
be that which it really is, a hearing.

This dethroned queen doth not stand as doth a criminal, but
rather as any one, queen or common, who asks our assistance in
a matter where we are to act as becomes Christians who would
temper justice with mercy. These foul rumors, which do so offend
and grieve us, may or may not be true, yet common justice to
ourselves and to our realm would demand, and must have, a fair
understanding of this most grievous question. We may not
know the whole of truth from the proposed hearing alone of
those who make accuse; nor is it right to give judgment until
the accused herself has been heard, either by her own pleading,
or the testimony of such friends, if happily these she may have,
who be willing to proffer some kindly word that may lighten the
weight of reproach.

Lei. Your Majesty has so well outlined the course which wisdom doth approve that the task of preparation is light. There
remains now, your Majesty, but the naming of the court to complete the full arrangements for this important hearing.

Q. Eliz. I pray you, my lords and gentlemen, that you retire to the office of state, and there prepare this affair as doth
become papers of this kind. It is my desire that you acquaint
me with the full reading when drawn.   [*All rise.*

Cecil. It shall be as your Majesty desires. I will submit it for
your approval when rightfully drawn.

Q. Eliz. I would have you immold not a little tenderness

and compassion into your stark, legal paper. The *juste milieu* is the better. My lords and gentlemen, you may retire.

[Exeunt council.

How swiftly flow the moments of the day. Action makes the hours seem short. To those who wring under sorrow's infliction the moments run with sluggish drag, if they feed the time on their grief alone, but if they mold their heart-aches into acts, and shape their sorrows to trend the events of the day, they will rather seek to stay the moments than note the slowness of the hour.

Enter EARL OF LEICESTER.

Lei. Your Majesty, I do return that you may make to me the fulfilling of the promised grant of a free and unrestricted pass, and your gracious permission to follow my own bent, touching the matter of watching and crossing the plans and ends of your enemies, who seek to advantage by the Scot's presence in your realm.

Q. Eliz. My Lord, if I do grant to you this *carte blanche,* how know I that you will not use it to my hurt?

Lei. Your gracious Majesty, only this: Look with your deep searching sight into the chambers of my soul, and there read the unselfishness of my purposes, and the honesty of my aims. I do but ask this that I may the better protect your Majesty's interests, and keep informed of the moves of your foes. With this, your permit, I need not inform other gentlemen of the council when I feel it is for your interest to act, and thus proceed as your agent alone. Did I not know, your Majesty, that you fully trusted me, I would not ask this thing. But with such a bond between us you cannot doubt me. No! The swimming of your eyes brings in the tide of your sweeter self. I am answered. Your honest eyes have spoken quicker than your truthful lips. For your people and yourself, whose interests I serve alone, I thank thee, my Queen! For myself, I can but ask that you read in my eyes the full answer of my soul's thanks for your renewed trust in me, your slave.

Q. Eliz. Won again! won again! Foolish woman, weak queen. Yes, as you will. So now, as it always was, soft speech,

6

soft act.   Follow me, and I will make to you the fulfilling of my promise, if I harden not in my walk from here.   Lead on, lead on.   Poor fool of a queen, how you do barter the graces of your station for this thin seeming; yet so starved is my heart that I do go blindly, knowing that I am but duped, while I make a treasure of that which, had I the real, I would spurn to hail.

[Exit Elizabeth.

Lei.   First the heart, then the will.   If heaven's joys could be had by lover's suing, I might gain eternal bliss by my play at wooing.

[Exit Leicester.

SCENE IV.   *Great Hall, Buckingham Castle.*
Enter Servant.

Servant.   This grand room, which hath so oft tossed laugh about, and made echoes of boisterous mirth, is now to be saluted with graver preach.   See, here will sit my lords and gentlemen, clothed with dignity and wrapped in power, grave as owls, with intent within their hearts, and purposes high or low, which none but God may know.   And here the broken Scot will take her place, and strive, and plead, and make denials long delay.   There's something strangely out of place in making this gay hall a scoring-room.

Enter SIR WILLIAM CECIL, EARL OF LEICESTER, SIR CHRISTOPHER HATTON, EARL OF ARUNDEL, EARL OF PEMBROKE, SIR THOMAS SMITH, SIR WILLIAM TAIT, LORD CLINTON, DUKE OF NORFOLK, *and others.*

Cecil.   I pray you, my lords and gentlemen, be seated.   If there can be comfort in this unhappy business, pray tax your ingenuity and find it.

Lei.   One can hardly expect to find even ease of body, when the mind is so disquiet.   O, that the world would make its petitions to heaven so earnest, that they might draw from the throne of God such a desire for rectitude, as to escape the sin of hot ambition.

Duke of N.   Ambition, my Lord, whether hot or cold, is a plaything that not a few have toyed with.   Those who have been most successful in its direction, are those who have shaped ambition most for other's good.

Hatton. My lords, there are so many kinds of ambition, that I do tire in my efforts to make a proper rate. I know an earl whose ambition's in his buskins, and with such labor doth he adjust the coverings of his feet, that, indeed, his ambition hath bent him sore. And I know a lord whose ambition for set of breeck hath so taxed his brain in contrivance of look, that he hath crossed both his eyes in spying set of seat. And other men let ambition run to hose and ruffs. And women folk, heaven help me find the pitch, have so much ambition in cut and fit, farthingales and bishops, without a word of puff and stuff, that by my rapier, in ambition's train they lead the march.

Duke of N. What vast difference there be, gentlemen, in measuring ambition's end. Some men aim under ambition's goad to stride a kingdom; while another, with full as much strain, may cope with the latitude of a feak. He who sees in ambition's field the gateway to a fortune, may, when he's forded o'er the moat, assail a gaudy bubble. To-day may prize an act that to-morrow may stamp as treason, and to-day's treason may be to-morrow's devotion.

Clinton. My lords and gentlemen, are we here to soliloquize on modes and follies, and guess at life's poor tangled riddle? or have we met by royal command to regard the affairs of state?

Lei. [*To Norfolk.*] Your Grace, a word with you privately. That we may the better adjust this affair so as not to discover the purpose of our intent, I pray you that you make listening eloquent, and speaking a rarity; for, however carefully you may shape your words, the delivery of them will betray your heart. And, if it come to points over soft, avert your face, that your eyes may not play you betrayal.

Duke of N. I trust, my Lord, I shall not lose sense of my duty in the depths of my emotion. I have so cultivated my instincts that my faults do not herd as wolves with my better desires, and so prey upon them that I may become bewildered in an honest cause. Such leaning as I have toward the Scottish queen hath the assurance of my approval, and my approvals are the fruits of my intercession with God.

Lei. Your religion, your Grace, may indeed serve you well at church, but in matters of this kind your dependence should be more upon wit.

Duke of N. I will follow your directions, my Lord, so long as they lead to the hill of right, but when they pad the valley of doubt, I shall trust alone to the sense that never played me false.

Lei. It is well, your Grace; let us to the hearing.

Cecil. If you have done your fine speeches, my lords and gentlemen, we may try the virtue of compliance with the queen's commands. [*To Serv.*] Acquaint my lord the Earl of Murray with our readiness; and with our compliments, say to my Lady Shrewsbury that her charge may be forthcoming. Gentlemen, my lords, I pray you that in this matter we do follow the direction of her majesty the queen; and that we may escape disorder, let us move straightly.

Enter EARL OF MURRAY *and* LORD NORTH.

Earl of M. Me lords and gentlemen, we salute you.

Cecil. I beseech you, gentlemen, that you find comfort, at least such as this distressing affair may afford.

Enter MARY, QUEEN OF SCOTLAND.   [*All rise.*

Madam, such accommodations as the queen our mistress has provided, we offer you. Pray be seated within the inclosure.

Q. Mary. Why this inclosure? I am not a criminal at the bar. My presence here is in violation o' my protest.

Cecil. I pray you, madam, protest not in the beginning overmuch; for this convening is, indeed, the outcome of your own request.

Q. Mary. I did, sir, make mine earnest while in the maze o' bewilderment, but in a more fortunate season I did seek to withdraw my consent, but was so hotly refused that the naming o' it was counted an offense.

Hatton. You should not, madam, forestall judgment by belittling your judges.

Q. Mary. My judges? My lords and gentlemen, this assembly or any part o' it is not o' mine own choosing. The rule at

common law would hold that even the meanest should in trial
be voiced in selecting his jurors.

Lei. Madam, this is not a trial. The graciousness of the
queen her majesty hath, in royal goodness, afforded you this
opportunity of acquittal, if happily your denials be of that
weight.

Q. Mary. That I am not charged with wrong should estop
trial. One may not deny, at least without danger o' suspicion o'
guilt, that wherewith they have not been lawfully charged, note
you, my lords and gentlemen, lawfully.

Earl of A. Madam, the putting down of the charge was a
matter intrusted to proper hands. The denial of the knowledge
of the charge on your part doth not speak well for the strictness
with which you may answer the inquiry.

Q. Mary. I am, my lords and gentlemen, alone. I would
not so display a plea for pity as to wry your judgment; nor
would I ask other forbearance than that which one Christian
should give to another. But my very loneliness doth warn me
that the lines o' my speech must run in directions not heart-
ward, but rather in sterner moods as may the better make for
me a force o' pleading that shall stay myself an' cause.

Duke of N. My lords and gentlemen, that we may not take
over advantage, I pray you that we proceed first upon the merits of jurisdiction, which, if it hold, we may then proceed to the
os of the matter.

Earl of A. The principles of law would make no question of
the jurisdiction, your Grace; the command of her majesty the
queen has affirmed that, for it is based on a full knowledge of
the statutes.

Q. Mary. The queen your mistress hath small right to attempt to force me against my will, seeing I am no subject, to in
any manner answer slanders that the harboring o' doth ill become her, and which are but weakest hearsay.

Cecil. Our loyalty to her majesty the queen would halt
seditious speech.

Duke of N. My lords and gentlemen, I trow there be need
for a most careful beginning in this case, to the end that we
meet the full approval of our own consciences, and likewise the

fair assent of the party most interested in the hearing, that we have acted justly.

Madam, howbeit, there be not a few among your own people who hold the scandals wherewith you are charged of sufficient weight to be admitted as true. And yet I am in honor bound, as doth become fairness, which I would make my chief stay, to declare unto you that the proof of your guilt is not now strong enough, at least at this distance, to warrant the just in accepting the full burden of the grievous reports objected against your good name and fame. I hold it not as a secret that I have within my own heart such whisperings of doubt as do most earnestly plead with my sense of justice for a fuller hearing. And there be those assembled with me here, by the queen's command, who are nobles and gentlemen, who have, as was right and proper, acquainted me with their like feelings. That we may, therefore, madam, the better tend to the solution of our own doubts, as well as to assist you in the establishment of your innocency, we would pray that you waive your claim as a princess, to the end that as queen, not ·yet without hope of restoration, you may silence slander and shame envy.

That you have not an advocate of your own choosing, doth the better testify to the confidence of the queen our mistress in the fairness and uprightness of these her chosen commissioners, who, by her royal command, would, without prejudice, arrive at such a conclusion as shall establish and maintain amity and sweet friendship between the queen our mistress and yourself.

Make, therefore, no further objection, but lend us that kind aid which shall happily discover the grounds of your innocency, and the confusion of your accusers; to the end that you may be received by the queen her majesty as doth become your royal blood and close relationship.

Q. Mary. My lords and gentlemen, I drop all parley, and imitating your weapons, I urge your farce by defiance.

Lei. Madam, more of the Christian spirit that has graced your afore speech would ease the weight of our duties.

Q. Mary. Give, I pray you, my lords an' gentlemen, my case that attention its gravity meeds, an' let not mine ignorance o' the rules o' such procedures baffle your conception o' duty.

Earl of A. Shall we not then proceed?

Cecil. You have heard, madam, the reading of the special charges. Do you deny them? For on your positive denial are we to base the further proceedings in this legal hearing.

Q. Mary. I make no acknowledgments, nor yet denials; for how can I, seeing that I am hedged by a maze of misunderstanding that doth hide mine innocence and cloud my rights, so that if I make either denials or acknowledgments over broad, I may lose the weight of such favor as would stand to mine acquittal.

Cecil. By your own request, madam, and your own free will, save as conscience made prayer, you did ask for opportunity to prove by denial of self, and the support of evidence, such as your friends might offer, that you were not a party, either by act or knowledge, to the unholy taking off of your late lord and husband, Lord Darnley.

Q. Mary. My lords an' gentlemen, look at these, mine hands. By your keenest discernment, can you discover blood on them? Blood! Yes, blood! My God! The blood o' mine own husband. Mark my voice, hath guilt disturbed it, or thrown it into tremulous tones that accent crime? Doth my face or manner bear the stamp an' mark o' a murderess? O! My God! Am I the accused o' so great a crime?

That I hold mine anger in check, and make o' my resentment good stays to my sense o' wrong, doth the better speak for the sweet influence o' mine holy religion, an' the purity o' mine afore life. Murder! Murder! My God! Murderer o' mine husband, the father o' my child. Did e'er envy or spite forge so cruel a shaft to pierce the soul o' innocence? However dark the circumstances, however thick the plot, should not the judgment o' those akin, if not kind, call halt to policy's drive, and treason's spite.

What need had I to slay my lord? Was he not o' mine own choosing? Not he chose me, nor raised me to his station, but I raised him to mine. If the distemper, which might prompt so foul a deed was o' older growth, an' did thrive long ere the sad taking off, howbeit, my lords an' gentlemen, that I did hazard mine own life in mine attention as his nurse, while he lay smitten by pestilence? Had mine ambition for change o' bed so mastered my sense o' right, as to harbor the wish to speed my lord's death, I had only to wait, for the stroke which had marked him was but suspended, an' would have dealt the blow that made me widowed, but little lagging the fell infliction that misfortune saw fit to use.

Cecil. A plain denial, madam, would better answer this clause.

Q. Mary. If I be unspeechful, my lords an' gentlemen, an' but turn my face to you, you must read in the reflection from my soul a full denial o' this unnatural charge. Have I need to again ——

Cecil. An undisguised no, or yes, would as well meet the ends of justice as will this overflood of words, which but awake or foster bewilderment as to your intent, while it does not remove suspicion.

Q. Mary. It were well, my lords an' gentlemen, if it be your intent to conduct this hearing thus shortly to have made mine answers for yourselves, an' allowed me to have saved myself this shameless hurt.

Hatton. Madam, the word bewilderment has been used, and it doth well tag my state of mind. I fain would dissolve the thickness of your meaning by plucking your over-speech.

Q. Mary. Had you, sir, spent more time at your prayers, an' less with your valet, an' in your first years taken with your milk more good sense, an' in later years had less o' balancing, you might now have graced your present station a bit, rather than exhibit, as you do, your desire to wound. Sir, if you were deprived o' queenly favor, into which gossie doth quoth you did dance with domino down, your havior would far better fit you for the antics o' a zany.

Hatton. I have gathered in my lifetime, madam ——

Q. Mary. Your gathering, sir, doth make poor exhibit when out o' proper place.

Cecil. Madam, you are charged, second, with wedding unlawfully with the Earl of Bothwell.

Q. Mary. In mine own land, sir, wedding be not unlawful.

Cecil. In the land wherein you now are, and whose representatives we are, it is not lawful to turn funeral hymns to wedding marches.

Q. Mary. Are there not stresses, my lords an' gentlemen, that the weight o' a kingdom doth lay upon one that she may be so forced to shape her course that the necessities may change common usage?

Cecil. The laws of this land are so drawn and framed that necessities make unto themselves only such forbearance as shall not conflict with common good.

Q. Mary. It was the common good, my lords an' gentlemen, that drove me to this appearance o' evil. But I admit not that the act was other than that which did meet the full approval o' heaven.

Earl of A. If you do look to heaven for approval of your most unwomanly acts, it were well to sue death for acquittal, that you might know the grounds for your hope.

Q. Mary. I fear, my lords and gentlemen, that you do judge as my portion death without my suing. If I make careful scanning o' your faces, save two, I catch the reason o' my slandered life, an' miss that fair that doth temper justice.

Earl of A. I pray let us proceed, my lords and gentlemen. We do tax the time with parley.

Cecil. Madam, I am not able to record your answer to the second charge.

Smith. My lords and gentlemen, are we to pass simply upon a quick denial the first of these grave charges? I fear we shall miss the ends of even mercy did we enter verdict without separation of proffered testimony, which we have at our command.

Cecil. It was my purpose, my Lord, to first read the charges, and record the defendant's answers thereto, and then return and submit said answers to the crown's rebutting.

Lei. That we may consume no more of the time than is necessary, could we not fully touch all the requirements by noting each charge, *pro* and *con*, as presented?

Earl of A. Justice makes no note of time, save that it be employed in meeting the ends of fairness.

Cecil. If it be the better thought, we will return then, and continue by clauses.

Q. Mary. Will oft-repeated denials, my lords an' gentlemen, make more positive mine innocency? If there be a happier thought, as yet unspoken, that I may make more apted to my distress, an' so ease my plight, I pray God that you help me find it; for mine appeals seem useless, an' naught but God's interference may help me.

Cecil. The denial in the first clause has been recorded. Doth the accused rest her denial upon her afore statement?

Q. Mary. I may not further alter it, but I wish not to surrender any advantage that may present in the further unfolding. I would restate my position: I am no subject.

Cecil. If your further answers are but vain interferences, it would be better to think of curtailment in your speeches.

Q. Mary. It doth occur to me, my lords and gentlemen, that with so great advantages on your side, I should be granted such liberty of answering as, in my weakness an' ignorance, I may feel as helping my case.

Cecil. Madam, you deny then, any participation, by knowledge or otherwise, in the cruel murder of your husband.

Q. Mary. My lords and gentlemen: If I do lose myself an' forget my station in this, my sea o' trouble, I pray you extend to me, as men whose years should have brought the milk o' kind forbearance, such forgetfulness o' my hot speech, which this oft probing doth force, as will credit your years. I am a queen, who, by policy's turning, am absent from my throne. I stand before you cruelly accused, an' sadly bereft. I would so reinforce my denial o' this most sad an' wicked crime, that it may save me further reference to so dark a horror.

My lords an' gentlemen, once for all, an' I do most earnestly ask God to witness my words, I deny any an' all foreknowledge o' the wicked murder o' my late lord an' husband.

Earl of A. My lords and gentlemen, now that we have at last a positive denial from the accused, may we not meet the denial, at least in part, by the presentation of the proffered testimony offered by the Earl of Murray, and also the hearing of other important witnesses? To sustain the charge of foreknowledge of this suspected murder, it is necessary for the prosecution to establish both a motive and an incentive, and also show that the defendant was influenced by the parties, or party, that actually committed the deed.

As the Earl of Bothwell be not here to answer the questionings of this commission, and as vulgar opinions do credit him with planning and directing this foul murder, it be but necessary to establish between the accused before us and the guilty earl such a bond of regard and understanding as would make, by common consent, the accused privy to the designs and purposes of him who hath already been publicly condemned.

Cecil. That we may arrive at a full understanding, and give this denial its just weight, it is proper that witnesses from the accused's own country be heard herewith.

Q. Mary. I did flee mine own country to escape persecution. Is this a Christian act, to import hither my relentless foes? An' I see that you would call even mine own blood to rise up against me.

Cecil. Until the meeting of your denial, there be not further need of your interruptions. My Lord Murray, have you the papers and letters which you submitted?

Earl of M. I hae me lords and gentlemen, submitted nathing. By favor I did say her majesty the queen your mistress an' her council, privately, that I hae in me keeping letters that did pass atwixt the Earl o' Bothwell an' me sister wha is before you.

Q. Mary. O Brother! hast thou forgotten how in youth we made the bond o' love the clasp between us? Thou an' I were loving an' true as brother an' sister; shall now this hateful shift o' policy rise between us? Canst thou, O brother, thus coldly forge an' hurl cruel irons o' hate to pierce my soul?

Turn back, O brother, turn back, and read with eyes o' love on memory's tablet an oath for yet better deeds than this.

Cecil. Madam, your mature years, and not your youth, is now the object of inquiry. [*To Murray.*] My Lord, do these letters which you possess relate to time while yet the late Lord Darnley was still alive?

Earl of M. They do, me Lord.

Cecil. It be counted no violation of privacy to further the ends of justice by any means. May I ask that you read first such letters from the Earl of Bothwell to your sister as might, by inference at least, exhibit an intimacy that would furnish the motive for the committing by one party, and sanctioning by another, of a deed or deeds, of such gravity as to hold the parties amenable to law.

Earl of M. Me lords and gentlemen, I winna gainsay you do urge me to a maist clinty thing. I do, in truth, herein hald letters whilk need the fullest explate frae the rackless writers to dight them o' an acknown aware wi' guilt. To read them mesel, me lords and gentlemen, is a taz to me maist laithfu, an' did I obey the dehorting lane o' me safter thoughts, I wad hae stayed me presence by excuse o' kinship.

Earl of A. Your presence, my Lord, doth vouchsafe the expectations of the commission, in that you have promised submitting the guilty letters. Kinship furnishes no excuse for shielding wrong; none but participants seek to hide guilt.

Earl of M. This whilk I hald in me han', an' whilk me desire for the hale truth aboon a' things, an' me wish for the right weers me frae wi' halding, doth hae the date ——

Q. Mary. My lords an' gentlemen, if you have so far forgotten the dignity o' your station, an' the due to decency, an' the respect o' my rank, as to descend, in your deliberations, to the listening to forged an' stolen private correspondence, you have sunk to such depths as to forbid my further participation in your wanton an' cruel mockery, which you attempt to dignify by naming it a hearing. Your eagerness to avail yourself o' this last foul means, deprives you o' the right to expect from me a request for permission to retire. As I am to be adjudged so unfairly, my absence will not affect your verdict, nor can your verdict affect mine innocency. On entering your assembly I declared I was no subject, neither am I; but as an independent queen, I display my disapproval o' your unlawful an' unchristian proceedings by thus retiring. [*Exit.*

Cecil. The retiring, my lords and gentlemen, of the accused doth not meet fully the ends of our inquiry, except the act be taken as further evidence of guilt.

Earl of A. Should we not listen to the reading of the guilty letters in possession of the Earl of Murray?

Duke of N. My lords and gentlemen, would it not be more becoming, now that our harshness has compelled the retirement of the Scottish queen, that we do adjourn until sleep or prayers do the better frame our further inquiry.

Earl of M. I trust, me lords an' gentlemen, that you will na wyte me for this unco behavior o' me slid sister; but I winna hald back frae ye that I did fear this very skyt o' her. This mischance do stay me frae further expose, at least sae near to her presence. The mirk guilt an' het temper o' me sister wad haste to impeach this maist leal hearing.

Within this casket be letters o' fu' an' plain evidence, whilk do sae fix her guilt that naught save the sweet mercy o' heaven wad remove the awsomeness o' hersel acknown connect wi', na' anly the crime that vulgar rumor do ding her wi', but mony ithers yet mair mirk an' devilish.

Earl of A. The rules of law would forbid further proceedings, at least in form of trial, without the presence of the accused; we may adjust this matter to the end that we may make a proper report to her majesty the queen.

Duke of N. There be about this such a taint of unfairness that I no longer submit to this strain upon my better sense by further participation in your deliberations. And I crave both of my queen and you, my lords and gentlemen, that forbearance to my refusal as the honesty of my convictions doth entitle them to.

Earl of A. Your Grace, you may not withdraw thus freely without royal consent, by whose command we are convened.

Duke of N. As the accused hath withdrawn, a further hearing would be in form of council. My warrant from her majesty reads: " To attend in person the hearing and full answering of the accusations against the Queen of Scotland." As that person has retired, there is naught in my warrant that directs my further attendance.

Cecil. I do join the Duke of Norfolk, at least in part of his stand. What remains of this hearing may now be conducted, and I affirm with better propriety, in our capacity as a council.

The churlish retirement of the accused, together with the undisputed statement of the Earl of Murray, have surely determined the verdict.   There is left to us, therefore, only the drawing of the report to the queen her majesty.

If, therefore, there be no further answer, I do, by authority in me invested, declare this hearing closed; and the convening of its members will be subject to the command of the queen.   [*All rise.*

I pray you, gentlemen, that the outcome of this convening remain as a state secret until such time as it becomes public by authority of the queen her majesty.   [*Exeunt omnes.*

SCENE V.   *Room in the House of the Earl of Leicester, London.*

Enter EARL OF LEICESTER *and* SIR NICHOLAS THROGMORTON.

Lei.   That you have, my good friend, just cause for offense I do allow.   This thing of which you do complain is but a single act.

Throg.   Pardon me, my Lord, I have not so made measure of this most grevious hurt in that it be encompassed in a single act.   So long and slow hath the agony of this slight dragged itself through my mind that it hath grown into an hundred affronts.   Why, look you, my Lord: Stood I not fully accredited with her majesty the queen, and was not the path of preferment as open to me as to this man, her minister?   Did he not drag me from mine estates, and so make report to the queen that she did consent to my recall?   True, my Lord, this was but a single act, but look you to the monstrous progeny it doth bring forth. Not only am I weighted with the loss of my preferment, but so slender are my opportunities that I am even less than those who made yet smaller office in the affairs of court.   And to such depths doth this assign me that I am, of truth, afflicted in mind and estate.   And having lost good favor, you yourself, my Lord, know how steep a thing it be to gain anew that which doth grieve us in the losing.

Lei.   I would not make yet smaller your affront.   This man of whom you do complain hath worked me not a little harm, and I would count it small loss if I were to grant unto him yet more of my peace, if thereby in the end I might improve myself.

So oft hath he stood 'twixt me and my ends that I have, alas, full use for all my Christian grace to hold in check my hot resent.

Throg. Be there not some way, my Lord, whereby this lofty cock may for a little be unplumed? I like not to be sheriff-posted over much, but I have mind to make so much tempt of fortune as shall assay to curtail the power of this proud counsellor.

Lei. Have a care, have a care! In these times there are not a few who have made their bed in the tower for less proditorious speech than this.

Throg. It is not my purpose, my Lord, to make yet so careless a plan as shall bring dis-ease to the snarers and snared.

Lei. So thick is the air about the court with plots, that you will have good need for all your conceit to work hurt without being hurt. In these cold, unchristian days, every man's hand is against his brother, and there are hardly two among the council, nor yet in other offices of court, that do trust one another. So dark and travailous have these times grown, that my prayers slowly rise to God, so heavy are they with my laments of these unchristian intrigues.

Throg. I do reverence your earnest piety, my Lord, but think you not that sometimes God may make use of human instruments to work out His diviner plans?

Lei. That it is so, doth encourage me to hope that some of these monstrous wrongs may be righted by us.

Throg. Did I not hear you say, my Lord, that the Duke of Norfolk had grown not a little tender towards the Scottish queen?

Lei. Whether this be a tenderness of the heart, or a stroke of policy, I know not.

Throg. From whatever soil this weed doth spring, think you not the nursing of it will be an advantage?

Lei. How?

Throg. If his grace the Duke of Norfolk be but gently urged, and escape that hinder which would check his softness, think you not he might enter into plans with the Scot, looking to her restoration and his own elevation?

Lei. Be there need to involve the Duke of Norfolk, that we may yet reach within the council?

Throg. If the chief within the council could be wrought upon, by promises of the settlement of this vexed question of how to dispose of the Scot, and the smoothing over of other yet lesser troubles, think you not that he would look with a degree of favor upon an alliance of the duke with the Scot?

Lei. I do but half see the drift of your reach.

Throg. Well said, my Lord, for I am but half cited.

Lei. If the unsaid of your speech doth not have in it more promise of the fulfillment of our mutual wish, you might well pronounce "*finis*" now.

Throg. I pray you, my Lord, stay both your judgments and your jests, until my designs call for one, or my slips deserve the other. If I am a marplot, my Lord, let my words canvass it.

Lei. Has this scheme the merit of maturity? or be it rather the conception of the moment?

Throg. It hath well taxed my mind, my Lord, even from my first rack, and it hath bedded with me so long that it is no unproportioned thought.

Lei. And now to better nurse your unease you ask me to tie my resent with yours, and take the smart of your hurt for my cue. By my faith, you must have sucked your philosophy from stones, and lost sleep in the labor.

Throg. I do assure you, my Lord, that in my waking I have matched well the diverse bits of this which I do now unfold, and such labor have I made of it, that sleep, of truth, has been a sly visitor.

Lei. If you have lost sleep to plan, who can so much deviltry set afoot when awake, God and the angels protect him whom you do seek to encompass.

Throg. That I am not fat-brained, my Lord, my foes will oath. In mine office, as ambassador, I did learn both by listening, and my own experience, that the deepest plans had fewest details, and if you bear with me yet a little, I will so clear this affair, wherewith I would fix your attention, that it shall not miss your approval.

Lei. By listening I do not commit myself.

Throg. That you do listen, my Lord, doth give me assurance that whatever the plans be, the end aimed at is the same with us both.

Lei. I have not yet so assented.

Throg. I trust, my Lord, I do not bootlessly wait for your assent: I have afore read so much of your sweet mind, that I did make no disquiet with myself as to your consent, feeling that you, as well as I, would relish the cleaving of that power that has slighted us both.

Lei. You do plead with such earnest force, that I do hold in check my judgment to hear yet further whereof of this matter you would speak.

Throg. You have made good use of your judgment, my Lord, and I trust I offer not stale refreshment for the good entertainment of such gracious willingness. If the Duke of Norfolk, who hath already absorbed not a little of the moon in his nature, be but gently urged, he will take upon himself the full office of a knight errant, and strutting beneath the starlit cope, make such lament of the sorry plight of his lakin that he will forget both religion and realm, and so thirst for knightly tilt, to loose the bars that cruel hold the object of his fire, that he would slap his thigh and commit some such act of rashness, as would awake in her majesty the queen the force of her asperity.

Lei. But you forget that the Duke of Norfolk is not her majesty's counsellor, Sir William.

Throg. True, my Lord, but the duke be but one link in this, my chain of circumstance. Think you not, my Lord, that there be good words enough, that by cunning shaping, one might win the approval of a man or two of the council to this plighting?

Lei. You have a good head, and if you had yet more grace than cunning, you could cure more souls than Knox.

Throg. That I have not the gown, my Lord, doth not wholly check my winning men.

Lei. But how can the " man or two " of the council be sized in this affair? For they who assent to this union must not feel unfavorable to the Scot, and what favor the Scot doth have of theirs, the queen her majesty must lose, and she takes not over kindly, even the missing of a grain of favor. And if it do come

7

to her ear that there be those among her council, or even about
the court, who would attempt, by act or assent, the interest of
the Scot, they would quickly find themselves face to face with a
searching questioner.

Throg. You have approached, my Lord, the gate whereof I
have labored to throw open and make inviting the view, that
our friend Sir William may the easier enter fields, in whose
greenness he would become a conspicuous trespasser; and when,
at last, he hath strayed so far from the entrance that seemed so
pleasant a chap, and offered such good excuses for his coming, he
will be suddenly called upon to explain the object of his presence
on forbidden ground, and will become so confused that his poor
gambling would betray his loss of loyalty to her majesty the
queen. Then, while he doth strive to armor his weak slip, he will
be the more easily plucked, and by the queen reduced. Then
we, my Lord, yea! even you and I, can, in the future, when
meeting this now high cock, keep our reverence for those who
retain without abuse their lofty station.

Lei. How? My good friend, would you assay to so train the
fates that you might sweep in with one fell, cunning stroke all
at court, who, in their serving her majesty the queen, have
nicked your proud sensitive self?

Throg. Your comprehension, my Lord, of the plan is good;
but I have not laid so deep a scheme as will reach beyond our
friend, Sir William, except it break a hanger on or two, who in
their blind dancing to his dull piping, would not lose their step
even in the crash of fortune.

Lei. Think you, good friend, that if mercy be so small a part
of this your smart plan, that in the reckoning twixt God and
you, He will hold from you the full measure of that you would
turn from another?

Throg. I have not, my Lord, your prophetic sight, nor yet a
vision beyond our present need, and so only deal to overthrow
proud flesh here, that in its rank struttings has pruned without
mercy, and sullied without stent. If in this attempt to even the
digs of spite, this stiff lump be toppled, and in his trip he do
tumble a kin or two, they but receive that reward due the weak,
who too blindly claw for hire. It be my intention, my Lord, to

so present this matter to those whom we would introduce, that they shall safely land in the web before they fully catch that they have favored the project.

Lei. Think you not that there be safety in counsel? There be those even now who, from coldness, lukeness, or self-ends, could be mustered at once to encourage this fetch.

Throg. If there be such within call, my Lord, I pray you that we may dish this out to them while it be hot.

Lei. [*Rings bell. Enter* Page.] Say to my Lord Lumley that an affair of interest doth require his presence, and, if it be his good pleasure, I would he should attend us here. [*Exit Page.*

Throg. My Lord, if you have not lost sleep in this matter, you have forsooth made good use of your wake-time. My Lord Lumley has indeed good reason to join us in this move. I will remain silent, for it is more fitting that you do approach our *homme-de-bien.*

Lei. I will acquaint his lordship with the outlines of this matter, and, when you see the tide full run, you may plunge and swim with us.

Enter LORD LUMLEY.

The sun, my Lord, must have smote you full at peep o' day, for so good a smile did he grant you that you have worn it even now past mid-day. Your health is too well fixed to need asking, and your lady and goodly sprouts have so much of blessing that it were waste to wish them more.

Lum. Now, good Earl, it were poor taste to offer me this dessert on an empty stomach. That I am sent for doth of itself proclaim that you would make a communication not a little out of the ordinary, and that you do so graciously salute me, doth clinch the guess that your communication be not for public rehearsal. Good Earl, I pray you, if you have a mind to break to me that which would even temporarily disquiet my soul, that you swear to me that if I soil my hands in your office, you will sue the queen her majesty for cleansing.

Lei. My Lord, if you were not of good blood, and had not your house worn their crest, even back to Alfred, I would swear you were a gypsy.

Lum.. How so, my Lord?

Lei. Why! before I had cracked a word you did seem to smell adventure. My Lord, if you were made finder, in less than quarter year not a witch would mumble in all our queen's good land.

Lum. Your compliment, my Lord, doth of truth bewitch me, but I do fail to find its wit.

Lei. My Lord, what think you? Doth the Duke of Norfolk really love the bonny Scot, or has he allowed his mouth to run at sight of face?

Lum. Think you, my Lord, that I am sitting up o' nights making note of lover's prate?

Lei. Then you adjudge the good duke that he be a lover?

Lum. It be not so long ago that I did sigh and swear by luna that I have lost the memory of the stare that swains do wear. If his grace the Duke of Norfolk hath not for the filly Scot the lover's yuke, he hath, then, no excuse for that dreamy, far off look in his blue eyes.

Lei. So you have noted this, my Lord?

Lum. Who hath not? I trow you there be not a maid or page that meets the duke but hath smiled at his lovesick looks.

Lei. My Lord, you have been a closer watcher than I; as good even as our friend here.

Throg. Pray, my Lord, do not appeal to me in matters of this kind. It doth not become me to nose among the love affairs of court.

Lum. Not your nose, Sir Nicholas, but your eyes would fully compass this blunt affair.

Lei. I trust, gentlemen, that it be not envy that doth pepper your speech.

Lum. My Lord, less of grum in your words would clear them of the suspicion that they are prompted by the green-eyed.

Lei. Fie! gentlemen, fie! I trust we old hay-stacks need not take fire at the sheen of this Northern Siren's eyes.

Lum. Not fire so much, my Lord, as faddle.

Throg. What think you, my Lord, be there those in the council who would frown or smile if his grace the duke should prove in earnest?

Lum.   If the duke be in earnest he would make little of the frowns or smiles of the council, or yet the crown.

Lei.   Think you that he hath so stiff a neck?

Lum.   That he hath, doth the better grant me the license to announce that he be not easily blown about, unless the breeze do please him.

Lei.   You have, my Lord, so much mind of the duke's bias, pray have you mixed with it a bit of ween of the Scot's bent? Doth she lean toward his grace the duke?

Lum.   How much of melting this giglot has for the duke I know not, but I have read in rhyme of a bird, not cage-bred, that so pined for flight that it coupled with a hawk to gain its welkin.

Lei.   Think you the Scot doth put more weight on flight than on the means of gaining it? and that she would tarre the duke if thereby she might slip her present closeness?

Lum.   But, my Lord, are you not over-rating the duke's soft-ness and earnest? Or perchance, you may have lost your scor-ing in his make-up.

Throg.   Gentlemen, we may measure but poorly how much of earnestness the duke may have, but we are most concerned that he shall go blindly and swiftly, for I hold that a man who loves blindly has pawned reason.

Lum.   You have, good Sir Nicholas, I trow, all of reason on your side.

Throg.   Such reason as I have, my Lord, I do bend it to your better judgment.

Lei.   If you could hunt hares as you can claw, I would of choice ride with you a day.

Throg.   It's not the hunting, my Lord, that doth testify the profit, but the bagging.

Lum.   This game that you would bag is sly.

Throg.   I would, my Lord, that you did have a better under-standing of that whereof we have conversed.

Lei.   I will acquaint his lordship with the drift of your scheme.

Enter Page.

Page.   May it please your Lordship, a gentleman doth attend who would speak with thee privately, and as an earnest doth bid me hand you this bill.   [*Exit.*

Lei. Gentlemen, grant me your indulgence. A matter of private import demands my attention. I pray you, during my absence, look to the details. I will join you quickly.   [*Exit.*

Lum. His lordship seems strangely agitated in the reading of this note.

Throg. I think, my Lord, it was some matter of church or charity.

Lum. Of church? Pray what church doth hold so thin a creed that it may honor the Earl of Leicester with fellowship? By my word, if he hath a church the prince of darkness is the curate. Was it thus [*crosses himself*] we did for grace, under the old?

Throg. If your Lordship doth make inquiry on matters religious, I fear my answer would not enrich you. I set so small a store on all this rasping over creeds, that I scarce do know which be up and which be down. I hold that's better policy to praise the ups and parole the downs, but do both my praising and my promising with such a degree of indecision, that if the downs were up they could not swear which were praises and which were promises.

Lum. You should be Lord Chief Justice, for one so nicely balanced as you would decide a case purely upon its merits, that is, if its merits were to your liking.

Throg. I would not be Chief Justice, my Lord, but yet I would, had I a good opportunity, so cheapen justice that all might, at least, have a taste of it.

Lum. Have the earl and yourself yet brought your plan to full maturity?

Throg. I did but this hour, may it please your Lordship, enter upon its consideration.

Enter LEICESTER.

Lei. Lord Lumley will you be kind enough to lend me your presence. So thick hath this matter grown that it be necessary that I do acquaint you with that which hath been aforesaid.

[*Exeunt Leicester and Lumley.*

Enter Felango, *cautiously.*

Throg. If I mistake not, you shall have such good field for your peculiar wit, that you should win right royally the applause of your master.

Fel. If there be more cunning than my good Maëstro hath yet attempted, I shall, of truth, have need to acquire not a little freshness that I may meet fully the ends whereof he doth plan.

Throg. Have you yet clapped eyes on this trig Scot?

Fel. That I have doth give me good reason for this flutter of my heart.

Throg. Your heart! Why I have read, or have been told, that in your country the men have not hearts.

Fel. You have listened to a slanderer, for in mine own land we not only have hearts, but they sometimes break.

Throg. That such as yours do not break may be the reason for this rumor.

Fel. Thy heart must be near to thy stomach, for I have noticed that thy nature doth change in fasting and feasting.

[*Exit Felango.*

Enter Lumley *and* Leicester.

Lum. I will so identify myself with this affair that it shall be my office to see the Earl of Pembroke. It were necessary, at least it were good policy, that we do win his favor in this most delicate business.

Lei. It be understood, my Lord, that there be used only such representations as do conform to exactness. We have good need to so conduct this matter that we may not miss the favor of heaven.

Lum. If you have, my Lord, such familiarity with heaven as to command its favors in affairs of this kind, I trow you might have angels to work your croft, and bid Gabriel shie your foes, and even lend help to me in this, your bidding.

Lei. If I did make employment of angels it should be my aim to see that they had as fellow-workers such as had a prospective hope of future companionship.

Lum. Such conditions would exclude their employer, I fear.

Lei. Not angels, but men do most concern us now. Look you well, my Lord, to your agreement. I will more of this matter, when it shall yet be more happily arranged.

Lum. I do trust your better discretion that this matter come not to the ears of the queen until such time as there be necessity for it; even then, my Lord, you are to stand between any royal displeasure and myself. As your salutation was so sweet on my coming, I pray that I may use the remembrance of it to speed my parting.

Lei. Such good wishes, my Lord, as welcome did offer to your approach, have increased during your tarry, and I check not your remembrance of them, but repeat with interest for your departure their sense, adding: may heaven's best grace accompany thee.

Lum. So noble an *adieu*, my Lord, merits speedy *exit*.

[*Exit Lumley.*

Lei. The undercurrent of this matter should of need be kept within bounds. I have surfaced his lordship, and shall make such use of him as can with propriety be done without throwing down the bars of concealment necessary for the success of your enterprise.

Throg. Your prudence, my Lord, bespeaks much for success. It were well that there be not too many hands in the glove.

Lei. It, then, is understood that the duke is to be urged in his fancy, and that as many of the council as we wish to blind, not omitting our friend Sir William, are to be baited into its encouragement. Then, when we have them fully committed, we may, by accident, mind you, by accident, loose ourselves for the queen's hearing.

Throg. To the better push our plans, it be necessary that the Earl of Murray should be made a party in this dance of circumstance.

Lei. I hear at court that the Earl of Murray will soon visit her majesty the queen by invitation.

Throg. Fate and fortune have indeed tumbled our dice.

Lei. Is it then so fortunate a thing that the Earl of Murray's presence do grace this scheme?   [*Ring bell.*

Enter FELANGO.

Throg. Of grace I say not, but of policy I think it fortunate.

Lei. [*To Felango*] It be my pleasure that when it be announced that the Earl of Murray hath arrived, you do fully inform yourself of his mission, and whatever passes between him and those with whom he doth converse, acquaint me forthwith.

Fel. The details of this, Maëstro, should be arranged yet with more care.

Lei. I will make further speech with you when it be more opportune. Bethink you I am daft?

Throg. My Lord, I think it meet that I do betake me to the office of the secretary, and there smooth the way for the introduction of our train.

Lei. As you are a Christian, see to it that you do not bend unholy means to your ends, for whatsoever you do more than the license of holy writ, you shall be called upon to answer for to heaven.

Throg. I will, my Lord, so carefully mix the ingredients in this affair that there shall be no offense to heaven or hell. In my departure I do leave further audience with you at your pleasure, and the need of our mutual ends.   [*Exit.*

Lei. How now! So full of cares am I, and so loose have the ends run, that I am in danger of strangely mixing my tantles with tragedies to my expose.

Fel. I pray you, Maëstro, in the nobler affairs keep your own counsel, in the darker, trust to me.

Lei Trust to you! That I have trusted to you hath so licensed the evil within me that it hath blighted the good.

Fel. Say not so, Maëstro. There be now only such need of patience as shall dispose of your last unfortunate slip, then, make such installments of prudence as shall assure you yet longer draughts of pleasure, without the risk of expose, and all shall be well.

Lei. This be but a hoot snatch. What of the maid? Did you entice young Howard to your liking?

Fel. More to my liking than to the maid's, Maëstro. Of truth she hath such heaviness of heart, and of body too, that she doth illy take to love-making.

Lei. Fie on love! Give this young dolt, Howard, full swing of encouragement, and in his fire he will forget conscience; and so sore of plight is this wench that it be not an over hard labor to break her stiff will, and so change from me to Howard the consequence of this weak folly.

Fel. I fear me, Maëstro, that the lady doth make suspect of some such deal, and hath grown shy of the approach of men.

Lei. It were better for her were this shyness not so new a thing.

Fel. But, Maëstro, was not her shyness o'ercome by the fervor of your suit?

Lei. It doth not suit me that you should pick apart these warm affairs of my heart. I have done with this wench; she hath in her too little discretion to meet my ends, either of tool or toy.

Fel. True, Maëstro, but the results of your favor may not be longer concealed, and already the lady be so wrought upon by the fear of her situation that the lock of her judgment may be broken by the dread of her plight, and she be open to peach.

Lei. I know of no Christian way to settle this miserable affair, and to meet such emergencies as this did I make attachment of your peculiar office. If this wench will not submit to your directions, and thus avoid my expose, I pray you adopt such means as you have found expedient in your own country for the settling of these tort slips. But look you! I have a horror of blood. If this wench be so foolish as to refuse the better part, I pray you, Felango, see to it that there be a hush put upon her blab. Have I not read of how you Italians can chase away the breath of life and leave no mark of the chasing?

Fel. In matters of this kind, Maëstro, it be customary to fix the sum which shall recompense the remover in proportion to the need of the snuffing out of the removed.

Lei. O man! pounds and pence are the motives of your soul. You do prate of the cost of this thing as if it were a bag of corn [*gives him a purse*]. Here, I have no desire to know the fee I pay for this necessary hitch. Be it much or little, I pray you let me not know how 'twere done, only that it be well done.

Fel. One word more, Maëstro; Lady Sheffield did instruct me to acquaint your Lordship with the appointment for to-night.

Lei. Ah me! I had quite forgotten that. How took she the missive? When she read it did she blush as modest maidens do? or did anger hang its banner out?

Fel. You have nothing to fear, Maëstro. I have every reason to believe my lady be ripe, and that this appointment be to her liking, but I would caution that your earnestness be well assumed, for if my lady doth suspect, I fear your bird may fly and leave you empty handed.

Lei. No fear, I love a little shyness. A suit that doth end with little urging soon grows cold. Where, then, am I to attend her?

Fel. The lady did consent, Maëstro, to your trysting, and will carry in her hand a red rose.

Lei. I will match her red rose; no fear! Get you now to your employment. Mind you that there be nothing vulgar, and no outcries to endanger expose. I do abhor a scene, and you would offend heaven by over much noise.

Fel. With no more loud speech than at her coming, will be her departing, Maëstro. If this maid still persist, and think she hath not enough of your attention, she shall exchange disease for a long, long sleep; thus! thus! [*Imitates strangling.*] [*Exit Felango.*

Lei. Sleep! sleep! O thou blessed balm for tired souls, thou art God's sweetest gift to those who miss awake the fulfilling of hopes born in the enchanting folds of thy poor counterfeit. [*Exit Leicester.*

ACT III.

SCENE I. *Room in the house of the Duke of Norfolk, London.*
DUKE OF NORFOLK, BISHOP OF ROSS *and* SIR NICHOLAS
THROGMORTON *discovered.*

Duke of N. Gentlemen, so much at heart have I this matter,
that I count not any sacrifice as loss, if I may, thereby, relieve
the oppressed, or render assistance unto the queen my
mistress.

Throg. My Lord, it is to that end that I have bethought me
of this. The presence of the Scottish queen within the realm
of her majesty our mistress doth engender strife; and, as the
queen our mistress doth the more desire peace, it of right becomes her loyal subjects to so shape their acts that they may
assist their loved mistress in maintaining that sweet calm which
has so far blessed her reign.

Duke of N. So little of self have I thought, but so much of
the good of queen and realm, that I am bound to sag at nothing that will impeach disquiet, or further success to England.
I have given not a little thought and prayer to the affairs of the
queen of Scotland, and trust I do not slur my loyalty, nor invite
a question as to my devotion to my faith, if I display a desire to
succor the distressed, when, in so doing, I would strive to lift a
burden from my sovereign's heart.

Bishop of R. In so sore a plight is this poor queen of Scotland, that I do think the ends fully justify desperate means.
If the queen of England will not be softened by appeals, we,
who see the right, should not hesitate to act. In my heart I
feel that if your Grace will venture upon such troubled seas, as
are the affairs of Scotland, and give, by your alliance with the
Scottish queen, the weight of your position, and the strength
of your mind, we shall, ere long, gain that tranquility so much
prayed for by the lords and estates of that distracted realm.

Duke of N. But how think you the queen my mistress and
her ministers would judge this, my open avowal at this time?

Throg. So great a burden hath this northern queen become by her presence, that it will be no mighty task to side the ministers of the crown with this righteous move, which promises such happy delivery from unease.

Duke of N. Have you, then, Sir Nicholas, uncovered this scheme to any within the council?

Throg. That I am here, my Lord, doth testify to my authority to speak. The tenderness of this matter demands such prudent concealment as shall save all from danger of too previous a betrayal of the ends sought.   '

Duke of N. If this matter be honorable, wherein is the necessity for concealment?

Throg. Your Grace, prudence be no less a companion to honesty than it be to trickery. There be those among the council who, if this thing be too bluntly broached, would not list, but would retard the good work by a too thoughtless condemnation; yet these same persons, if carefully lured, would adopt it right heartily if it smelt of royal favor or displayed a shadow of courtly approval. Your assent, your Grace, would stamp this affair with a degree of righteousness that would prevent its over hasty rejection by those who suck policy and fatten on chance.

Bishop of R. I am powered to announce, your Grace, that if the Scottish queen be restored, and it be through your happy offer, and her restoration include her wedding with yourself, then the crown matrimonial would be a part of the fruits of this most honorable draft.

Throg. I pray you, gentlemen, let us speak lightly of the fruits, but make such happy display of our good motives as shall forestall the assaults of our enemies. That his grace should wear the Scottish crown is but right, but that the Scottish crown should appear as the motive to the act should be concealed.

Why should we run to meet the date of biting envy ? Why forestall that we would escape ? If we display the ends as selfish gain, we lop ourselves the good that heaven designed should fall to the deserving.

Duke of N. Thy words have in them the sound of diplomacy.

Of that I do not object, so long as the ends be pure and the means honorable,

Throg. I have not the heart, your Grace, to bring to you. even were I so inclined, aught that would miss your approval.

Bishop of R. I have made good canvass of this affair among those of better judgment, and I have gathered such opinions as fully bear me out in urging you to accept, your Grace, this that heaven doth seem to offer.

Duke of N. Prudence and loyalty would seem to dictate that we should acquaint the queen her majesty with this affair, and our intent.

Throg. Not so! your Grace, not so! Rather it be good prudence that we do first enlist upon our side so tall a company, that the queen's resentment will be impeached by such array of advocates that she may thereby be recomforted, and her anger turned to sweet assent.

Duke of N. The queen our mistress doth the more kindly take to any project when she be privy to its inception and mindful of its growth.

Throg. That this be so, your Grace, doth hold in all matters save this. We must not conceal from ourselves that this cast doth have in it so much of knack that they who helm it must, forsooth, be as wise as statists and soft as lovers; for the queen her majesty hath nursed not a little of that yellowness that doth gnaw womankind at large, and so palled her wit in the pout of envy that she be, alas, strangely askew in the settlement of this delicate matter.

Duke of N. If there be a misunderstanding by the queen her majesty, then there be all the more necessity that her loyal subjects do avoid an advantage that be the growth of that misunderstanding.

Throg. Far be it from me, your Grace, to favor or suggest that there be any beneath work in this matter; but anxiety doth so oppress the queen her majesty, that she has missed that calm which would assist a better settlement. As they who are sick wist not the drug they swig, but on the turn of strength bless the leech that gave it, so she'll favor those who mend her present hurt, though, if known, she might spurn the proffered balm.

Bishop of R. Would it not be a good stride, your Grace, if you were to visit the queen of Scotland, and take measure of her good pleasure in adjusting this delicate affair?

Duke of N. I had so made promise to my better judgment, and bethought me that it were meet that she be fully consulted, and our conclusions made to stand with her opinions. If there be no opposition, may not this interview be arranged quickly?

Throg. Think not, your Grace, that I have moved overmuch towards these ends without your assent, but with full trust in your good judgment, and feeling that it would not miss your approval, I have consulted his reverence, the Bishop of Ross, and the conference with the Scottish queen can be arranged at your pleasure.

Duke of N. Would it please his reverence that he first acquaint the queen with the object of my visit? There should not be that suddenness in approaching the lady as would startle her.

Bishop of R. It shall be smoothly arranged, your Grace, and the better that my heart be in it.

Throg. Yes; smoothly, your Grace, smoothly.

Duke of N. Then, gentlemen, I will stay my further movements until advised by you.

Throg. At this stage, your Grace, prudence be so fine a jewel that its lustre should not be tarnished by an over-careless betrayal of the cause of its employment. It be, therefore, better that such thoughts as you have in this matter be between you and your conscience alone. In these times one may not know whom to trust, and your seeming best friend may screw your heart's secrets to your dire disaster.

Duke of N. As you have espoused this cause, good Sir Nicholas, I do trust your advice, and shall make this matter a theme of discussion, as you advise, between myself and my God.

Bishop of R. I shall so use my office, your Grace, as shall conduce to your best purpose. Let us so counsel together that both the ends and means shall not escape the approval of God, and deserve His blessing.

Duke of N. As I must needs have a friend who shall approach the Scottish queen in my interest, I know not one among all my trusted acquaintance to whom I could, with more safety, trust the sweet office of love's embassador than to you, good Sir Nicholas. Will you, therefore, take to the Scottish queen my tender solicitude for her welfare, and obtain from her, if it be consistent with her gracious wish, and do meet with her full desire, the privilege of an interview between herself and me.

Throg. That you do trust me, your Grace, to be the messenger of so sweet and delicate an approach, would force from me, even were I coldly inclined, so quick a compliance, that my resolve would be second only to your own. Your approof, your Grace, of my friendship merits most earnest effort in your behalf; and as your kind request meets fully my most heartfelt wish, I do the more readily offer my acceptance of your honored trust. And to discharge which, I would make the good excuse of my hasty exit, to the end that we may the sooner reap the fruits of our resolve.

Duke of N. This is, indeed, a proof of sweet friendship. With no vow, save that which should be between brothers of a common blood, I do accept your willing offer to lend me the safe tend of your valued assistance.

Bishop of R. God bestow upon all the fullness of his blessing, and grant such wisdom as faithfulness shall profitably use.

[*Exeunt.*

SCENE II.　*Room in Leicester's House.*

Enter BARNEY.

Barney. Sure, 'pon my soul but master's foxy. By the sound of his words he doth mouth the prayers of saints, but in his acts he doth more than meet the devil's task. Sure, he doth have such softness in his mouth that he doth make all at court his dolts. Sure, but he's as tricky as Judas, and this I say when out of breath of prayers, yet when I hear him preach, I'd swear he's fit for bishop's stole. Ah, welladay, welladay! What with that 'Talian devil, and master's tricks, sure, God's pity needs come to any those two fly at.

Enter FELANGO.

Sure, its you, is it? By me soul I just spoke your name, or that 'o your master. Sure, the word's not cold on me lips yet.

Fel. Why man, the Earl's is not so strange a name that you need harp a slur upon it.

Barney. Sure, the devil's no earl!

Fel. Devil! [*Crosses himself.*] How dare you proclaim the imp my master? I have within my heart such words of grace as would quit his presence; my life in its every act, makes too strong a wall for Satan's bolt.

Barney. Your life! Sure, but you're a fine scholar; but your glab hath not in it the goodness that the words would bring, were they your own; for sure, you get your tip from master, and you've not his good sense in choice of hearers.

Fel. Still your tongue man, still your tongue, and keep your chatter to brawl at cook. Is Maëstro in?

Barney. Sure, it's not public that he's out, leastwise he's not posted. If he was here he'd be home, and if he was home sure he'd be in. Hark ye! from the bang in the hall I catch the clepe of his coming.

Exit BARNEY.

Fel. There are two things that the fates have denied me. I am not handsome, nor am I rich. Heaven in its dealings has scanted me, and so slim am I in luring looks that maids are shy, and I am lone in their soft company. In gold I have so missed my deserts, that were my wits as thin as is my purse, I would have good need to feel with care, and stumble with rolled up eyes, and journey with a dog.

So loosely run the Earl's accounts, and so much have I them in hand, that I am dull indeed, if I slip this chance to hedge my poverty. [*Unlocks drawer in the table.*] I think there is, or should be, here, the warrant of my search. Could I make this my own, I could laugh at Jew, and fig his envied loan. Saints, it is here! For once fortune has favored the good. [*Conceals paper.*]

Enter BARNEY.

Barney. Here yet? Sure ye stick like want. Master'll not return for hour yet.

Fel. How! Sent he message?

6

Barney. No message, but an asking.

Fel. What was the inquiry?

Barney. As master bespok' for gentlemen you need have no uneasiness.

Fel. Man you should salt your wit, and keep it.

Barney. My wit's the kind that keeps without salting. Sure if 'twas as poor as yours salt would not save it. For a wager Signor, be you wed?

Fel. No, man, but why make to me such a put?

Barney. Then wait, good friend, till you're a dad, and learn how slim your wit will be when your first brat begins asking questions.

Fel. Tell me, Barney, was Sir Nicholas Throgmorton tagging your master to-day?

Barney. Sure, do you take me for a well?

Fel. Yes, and a dry one, and as you are dry, here's the price of a pint.

Barney. Sure, you're a sly one. Pence will fetch what blab wont. Yes, Sir Nicholas was here, and he and master blustered an hour. Sure, Felango, what's this new deal the earl do scud about?

Fel. Well, as I may give it to you, and know that it'll be kept, it's this: Your maëstro, the earl, has a bit of hump left from his slight the Scottish queen did send, and so to even up the cut, he'd make her shed a tear or two. And as he has, as all good men should, the praise of time, he would make a double hitch, and in his reach for the Scot bring down a lofty councillor or two. You, Barney, even in your dullness, must have seen the fire that flew when the queen's secretary, Sir William, jammed the earl a bit,— so your maëstro, now that this northern fill-gill has dropped within his stroke, would, by one well-measured rout, bring down a queen and councillor, as payment for his hurt.

Barney. So that's it! Sure he's a will of oak and a heart of stone, and ne'er forgets. But what's the hand of Sir Nicholas doing? Is he a tool or partner?

Fel. Why he, like the earl, your maëstro, nurses a bit of

greenness, and so he the quicker strides with your Maëstro to reach the foe that sized him up.

Barney. But sure, his grace the Duke of Norfolk hath not a grievance, nor hath he grown hungry to fang a foe. Sure, he hath not an enemy within the court; and one of such goodly heart would not consent to play for another that which would meet his scorn.

Fel. You are as innocent as a hen, and as dumb as a hern. Why, man, it is because his grace the duke is a saint that he will the better dance to the piping of your maëstro.

Barney. How so? Sure, you so mix saints and sinners, that I can't tell which be sellers or which be sold.

Fel. There's where you miss your wit, man. Why, if I had ears like yours, there'd be no sound that would slip me. With such highways to your sense, you should hear the stars talking to one another.

Barney. O, come down man! come down! Sure, it's not the stars I care for, I'm yuking to know what the earl my master is fixing for his grace the duke.

Fel. Well, this is it. The duke stands high at court. His faith is sound, and his loyalty to the queen bound, so that he may move even at a cross without suspect; and as he hath already shown some softness for the Scottish queen, the earl your maëstro thinks him well that he may be easily led, and if he be, and should avow and sue for favor with the Scot, and so entangle himself in love's silken net as to forget for a little loyalty, he would thereby draw the queen's resent. But to hold this off for a season, your maëstro will seek, with Sir Nicholas' ready help, to gain a member or so of the council in this plan, by pleading the stress of the queen, and the shifting of the burden from the shoulders of her majesty to the heart of the duke. It is his reach to slip the secretary, Sir William, in, and then, when he has fully consented, with others, to the alliance of the Scottish queen with the duke, he will betray all to her majesty the queen his mistress as if by accident. Then, slipping to cove himself, will smile when those who followed his tole, receive the smart of the queen's hot tongue. And 'tis his hope, based on the success of other schemes, that such a flood of wrath

shall flow, as shall sweep Sir William, with a hanger on or two,
smooth out the council chamber. And then, when like drown-
ing rats they trail to shore, he'll draw so much of vulgar gaze
to their sorry plight, that they shall lose all fitness for future
greatness. And in the tumble of these lords the Scottish queen
will get her dim; for the queen, to make good prevent of other
haps will quickly lop her head, and so the earl your maëstro
will by this stroke meet the sweetness of his wait.

[Bell heard without.

Barney. May the good Lord protect us! Sure, but master
has a head! Holy mother, but he's a sly one. But I believe that's
his ring.   [*Exit.*

Fel. Measure for measure; man for man. I, too, think the
earl a sly one.

Enter LEICESTER.

Good Maëstro, I have waited with some impatience your coming, because of the importance of the hour.

Lei. I have dreaded with some impatience your presence.

Fel. The gods, Maëstro, must have winged my coming.

Lei. Not the gods, but plainly your own interest. But
enough of " I. " Hark you, there be urgent need for your immediate presence in the vicinity of the Scot. First then, convey
to the Duke of Norfolk the full assurance of my friendship, and
say to him that I have counseled well to the furtherance of his
interests. Say, also, that I have so approached the queen with
the import of his desire, that I have partly opened the way for
its easy fulfilling. Say, also, to the Scottish queen, that the
queen my mistress may not look with disfavor upon this new
turn, and force home to her the largeness of my interest in her
affairs; but in the playing of your tongue forget not the use of
your eyes, and so keep your ears in readiness that they may
prompt your lips to rehearse to me the fullness of all that hath
transpired of interest in this matter.

Fel. Shall I go at once, Maëstro? How of the other matter?

Lei. Yes, at once; and of the other matter make abeyance.
This most needs the earnestness of our immediate intent.
Here's the needful pass. Show it, but do not deliver it up. On

your return, if you find me not here, send to me the import of your errand, if it be important.   [*Exit Felango.*

O words, O words! how many meanings have thy uses. That which to friend doth assure him joy, doth, without change, in an enemy's ears, shape offense. The " hallowed be " and " amen " of our prayers we oft warp to basest ends. If it thus be gain to so distort the weight of speech, he is best, at least outwardly, whose stock of words doth make the greater show; and knave may distance churchmen in the race, if he but have an oily tongue and smiling face.   [*Exit Leicester.*

SCENE III. *Room in Bolton Castle.*

Enter QUEEN MARY *and* BISHOP OF ROSS.

Bishop of R. May it please your most gracious Majesty, I am of truth pleased if my coming hath brought you pleasure.

Q. Mary. Your Reverence doth, indeed, by your presence and your holy words confer sweetest pleasure. So dully doth time drag, and so poorly decked is it with joy, that I am sadly off with this great lack of earth's poor joys. But your good and comforting words of cheer, your Reverence, stayed as they are by your words of tender piety, bring to me a sweetness long a stranger to my days of captivity.

Bishop of R. May it please your Majesty, as I may not prolong this interview, I would come at once at the fullness of my mission.

Q. Mary. I do the more cheerfully hear you, your Reverence, for the assurance of your holy office doth give me the knowledge that your offer of counsel shall not have in it other than that meant for my peace. I know and feel that you, your Reverence, can not bring me harm.

Bishop of R. Not harm, your Majesty, but balm I would offer you. Your friends, while they may not cast down, as yet, the walls that so cruelly hold you, are still mindful of your distress, and, in their prayers, they petition heaven for your speedy delivery. And, as if in answer to their supplications, there has arisen within the souls of your best and most tried friends a hearty desire to see you bettered. His grace the noble Duke of Norfolk, of good report and most elegant mien, hath joined your

friends with such earnestness that he hath bethought him most
prayerfully how he may best work for your Majesty's comfort
and peace.

Q. Mary.   His grace the Duke of Norfolk is, indeed, of most
noble blood, and, already, I have within my heart a strange
interest that he should think well of me.

Bishop of R.   Your Majesty, it be, forsooth, a happy turn that
you have this sweet interest in your heart, for it is his deep
concern in your affairs that has so warmed his heart.

Q. Mary.   Your Reverence, do you plead as an ambassador
from Cupid?   If this be the weight of your mission, think you
not that so tender a dint would fall with more softness, and be
more to the liking, if it were delivered alone by the heart that
prompted it?

Bishop of R.   Your Majesty, happy indeed would his grace
the duke feel, if he might be privileged to betray himself to so
sweet a listener.

Q. Mary.   One may not offer, your Reverence, except where
the proffer seems desired by act of the intended recipient.

Bishop of R.   Far be it, your Majesty, from me to attempt
the role of negotiator in matters where the heart is concerned.
But as in nature the grateful summer showers are oft forerun
by gusts of boisterous wind, so I, by my rude bluster, would but
herald the approach of a gentler shower of words from one
whom you have met before, but in the meeting had not tilt with
lover's lance, but fair and square in fortune's field, fought out
the fight of right and wrong.

Q. Mary.   Your Reverence, I am poor at spae.   Pray tell me
whom did I tilt with that shall now again measure lance with
me?

Bishop of R.   He whom I would summon, and who doth attend without, is one who, in fortune's turn hath lost his gilt, and
in the losing laid down his bond to claims of other days; and
now that he no longer serves a creature powered by wrong, he
hath renewed his honorableness, and so joined himself to your
friends; and as one still trusted in a measure by your foes, he
would audience with your Majesty, that he may bespeak the
good intentions of the honorable Duke of Norfolk.   From your

past experience, not knowing the salutations now borne to you by this, your new friend, you would ne'er call his name, save in dread. And did I not tell you that your distress hath softened even the hardest heretofore against you, you would " Oh! " when I tell you that without waits the past ambassador of the queen, your afore tormentor, Sir Nicholas Throgmorton.

Q. Mary. That man! Save it were your words, your Reverence, that gave me this information, it would pall me to know of his nearness.

Bishop of R. Your Majesty, that your distress hath won so stiff a man, doth exhibit how much the spread of this injustice against you hath worked within the hearts of all. This, your past adversary, would now siege your heart, and he doth bear on his lips the full desires of his grace the Duke of Norfolk, touching his interest in your affairs.

The sudden turning of your fortunes, and the falling away of men whom you had esteemed as friends, has taught me prudence. With the ding of bitter lessons, as a prompt to safety, I did listen to the approaches of Sir Nicholas. Of his grace the Duke of Norfolk I had little doubt, and less fear, for our good faith doth run in not a few of his clan. So, when Sir Nicholas did acquaint me with his mission, as speaker for the duke, I did but canvass his words, as was proper; and when they made no offense, either by the message they brought, or the manner of it, I did, by much labor, secure permission for his entrance into your presence, and now but need your royal sanction, and the evidence of your pleasure, to bid him break to you, as he can better do than I, that whereof hath met the approval of your friends, and hath from my heart the earnest of my prayers.

Q. Mary. If this agent doth bring, your Reverence, the hope of peace, and doth offer the succor of friends, I will, of truth, hear him; for so hungry is my soul for a bettering of my fortunes, that I would welcome any who might proffer to me a grain of hope. Bid this, then, your friend and my friend enter, and God grant that his message shall be the prelude of happier days.

Bishop of R. Your Majesty, before we hear this embassy

from his grace the duke, may we not learn what cheer our agent, Stephens, may have; for, by the providence of God, he hath safely passed all suspicion, and is now with us again. Will your Majesty hear him?

Q. Mary. Of truth, I will most gladly hear this, our faithful friend. God grant he bring me sweet cheer.

Bishop of R. Will your Majesty summon an attendant?

[*Mary blows a whistle.*

Enter Page.

Say to the first gentleman in the ante-room that her majesty awaits his presence. This your agent, your Majesty, has with much peril despatched your commands.   [*Exit Page.*

Enter STEPHENS.

Ah! Good friend, I bid you welcome, and as your presence doth bespeak the arrival of messages from friends, I can the more readily bid you salute her majesty the queen.

Steph. Most gracious Majesty, I read in your face an earnest longing for pleasant greeting. I would to God that such of merit as I bring were increased a thousand fold.

Q. Mary. I do bid you welcome, and as you are but a bearer of news, not a maker, I receive with grace your proffered offer, and your sweet wish. My heart has hushed its long-delayed hope of great fortune fast arriving, and so content am I with heaven's dealings that I do make even my small comforts a thanksgiving.

Bishop of R. Do you bring despatches?

Steph. Only such, your Reverence, as I may deliver by word of mouth. The heartless barbarity of your keepers, your Majesty, forbid my delivering such despatches as I had. Your Reverence, are we without listeners, save ourselves?

Bishop of R. In this room, yes.

Q. Mary. I know not what life these walls may have, nor what eyes do look upon us unbidden. I know but this, that from my long detention, and the strictness of the watch, I have learned caution. Whatsoever communication you have to make, let it not be over loud, for, if there be ears other than our own, they belong to those who have not kindly tongues, and they might, should their reasons demand it, so twist even the innocent babblings of a babe that in its rehearsal it would be treason.

Bishop of R. Has word been returned from His Holiness the Pope? What message sent the King of Spain?

Steph. We have from the Holy Father, your Reverence, first his blessing on our undertaking, and the full assurance that when once the blow has been struck he will render substantial assistance. The King of Spain may not openly send arms, but he gladly bears the expense of an hundred agents, and he but waits your sanction, your Majesty, to despatch a goodly number of trusty men at once.

Q. Mary. The fullness of the plan, your Reverence, hath not as yet been detailed to me. I do trust mine advisers, and only ask that this affair shall be so conducted as to avoid slaughter.

Bishop of R. Your Majesty, your friends who have planned this enterprise have first consulted, with deep reverence, your own immediate interests, knowing full well that in return of your better fortune, the church shall receive that recognition which it merits from your Royal Highness. It is our purpose to so interest the lords and estates within this realm, who still maintain their loyalty to the true church, that they shall see that in your liberty and rightful acknowledgment their interests will be improved. There be not a few, your Majesty, even among those who seem to accept the new order, that would, should your cause make a formidable showing, attach themselves to your interests. Among these we may first claim his grace the Duke of Norfolk. He hath afore manifested deep concern in your welfare, and hath gained for himself not a little of the queen's displeasure, because of his honorableness in dealing with your Majesty's case.

Q. Mary. His grace the Duke of Norfolk is indeed of gentle blood, and of such kindly thoughts, and so mildly mannered, that I do feel encouraged to hear you proclaim that such as he do openly defend me.

Bishop of R. Not only openly defend you, your Majesty, but yet more deeply doth he speak of yourself and your affairs.

Steph. The burden of my message, your Majesty, be not foreign, but doth partake of matters relating more nearly to the Duke of Norfolk and his interest in your Majesty.

Q. Mary. I will hear you, and as you have promised that your message contained a little cheer, I do trust that you are to make disclosure of that whereof I had hoped.

Steph. Let me say first, your Majesty, that in the North countries, around about my Lord Northumberland, there be many who have banded themselves together in your interest, and but wait a favorable moment to strike the blow that shall restore you to liberty and your throne. And hereabouts there are those who do meet secretly, and are so strongly bolstered by your friends in France, that they do even now labor to restrain their spirit, and but need to receive the promised help from the North to lead them to make the move that shall restore you. From long closeting, and after much counsel, your friends have decided that it were better that you do hold convent with the Duke of Norfolk. I am assured that he has not only healthy plans for your betterment, but he has also the means for executing them. In proof of this, I have but to crave of your Majesty permission to introduce a gentleman, who in this matter acts as his agent, and who waits without subject to your pleasure.

Q. Mary. Your Reverence, is it meet that I do receive this gentleman?

Bishop of R. Such, your Majesty, is the better thought of your friends.

Q. Mary. As I have trusted my friends thus far, I may not endanger myself by a further exhibition of confidence. Doth this gentleman await within summons?

Steph. Your Majesty, he doth but tarry without the door.

[*The queen blows whistle.*

Enter Page.

Bishop of R. Say to the gentleman who doth await, that it is her majesty's pleasure that he do enter.

Q. Mary. Your Reverence, if I do exhibit a lack of quickness in meeting the speech of Sir Nicholas, I pray you make not too great a note of it, for so oft have we rode at arms, and so freely have we struck, that I may, from force of habit, so exhibit my guard that in our first round we may seem more like knights with prize in sight than friends who would seek a conference of loving proffer.

Enter THROGMORTON.

Throg. Most gracious Majesty, I had it on my lips to salute you by proffering lamentations for your sad plight, but the sweetness of your face and the royalty of your grace do disarm all small pity, and loudly call for the full marshaling of friendly homage, and earnest reverence for this your exhibition of noble comity. True royalty may not be dethroned; and while misfortune may for a time encompass honest worth with distress, the divinity of truth and the providence of God shall vouchsafe the happy delivery of one so deserving, who is the embodiment of royal worth.

Q. Mary. Your words, good Sir Nicholas, have in them a far different tout than had they when last we met. I may not question your honesty now, if the remembrance of your aforetime coldness will but continue its march into the dim distance of friendly forgetfulness. As you are introduced by friends, you are a friend; and as such I give you the full welcome of mine heart, and such cheer as the narrowness of mine accommodations affords.

Throg. In behalf of him for whom I would well wish that I might more elegantly say, I accept the proffer of your welcome; for myself, I do count this as a golden hour, for it be the preface of my earnest to undo the coldness of the past between us two.

Q. Mary. As you did act but as an agent, I will not remember you as having of your own accord sought to work me harm. And as the past bore me but little profit, I fear we shall find it still less of gain to dig among the ashes of dead hopes and buried joys. Let us rather bravely meet the present, trusting that the lessons of the past shall the better fit us to advantage whatever of blessings be in store for us.

Throg. Your Majesty, your long imprisonment hath not robbed you of happy speech, and your wit doth seem to grow with your days of sorrow. You have reached at one spang the very center of the matter wherewith I am commissioned; and, as I am limited in my stay, and, also, that I am blunt of manner, and know not the softer forms of cunning, I would deliver myself plainly, and seeking to avoid offense, hold to such closeness of directions as will save me from the missing of anything of importance.

Q. Mary. Your approach, good Sir Nicholas, hath been so announced that you are well saved much bush-beating, and press of time can well excuse good plainness.

Throg. This, then, your Majesty, is the matter I have in hand. His grace the Duke of Norfolk, of whose interest you are no stranger, has, by the advice of friends, and his own inclination, commissioned me to crave of your Majesty the gracious privilege of an interview. And this he does the more boldly ask in that he has afore conferred with your friends, among whom stands first your most trusted embassador, his reverence the Bishop of Ross. I may not enter into the details, your Majesty, or even shadow the import of the designs and ends of his grace the duke. These have been so freely discussed among your friends, and you have been kept so well informed, that, mayhap, you have this matter better in hand even than I. My office only includes the soliciting of your approval to the interview. When this I do happily possess, and the naming of a suitable day, at the pleasure of your Majesty, I may well consider the success of my mission as having been abundant.

Q. Mary. Your Reverence, hath this matter been concluded between the friends? And be there no overreaching of propriety in my granting this reasonable request of his grace the Duke of Norfolk?

Bishop of R. The matter, your Majesty, hath been fully discussed, and the conclusions fully meet the desires expressed by Sir Nicholas.

Q. Mary. That I may exhibit my confidence in my friends, and display my trust in his grace the Duke of Norfolk, knowing full well that one of such gentle blood and noble Christian spirit must bring me great sweetness, and much peace, by consenting to interest himself in my poor affairs, I, therefore, fully second the advice of my friends, and freely grant the noble duke this interview, and leave to you, as his agent and friend, such arrangements as are necessary to meet the designs. This I do without exacting a pledge, believing fully that one of such

Christian nobility as his grace the duke, would scorn a selfish advantage, and refuse an unfair deal.

Throg. This, indeed, fully meets the expectation of your friends, and the hopes of his grace the Duke of Norfolk. And now, that I may not awake suspicion that shall cloud this happy·issue, I would crave, your Majesty, your sweet indulgence for my speedy departure, to the end that I may bear quickly your gracious consent to the anxious duke.

Q. Mary. I do, indeed, grant you your withdrawal, and praise your faithfulness. Say to his grace the Duke of Norfolk, that I do send my heart's best wish for his good welfare, and bid him accept the assurance of my poor prayers.

Throg. Your Majesty, that I may not disturb your hallowed wishes, I would, in going, crave that you do remember me, not as of old, but as your friend.   [*Exit Throgmorton.*

Q. Mary. God grant that this move hath in store for me a promise of brighter days.

Bishop of R. God give to thee the fullness of thy hope. Your Majesty, may we not now prepare the reply to the messages?   [*Exeunt.*

SCENE IV.   *Audience Room in Richmond House, London.*

Enter Queen Elizabeth, Lady Knollys, Lady Sheffield, Lady Francis Howard, *and* Countess of Nottingham.

Q. Eliz. Your good words do set me so fine a note that I am more than half inclined to humor you silly bilkers.

Countess of N. May it please your Majesty, of this suit I have, in your interest, made earnest canvass.

Q. Eliz. If you have made yourself over busy with this my affair, you have jarred that which should have run with sweet glabrity.

Countess of N. Only so far, your Majesty, have I spoken in this your cause, as would give me audience with your own court.

Q. Eliz. My own court have not all of them such an overburden of prudence as would give them the full liberty of my affairs, and more especially in *affaires d'amour.*

Lady Shef. I pray, your Majesty, make unto us a yet more open avowal of the duke's pleading; it hath in it so much that doth awake the tenderest depths of our souls, that we yearn for more; and envy of your lot is but checked in us by the remembrance of the royalty of the lover.

Q. Eliz. These French do most bewitching exhibit their tenderness. The royal duke of Anjou doth, indeed, most stoutly display his passion; for, such words, such stringing together of tender phrases do well nigh shake my resolve.

I do acknowledge my trust in you, that I do permit this taste, and mind you, but a taste, of French *delices.*   [*Reads.*

" *Your Most Gracious and Grandly Beautiful Majesty. So long hath my heart made its hopeless siege, that the army of my blood is well nigh stricken with the poverty of waiting. Lulling sleep hath forsaken my eyes, and I am become as one stricken. My days are so filled with the longing of my soul, and the necessity of thy presence, that I have forgotten the changes of day and night, and night and day.*

" *In thinking of thee I am drowned in a sweet sea of expectancy. O, make to me some signal that shall bridge the space between us; for so rebellious hath my heart become with the restraint of its unsatisfied longings, that it will turn and devour itself if it cannot, in thy dear presence, plead its loving cause.*"

There, I will read no more; such as this is not for you. You two have had your tastes of sweets, and now are far too dry to relish this, only as a bit of gossip. Mind you now, I have made such a show of this affair as doth but poorly display how far the honorable duke hath prospered in his suit. There be in this, I have read, nothing that doth betray how great a breach the duke hath made in the citadel of my heart.

Lady Shef. Your Majesty hath left us so unsatisfied that we have, indeed, good need to re-collect some stray straws of lover's gleanings in other days, to fill the space we did make for a yet fuller hearing of the duke's most tender and loving avowal.

Q. Eliz. You have no need, my lady, to go back into your tender years to search for straws of love; for so careless have you been in your recent gleaning, that not alone the straws of your stolen sweets do betray you, but the field of your garnering hath been so near, and so thoughtless have the reapers been, that they have dropped a straw or two, and so exposed their over-burden of stolen sweets.

Lady Shef. I fear, your Majesty, that poisoned scandal, disguised as harmless gossip, hath prattled to you over much.

Q. Eliz. Not over much, but to your liking over plain.

Lady Shef. I pray, your Majesty, that your allusions be yet the better plained, to the end that, if I recognize any grain of truth that be mixed with this chaff of falsehood, I may so testify, that I be not in danger of losing your Majesty's esteem.

Q. Eliz. [*To Lady Howard.*] Go you, my dears, to the ante-room, and there arrange my frame; and at my call have it brought hither.

[*All exeunt but Lady Sheffield.*

That we have brought this matter to such a degree of understanding that I can the further exhibit my mind, doth, indeed, occur most fortunate. It is my fast intent to so frame my words that the meat of them shall be food for your consideration.

Lady Shef. I pray, your Majesty ——

Q. Eliz. Save your prayers, that they may the better console your awakened reflections.

Lady Shef. How? am I to offer no explanations?

Q. Eliz. Explanations when demanded, excuses none!

Lady Shef. Such excuses as I have ——

Q. Eliz. You may keep to prop your own lamentings. It is my pleasure that you do hear me out, and vouchsafe only such replies as answer my intimations. It hath not escaped my notice, nor yet duller eyes at court, that you have often so far forgotten your station and surroundings as to not only permit, but encourage, the amorous advances of the Earl of Leicester. The surfacing of your guilty blood doth prove my accusations, and your eyes do yet more plainly speak the truth in your shame's language. Much hath been repeated to me that I have credited to idle gossip, but what mine own eyes have seen I must perforce believe. Look you, as you and the earl, in company with others, did quit my presence yesternight, think you my eyes failed in their office, or that my senses deceived me, when I not only saw the earl's tender looks, but the guilty answering of your own over-ready passion?

Lady Shef. But, your Majesty, have I control ——

Q. Eliz. Of your own person, yes; because you do admire your rounded neck, and do waste your hours in training for a more amorous expose of your acquired charms, think you that thereby the Earl of Leicester hath privileges which should belong alone to thy wedded lord?

Lady Shef. But, your Majesty, I have no lord, being widowed.

Q. Eliz. That doth but the better assert your need to yet even more modesty. Think you that you can toy with this vain man, and yet escape a greater hurt? See to it! If you do not make the earl a stranger to your flame, I shall so snuff out your light that you shall have need to seek in other fields a lover less near the court. [*Rings a bell.*

Enter Page.

[*To Page.*] Conduct Lady Sheffield to the salon.

[*Exeunt Page and Lady Sheffield.*

[*Taking out the letter from her bosom.*] O, words that warm my heart, O, lines that answer the longings of my soul, come, dew my eyes again with thy loving breath. O, realm, O, crown, O, power and pomp, all your incertain grandeur have not in them the sweet content for woman's heart as have these words, if they be true.

Queen, thou art swallowed up in that yet sweeter word — " wife; " and king, thou dost shrink to naught beside the tenderness of that other name, sweeter still, " husband." I look about me and see, within my beck and call, that for which the world doth strive, and seek to gain, and in the gaining count it prize; and yet the weight of this, and all the power and might of this royal station would I glad exchange for one true, faithful, honest, loving heart to call my own. These who dance in mockery about my throne, and bow and cringe with borrowed reverence, do small favor to my better self.

He who to-day doth pawn his soul to gain royal favor, would, to-morrow, barter away that favor that he might gain the smile of some new face, even if in his gain he encompass me with

harm. Who have I, that with unselfishness loves me? They
whose ends I meet, and whose plans I urge with friendly zeal,
do lend me but the semblance of love; and so thin a thing is it,
that the mere approach of disaster doth shatter the sentiment,
born but to deceive.

O, earth; in thy busy round be there not some place where
mortals do remember something of their god-like nature? and
keep sweet and pure the peace of heaven's love? O, that there
were some clime where deception had not tainted all, and where
the eye in its answering look would speak alone the truth.
[*Puts letter into her bosom.*] Thou herald of what should be
true, nestle close within my heart. If fate doth rob me of a
fuller knowledge of thy better essence, heaven grant that naught
may transpire to mar the remembrance of my more charitable
thought, that he hath writ the truth.

But what matter if this boy doth or doth not love? Have I
not here at my very feet a lover yet more tender? I do let this
French boy prattle, for his lines do prank an idle hour, and by
my show of interest I bind the eyes of envy, and still the speech
of scandal. But my heart is afire with an unholy anger that
doth eat away my ease.   [*Rings bell.*

Enter Page.

Say to my Lord Leicester that I do desire his presence.
[*Exit Page.*
O, God! calm my aching heart and troubled mind.

Enter Leicester.

Lei. Your Majesty, I attend upon your gracious pleasure.
Make to me a command for proof.

Q. Eliz. My Lord, see you not in my eyes the throbs of my
breaking heart? This play at words between us doth sorely
hurt. Your soft parry doth but increase the smart. [*Taking
his hand.*] O, my Lord, this poor seeming hath in it but the
shadow of satisfaction. I pray you, throw off this pomp of
court, and give me that for which I long, the realness of your
honest self.

Lei. Your Majesty, the affairs of state require such earnest
thought that I do lament the need of this poor seeming. If

your words to me do grieve your heart, how think you they rest within my bruised soul.

Q. Eliz. You are yourself, my Lord, not so much to be pitied for this hurt to your heart, for it is common gossip at court that the Earl of Leicester doth wear his heart upon his sleeve, so it is ever within easy reach of hurt.

Lei. If it be true, your Majesty, that my heart be upon my sleeve, it hath but crept from its hiding place that it may the nearer be to thy dear self.

Q. Eliz. O, good Earl, if your words were as true as they sound, I would well change my throne for a continuance of thy companionship; but, true or false, they be indeed, such words as the good and true do use, and so I make of them the most their sound doth imply. But tell me, within the hour have not other ears than mine heard this same speech?

Lei. I pray your Majesty, make no jest of this, my most earnest thought. Have I not made proof of the full strength of this, my interest?

Q. Eliz. O, that mine ears were deaf to other words than these. So sweet is this your avowal, that I could well wish no harsher news had offered. I would, indeed, prolong this span and crave repeating of your tender speech, but so loudly doth the clamor of gossip assail my sense, that I would do violence to judgment did I keep back the exhibit of the report borne to me.

Lei. How oft, your Majesty, shall I cleanse your mind from rude slander and false report. If the envious do so offend as to salute your ears with base untruths, your patient listening doth but encourage the sin.

Q. Eliz. Nay, not alone what I hear doth hurt, but what mine eyes have seen doth grieve me most.

Lei. Seen! pray who hath bewitched thine eyes?

Q. Eliz. Nay, rather, who hath bewitched your heart?

Lei. The answer to your question, your Majesty, doth leave mine unanswered; but as your wish is a command, I can but say I am bewitched of thee.

Q. Eliz. O, fool that I am, to maw this cloyless sweet that must ere long prove bitter. But no, I will unburden. So long hath this sting made pain in my heart that it hath winged to my

lips this my right protest. Look you! seek not to soften, either
by words, of however sweet a sound, nor yet by leaking eyes,
the full weight of my accuse.

Lei. I pray, your Majesty, let not the foulness of this slander
so heat your words as to urge the sweetness of your soul into
use of words that to-morrow may bring regretfulness; rather let
me thus [*puts his arm around her*] assure you of my willingness
to faithfully do your bidding, and show how much I am your
slave.

Q. Eliz. Slave! nay I am the slave. Slave to this poor weak
heart of mine, which, in its sickening thirst for forbidden love,
doth assume a weakness that doth unfit my soul for the sterner
tasks of my exalted station.

Lei. Not so, your Majesty, not so; your crown doth exhibit
your royalty; but this glimpse of your true woman's heart doth
show more of greatness than all the pomp of throne.

Q. Eliz. O, you do half tempt me to be what this poor weakness doth prompt. But no, if I forget all that hath within my
presence been broached, I still have the evidence of mine own
eyes, which, alas, your soft words cannot blind.

Lei. I pray, your Majesty, what be this thing that hath so
offended, that even soft appeal when forced by truth and can-
dor's might doth yet so sore perplex you?

Q. Eliz. Look you, yesternight be not so far away that you
have need to tax your memory o'er much to recall that it was in
this very room, at close of hour, you did escort my Lady
Sheffield from out my presence. Think you my eyes have
grown so weak that they see not beyond the draperies of yon
door?

Lei. I pray, your Majesty, let not the uncertainties of shadows,
and the mistake in person so bewilder your recollection as to
make accuse of so simple a thing as my retiring in the company
of Lady Sheffield.

Q. Eliz. Not so much in the retiring, my Lord, as the manner
of it.

Lei. How?

Q. Eliz. Gallantry, my Lord, doth in this court meet my

hearty approval, but there be bounds which even a knight must not pass.

Lei. If I have without intention ——

Q. Eliz. Not without intention, but it is the with intention that doth grieve me. But O, my Lord, make no further parley. I saw your soft caress, and read that look within your eyes, which I was fool enough to think I alone could well. Had another disturbed me from my dream, the awakening would have had in it so much of doubt, that I might yet have had a grain of pleasure left; but this rude awakening evidence of mine own eyes, robs me of the kind shift that doubt might have brought, and forces the cruel iron into my very soul.

Lei. The evidence even of queenly eyes, when dimmed by tears, may not always be such as would meet full approval in more sober moments.

Q. Eliz. Your acts, while yet in sight, did but hint the broader scope of your intent when in the field of fuller liberties.

Lei. This is my field, and you are the giver of my opportunities. I have no longing for other fields, nor lament the absence of more golden opportunities, save that the decrees of fate do so much keep me from thy side. I feel the loss that you are so much by cares of realm engrossed that I must at a distance gaze and worship the object of my heart.

Q. Eliz. O, poor, weak woman! and I the weakest of them all. O, what hunger hath my soul that it doth feast on these poor, stale crumbs?

Lei. Not so, your Majesty, not so! These are the virgin fruits of this my heart. I pray you no longer strive with your better self. See [*puts his arm about her*], you are not weak; for in my pride I have oft dubbed myself as strong, yet I no greater exhibit make of my manly strength than this — the surrender of my heart and soul to thee.

Q. Eliz. I know not the terms that men at arms do use when they surrender all, but here, if this my speech be poor, it be not because it lacketh truth. By this act I make forget of hurt and harm of yesternight. I would not longer have you make denial, for in the denial you must needs repeat the act, and so ear again my soul; rather let me as a queen forget, but as a hungry-hearted woman feast on your soft words.

Lei.   Thou art now, indeed, your Majesty, more a queen than ever; and of all your willing, faithful subjects write me down as first and truest.   Now that sweeter, better thoughts do troop within your kindly heart, pray lend me a moment of this bliss that I may forge it into a shield for your own protection.   Know you not this Scot, that doth so trouble your ease and threaten the safety of your realm, should be more carefully housed?

Q. Eliz.   How so?   Are not the walls of Bolton Castle strong enough?

Lei.   Not their strength, your Majesty, doth give concern, but rather the easy ope of the gate, and the too free admittance of meddlesome herds.

Q. Eliz.   This Scot be so well guarded, at least such has been my command, that none may approach her save such as be loyal to ourselves.

Lei.   I would not add, your Majesty, to your weight of cares, yet I should doubt mine own loyalty did I seek to hide the need of closer watch.

Q. Eliz.   Such as are about this person are fully trusted.   If there be those who from curiosity, or yet baser motives, seek audience, they have not the means to do more than stain their own names by semblance of disobedience, and bending to sentiments of weakness.

Lei.   I make no question, your Majesty, of their weakness, and my testimony will bear witness to the fact that there be both weak and wicked persons who do visit the Scot.

Q. Eliz.   I am not ignorant of the fact that there be those who seek to use this wily Scot, that they may better their own advancement; but I hold that their plans have in them so little promise, that the striving for their fulfillment will but expose their weakness.

Lei.   Your Majesty has presumed to make full trust of the loyalty of those who may seek the presence of this your unwelcome visitor.   I pray you, think me not over harsh, or so tempered with suspicion as to misjudge those whom you have trusted.   Loyalty, your Majesty, hath in these days become so

strangely mixed with selfishness, that he judges himself most
loyal who is most mindful of his own interests. As an evidence
of my concern in the adjusting of this affair to your betterment,
I would ask the confidence of your attention.

Howbeit, there are those who are not of the faith even, nor
yet of the country, as is this Scot, and those, too, who have so
loudly proclaimed their loyalty that they are conspicuous in the
assemblies, as steadfast to your cause, who have yet so interested themselves in the affairs of this woman that honest men
have attributed their motives either to overzeal or to bewilderment, induced by such desires as influence the baser sort, when
brought in contact with dependent beauty in distress.

Q. Eliz. I pray you, why so loudly proclaim this weak thing
as a queenly beauty? Have you, too, had your head turned
by those dimpled cheeks, which, alas! but mask so deceitful a
heart? If you have no better name than beauty in which to
pronounce your reference to my thorn, I pray you make yet
further search within your store of words; forgetting for once
this vulgar craze that seeks to use in public mind, this poor
geck from the north, and give to me a meaning less fraught with
hurt than this you do so glibly fling.

Lei. I did but use the term, your Majesty, the better to
install your good sense with that wherewith, at least some of
thy courtiers, have caught moon-blindness.

Q. Eliz. What say you, of truth, hath this weak gadder
inflamed the hearts of England's stouter sons? I pray you, if
there be those who have bartered loyalty and right for smile of
deceit, make me acquaint with names and estates, that I may
with righteous visitation call back their better blood, that it
may flow again within the channel of loyalty.

Lei. My observation, your Majesty, hath, as yet, but
noticed feverish symptoms of weakly heat, not enough to warrant measures over strong, but yet sufficient to prompt caution.
I beseech your Majesty, that you do so far trust my discretion
as to grant me permission to so broaden my watch as to include
all within my suspect.

Q. Eliz. My Lord, give me the full depth of thine eye, nor
seek to hold back reflections of your heart. Answer me truly,

are not these words of yours such as the envious would make use of?

Lei. Your Majesty, if I have presumed too far in your interest, I will recall my suspicions, and so harbor my forces that they may protect my interests alone.

Q. Eliz. The words of your tame resentment to less trained ears might indeed force reproach upon my shadowed suspicion.

Lei. That I may no longer burden you with the care of watching a volunteer watcher, I will, by your leave, take discharge of this matter.

Q. Eliz. My Lord, by what means came you to the knowledge that helps your suspicions?

Lei. By this, your Majesty, am I to comprehend approval of my course?

Q. Eliz. Your term is too broad to meet sanction, without further explanation.

Lei. If I have incurred royal displeasure by so slight advances, I fear that greater hurt might follow yet deeper avowals.

Q. Eliz. I pray you, my Lord, make no further scatter, but so point your words that I may see their meaning with less waste of time.

Lei. I do admit, your Majesty, that as yet the shape of my suspicions doth lack definement, and, except in my own uneasiness, they have not so proportioned themselves as upon full statement to appear what my introduction would imply. But this with safety I may launch, and I crave your Majesty that you take no offense, for I do but state in terms of general speech the suspicion the presence of this Scot hath awakened. There be such interest in the divers turnings of her history that, when yoked with youth and comliness, a glamour is thrown about her that some judgments fail to break. And heads, not alone the young, but some with hoary crowns, have so been twisted out of sense's better path, that there be not a few who boastfully slap their thighs and prate of knightly tilt to free imprisoned youth; and others, too old for sentiment's soft sway, see, in this willing tool, a step to an empty throne, and, perchance, the renewal of popish sway.

Q. Eliz. If this be so, my Lord, there is, indeed, good need for careful watch; of truth, there can be none of mark who would so tempt fate as to tip lance in such unholy reach for glow.

Lei. I pray, your Majesty, take not to yourself an over-weight of uneasiness because of this new turn. Trust to me the plumbing of any scheme or plot meant to work you harm. If there be those who would lay to your disquiet, I would, by your gracious permission, discover them to their dire confusion. Already I do hold in abeyance my acts touching the suspected, because of the absence of your sanction.

Q. Eliz. That I do consent to thus commission you is a reproach upon my wit; but that I may again make trial of your constancy, I do give to you this whereof you do seek. See to it, then, that you bring to me fullest information upon this matter.

Lei. With this end in view, I would plan. So frail a pedestal has this churl hoisted herself upon, that could it be assailed by truth, the lured and enchanted might by exhibit of sickening sights of murderous details, be sided back to performent of right.

Q. Eliz. Naught save good of realm doth make me to consent to this unsavory drag; but as a prevent for greater ills I mind to use the less. But, my Lord, in the breadth of your statement, you have lost the singling of your suspicion; at least, I have missed the hearing of the suspected by name.

Lei. Lest I be impelled by my zeal to suggil the innocent, I pray your Majesty let me so keep lock upon this which hath prompted the asking, that I may the freer act, bolstering this request with the assurance that both early and full report shall requite your indulgence. And now, for fear that I have created an unwarranted suspect, I crave that you, your Majesty, free your mind of the awakened uneasiness, and let me close this interview as it began, by sweeter speech and dearest converse, that I may thereby so honey the remembrance of this interview, that we may with pleasure recall only its beginning and its ending.

Q. Eliz. I am warned by your words, my Lord, to still keep my wit on guard; for when you do make play with Cupid's words, I must confess judgment would preach " beware." But you do so flavor your words, and you have learned so well the paths to my weakness, that even my poor protest doth sound more like maiden's " no," that meaneth " yes." But what matter? As one at banquet, who, by force of etiquette must taste a dish he doth not wish, and so repeat the forms of breeding that when at last the sweets are brought, which better fit his taste, his inclination is crowded out by forced o'er feeding, yet he doth maw the dainties, though they cloy; so I, after your long, unwelcome, yet perhaps needful speech, do accept your proffered sweets, knowing full well they are not food, but only sugared bits that shall ere long missit on my satiated, sober thought.

Lei. Your Majesty's graciousness doth encourage the best within me. I have no need to form or forge words my heart would speak; for ready-coined within my soul are sweet, loyal thoughts, by thee as yet unmined.

Q. Eliz. Too long, my Lord, too long have we consumed the time. While here exchanging words meant for us two alone, the urgent needs of state do clamor for our action. Go, but so use your time that in your deal with weightier affairs you may find a thought of me, that shall at least be a shadow of this hour. Go, and in your going hold this for my dear joy and your good talisman. [*Gives him her hand.*]   [*Exeunt.*

SCENE V.   *Room in Bolton Castle.*

Enter BISHOP OF ROSS *and* DUKE OF NORFOLK.

Bishop of R. To your comfort, I would say, your Grace, that the broaching of this matter did meet with such good reception from the queen that I hold that you need more of gentle woo-ing than urgent suing to find the queen right buxom to your pleading.

Duke of N. I admit that I feel within my blood such moving of my better nature that I am nearly constrained to mend my purpose and sue for love alone. Think you a suit so proffered, with so poor a suitor, would meet with queenly favor?

Bishop of R. The queen, your Grace, hath afore spoken well in your favor, and so offered praise that you have but to recall her words, that they may lend their force to your suit. As happily you have already drawn the queen's esteem, when naught but affairs of the duller sort have lent their weight to your credit, may it not be now, when this more righteous show doth so fire your manhood as to display it to yet better advantage, that the approve you have had in calmer walks shall be so fanned by this more fortunate circumstance that words of praise shall not lag far behind words of laud ?

Duke of N. It doth concern me most that I do first righteously merit the love of your good mistress the queen.

Bishop of R. If you are seeking rewards, your Grace, for your deserts, I fear me that the Scots must plead a dearth of fitting returns for that which you so richly merit.

Duke of N. That you have mind to make of my poor virtues such friendly praise, I pray you that you do yet give further proof of your friendship by withholding not from me the just notice of mine infirmities. That your praise should indeed carry with it a conviction of your sincerity, it doth well need to be companioned with a reminder of my faults, to the end that I may so cultivate virtue as to lessen the weight of your censure, if such I need.

Bishop of R. At our age, your Grace, friends should not hesitate to rightly name not only virtue, but faults, and that I do acknowledge the rightfulness of this necessity, and as earnestly proclaim it, doth testify to my sincerity of praise and my truthfulness, when I affirm that you do but merit approval from me.

Duke of N. Let this act seal our friendship. If it be that fate hath not in store for us a yet firmer cementing of our love, let this clasp make of the present so holy a thing that it be not sacrilege to remember it in your prayers.

Enter Page.

Page. Your Reverence, the gentlemen in the ante-room, with compliments, signify their readiness to accompany you. [*Exit.*

Bishop of R. Your Grace, the presence of these gentlemen doth deep concern us both. Will you accompany me to the ante-room? And if it be to our mutual advantage I will make you party to our interview.

[*Exeunt Bishop of Ross and Duke of Norfolk.*

Enter LEICESTER *and* THROGMORTON, *cautiously.*

Lei. Have all been carefully instructed to observe caution, and maintain absolute secrecy? I have had a long interview with this queen.

Throg. They have, my Lord. All attendants, save those beyond suspicion, have been carefully sent to other parts of the castle, and my lord and lady are being so royally entertained by the latest bit of court scandal, skillfully mouthed by your agent, disguised as a foreign minister, that they will make no hindrance, and offer no obstruction to our conference.

Lei. My man Felango is indeed a valuable hound, he can preach and pray like a saint, and, if need be, can out-lie the very devil. To what depth have you plumbed his grace?

Throg. I have found, my Lord, that there be so much softness in his boyish attachment that he doth talk in poesy, and already prates of fitting gifts for his lady love.

Lei. Was your encouragement so partitioned from your true designs as to escape detection?

Throg. Fear not, my lord, I was pupil to too good a tutor to make trip on this my first recital. Why look you! ne'er lamb was more easily led than this love-sick duke.

Lei. Did you acquaint him with the order for this queen's removal?

Throg. Nay, my Lord, we may so inform them at some future hour.   *Enter* Page.

Page. The Queen.   [*Exit Page.*
                              [*Exeunt Leicester and Throgmorton.*

Enter QUEEN MARY, DUKE OF NORFOLK *and* BISHOP OF ROSS.

Bishop of R. Your Majesty, that wise God who doth order the affairs of man, hath in your great affliction shielded your dear face from the dire evidence of your woe. His grace the Duke of Norfolk, answering the sweeter impulses of his heart, hath sought this interview with your Majesty, with the noble purpose of devising means, with the approval of your counsellors, of not only lightening your burdens, but with the end, heaven grant, of restoring you to your rightful throne.

Q. Mary. Most noble Duke, this condescension doth herald

the nobility of your soul. For one in your station to take so kindly a thought for so sorely an oppressed prisoner, doth, indeed, prove not only your gentle birth, but mark your Christian grace.

Duke of N. The righteousness of your cause, your Majesty, hath given me opportunity to obey the dictates of my heart. I have so far considered your situation, that the attempt to mend it doth well meet with the approval of my better judgment. My loyalty to my sovereign, and my adherence to my faith do not bid me withhold such kindly office as doth but become one Christian toward another. The weight of your affairs, your Majesty, borne to me by the recital of your sorrow, has so woven itself into the nature of my better sense that not alone duty to my queen, but the wish to succor your oppression, doth prompt me to offer my poor assistance.

Bishop of R. For the better adjustment of this affair, I trow the principals may the freer act alone. If it please your Majesty, I would make such excuse of my going, as would haste the advancing of a sweet understanding between you two.   [*Exit.*

Q. Mary. Your Grace, the troubles of my realm have so wrought upon my condition, that I do the more readily accept the sweet promise of your offer to interest yourself in my behalf.

Duke of N. You do, your Majesty, seem bereft of friendly counsellors.

Q. Mary. Such as have it in their hearts, your Grace, to proffer to me kindly advice, do, from lack of opportunity, or fear of consequences, restrain their impulses, and leave but the slender shadow of their sweet thoughts for my comfort.

Duke of N. Your affairs have so mixed themselves, through no fault of yours, your Majesty, with the weaknesses of others, that it doth require most careful exhibit, that in offering fair tend to your necessities, one may not make encouragement to wrong.

Q. Mary. Your Grace, if I do make a most earnest recall of my past, I find not a day or an hour that hath not in it either the pain of a grievous hurt, or the sad remembrance of a bitter affliction. Even before my coming, fate had shrouded my cradle; and when that age came which brings to others so much of joy, it found me bargained in a quarrel, and betrothed to strife. And when at last my life was linked to a loving heart, the sweetness of that happy union was turned to sad bitterness by the briefness of my joy. Then, turning to those in whom I should have found that love and sympathy my tears had earned, I found alas, that where my sorrows began they had grown, and then, indeed, was I alone. With mine heart yearning for love's sweet trust, I sought, in a hope of finding a balm for my loss, to entice into the empty chambers of my soul a shadow of its former tenant. But my poor, bruised heart, filled with the holy echoes of the hallowed past, made poor banquet room for him who would revel alone in sense. So while but on the threshold, with no thought of the deeper, sweeter depths, he turned him back, and closing fast the door, stood sentry over the grave of my dead past, and with so little reverence kept he guard, that the sentry grew to a thing of hate. For not content with rude tramping o'er the graves of my sacred memories, in whose recalling alone I had joy, he with sickening touch sought to render the sacredness of love profane. Is it a wonder then, your Grace, that by contrasting the only love I knew with the wreck of that foresworn, I should grieve, and in my grieving so foster discontent as to barter judgment for hope of reprieve?

Duke of N. That your Majesty doth entrust me with these sad memories doth the better encourage me to propose such a turning in the current of your life that there may come back to you from out of your brief dream of joy, such a sweet aftermath that it may hide the grosser hurts that have sadly marred a life so fitted for its best joys.

Q. Mary. Your Grace, your words warn me that you have yet more weighty matters to acquaint me with.

Duke of N. I fear, your Majesty, that I do lack the courage to offer as free a lance in my own cause as I hope to lend to your good relief.

Q. Mary. Such courage as is yours by blood, your Grace, should not fear to enter any field, not barred by honor, nor fear to ride where the best may spur.

Duke of N. If in this field, where I do now make so poor a

show of valor, I might stride my mount, and so add his pranc-
ing mettle to my lagging resolve, I might indeed, ride swift with
borrowed boldness to meet the object of my desire.

Q. Mary. Are there not sometimes, your Grace, on fields of
justs, knights, who, from favor's lean, surrender without a push
of lance ?

Duke of N. That they do, your Majesty, doth the better encourage me, who am already pricked deep of heart, to sue for
the sweet healing of your smile.

Q. Mary. One so hurt should not longer contend, but by
right of honorable wound, quit the field, and claim the bestow-
ing of the gift.

Duke of N. Your words, your Majesty, do, indeed, stay my
constancy. And to prove that you are a sweet and prudent
leech, in matters of weak and halting speech, I would exhibit
the full return of my courage, by declaring, that my interest in
your affairs has so warmed my heart, that I find the fullness of
my resolve met, in the avowal, that, from pity's shallow tend,
my emotion has grown to love's deepest proffer; and so embold-
ened am I by the fervor of my soul, that I do thus [*kneels*] offer
you, your Majesty, my heart, and the assurance of my most
tender and devoted love.

Q. Mary. In my proffered advice, your Grace, I did little
think that I led to so tender an offer. That you do thus prove
your willingness to meet the dangers of so open an intent in my
behalf, doth indeed, testify to your courage and honorableness.
I do but regret that I have so poor a heart to return for so noble
a sacrifice. If in me you find, your Grace, the measure of your
honest desire, I can but bid you rise, and seal your plight by
accepting my bruised and hungry heart as freely as I do accept
the sweet offer of your noble love.

Duke of N. In this blessed convention I would gladly forget
all calls to sterner affairs, and basking in this hallowed peace,
offer prayer to heaven, that the future may for us be fashioned
from the model of this hour.

• *Q. Mary.* O, that I might forget strife for place, the gall of
power, and in this sweeter, dearer mood float out into a sea of
undisturbed peace, with faith for pilot, and love for master.

Duke of N. I do condemn myself, your Majesty, for rudely breaking the sweetness of this moment by my forced return to the consideration of the affairs of sterner sort, but time and sharp necessity, will not longer brook delay. And I do best show the depth of my devotion by seeking to mend your fortunes..

Q. Mary. I know the strictness of the watch upon the movements of all who do seek audience with me, your Grace, and, therefore, do accept this your concern as but further evidence of your regard.

How think you, will not this proposed move of my friends involve you, your Grace, to your hurt?

Duke of N. I may not burden you, your Majesty, with the details thus far arranged. As for myself, I do not look for favor, save from yourself; but hope by the uprightness of my ends to merit honorable consideration from those in power.

Q. Mary. I do best prove my full confidence in your Grace, by submitting to your loving hands the guidance of my fate. How far have my friends moved in matters that will be likely to bring about an immediate action?

Duke of N. The will of foreign princes, as well as the good pleasure of the court at Rome, has been fully gained. If need be they will make such show of arms as will do much to bring about a fairer consideration of your Majesty's case. It but remains now for your friends to make such careful selection of time for the move as shall disarm the suspicion of foes.

Q. Mary. I cannot disguise from myself the fact that the launching of this delicate affair will of necessity involve risk, mayhap draw the spite of the envious.

Duke of N. It is not my purpose, your Majesty, to act in this matter so as to awaken envy, or merit spite. It is not my will to transfer allegiance or renounce religion.

Q. Mary. Your leal nature, your Grace, would impeach disloyalty, and your piety would save you from cant.

Duke of N. It is my purpose, your Majesty, to so enlist the sympathy and good office of such as have a belief in the justness of your cause, that at the proper time, and heaven grant that the measure of that time be short, we can, with little noise, and less of arms, so press the fairness of your restoration that opposition, like whipped hounds, will slink to cove, and such as have a selfish interest in your restraint shall, by their own noisy strife, show the weakness of their cause.

Q. Mary. How, your Grace, will this assignation touch the queen my cousin?

Duke of N. As do other cases where her austerity has caused opposal, and her majesty was obliged to discede. To my humble mind she did first enter upon your restraint, taking upon herself a hope of aggrandisement through judging a queen. But now, feeling that the assumpt doth bring with it such a weight of care, that the dignity of the office will be more than swallowed up in the doubtful verdict, she would make a virtue of repentance, and slip her self-imposed task. While she would not with open over-readiness relinquish her hold, yet I do feel that she would give a goodly strip of fen-lands were she relieved in some such manner, that she might proclaim to foreign princes that you had asked for her consideration, but tarried not for its bestowal.

Q. Mary. Doth the queen my cousin so much regret my presence? I would that her objection might shape itself so as to determine the coming of my liberty.

Duke of N. It is proper, your Majesty, that we determine at once the full scope of our proposed actions.

Q. Mary. That this plan, your Grace, involves not the shedding of blood, doth the more readily claim mine assent.

Duke of N. May we not now summon the gentlemen, that they may witness this, our mutual understanding?

Q. Mary. So complete is mine happiness with this sweet discovery that I would indeed seek to advantage my content by sharing my joy with trusted friends.   [*Blows whistle.*

Enter Page.

Say to the gentlemen without that I do await their presence.

[*Exit Page.*

Duke of N. From conferences had with your friends, your Majesty, it hath been deemed wise and prudent that we do adopt in all correspondence, a secret cipher. This matter hath been intrusted to his reverence, the Bishop of Ross; he will acquaint you with all needed instruction.

Enter BISHOP OF ROSS *and* THROGMORTON.

Q. Mary. I have sent for you, your Reverence, that you might partake of this my great joy, which heaven hath vouchsafed to me, through the sweet resolve of his grace the Duke of Norfolk. He hath not only taken upon himself deep interest in the mending of my broken fortunes, but he hath so appealed to the tenderest emotions of mine heart, that I have surrendered to him the keeping of mine happiness, and granted to him the full right to maintain mine honor and defend my rights.

Bishop of R. May the blessings of heaven, and the attendance of angels, bless this most noble selection, and aid in the furtherance of this most righteous cause.

Throg. If the deserving are blessed by merits, the principals to this convent should receive liberally the tokens of heaven. But while we rejoice at this happy consummation, and for this sweet installment of peace, let us not forget caution, nor neglect to recognize the necessity for present concealment; for the powers do so hedge right, that it be, of truth, good battle to overcome their designs by temporarily using their own weapons against them.

Duke of N. The half truth of your statement, good Sir Nicholas, may not yet excuse the full weight of your insinuations.

Throg. I trust, your Grace, that words of caution may not be too great a tax on friendship.

Duke of N. Of caution, I make no complaint, but we do blaspheme if we ask the blessings of heaven upon duplicity.

Q. Mary. I trust, good friends, that the sweet understanding of this hour may so companion brotherly love, that there be no gaps through which inharmony may stalk.

Bishop of R. May it please your Majesty, we may not longer continue this interview without exciting comment, if not suspicion. I would, therefore, crave permission for our retiring, and as I may by so doing exhibit my office, I pray you accept the holy benediction of the church, for to your everlasting peace hath been granted the blessings of the holy father. In my going

10

permit me to extend to you, your Majesty, mine own humble
blessing. [*Places his hand on the queen's head.*] May God
grant thee the full measure of His everlasting love, and the consolation of His divine peace.   [*Exit Ross.*

Q. Mary. So rich is my soul with this peace of God, that I
have not the heart to tempt the mixture of affairs of earth with
the sweetness of the trust and hope of my soul. I pray you,
therefore, your Grace, grant me the liberty to continue this
most earnest longing for further intercession with God. [*Gives
Norfolk her hand to kiss.*]   [*Exit Queen Mary.*

Duke of N. [*To Throgmorton.*] Lead on, seek to add no
sound to the tender echo of her voice. Leave these walls to
whisper the sweet speech of her going.   [*Exeunt.*

ACT IV.

SCENE I. *Room in Earl of Leicester's House, London.*

Enter BARNEY.

Barney. Sure, but there be hatching and devilment enough about to feast the very old Satan himself. All the fine gents, lords, earls, dukes, and such gilt-edged trash that visit me master to night, are, I trow, bent on some prets, more for private ends than public good. And there's that wiley 'Talian, the foxy imp of evil, sure he's but a shadow of the master. What one thinks of in wickedness the other matches with his wit.

[*Exit.*
Enter LEICESTER *and* FELANGO. [*F. locks door.*

Lei. Well! Out with it! This is, indeed, ill time to harrow up my soul with this teen affair; but out with it man, out with it.

Fel. I did but your bidding, Maëstro, and having done it, it were proper that I did acquaint you with the deed.

Lei. Well! How was it done?

Fel. In this wise, Maëstro: I did yesternight acquaint the maid with your message, and did appoint the drawbridge above the ditch as the tryst.

Lei. Came the wench willingly? or had she doubts?

Fel. I, willingly, Maëstro, willingly. Such trust and love had the maid, that fire and smoke would not have held her back. She'd have followed you from Tweedmouth to Land's-end, and made no asking. I, Maëstro, it's rare to see such trust.

Lei. Fool! Make no soft speeches to me. Get me out the deed, and its doing!

Fel. I do, Maëstro; and with no more softness than the appeal of her poor eyes did put upon me.

Lei. Damn her eyes, and your loose tongue. If you have

147

yet more of this babbling, save it for your drab; do not sicken
my senses further by this your weak exhibit. To the point.
How served you the wench? How served you?

Fel. As you will, Maëstro. It was in this wise. The lady
came at the hour, which was nine, and, as you had directed in
your note, she wore her heavy cloak and wraps. When she had
reached the cliff, and waited at the spot pointed out, I did approach. In the darkness she thought it was you, and with such
quickness as her stoutness would permit, she made to embrace
me. And when she had her arms about my neck, I did thus!
and thus! and thus! [*Imitates stabbing.*] So heavy was her
stress, and such inroad had sorrow made, that she had not
strength for outcry; but with your name upon her lips, she sank
at my feet, and it was over. My God, Maëstro, but I have
blotched my soul for thee, and leagued it to eternal hell by this
foul deed.

Lei. Save your preaching man, save your preaching. What
did you with the corse?

Fel. It went out, Maëstro, with the tide; for I did so weight
it that it saw not the light again, but it floated out on the
slippery ooze of the river's bed, and hath ere now been
sepulchred in hungry fishes maw.

Lei. This overshow of virtue on thy part will cost me dear.
Not the deed so much, which was but the snuffing out of a foolish weakly light, which had more heat and trust than sense and
right. She would have made a failure of life's game at best.
But, go now. Remember my instructions. To-night the Duke
of Norfolk meets me here, and I would have you keep your ear
and eye ever within whisper rate.

Fel. I, Maëstro, thou dost pass from deed to deed, like bird
from twig to twig. I have not in my blood an overdash of
water, yet so sly and cunning are thy turns, that I do fear my
own good wyson.

Lei. Let your estimation stay your prudence.

[*Exit Felango.*

Well, here is another thorn removed; but I must sip more
shy. My Lady Alice, I trow, will not play me this hazard, for
she doth so temper her clips with prudence, that we may make

the play to our liking. What fools these ladies are! They sell their smiles for poor, weak chuck, and pawn their souls for the fleeting lend of love.

Enter BARNEY.

Barney. Me Lord, the Duke of Norfolk and friends do attend.

Lei. Show them in; and Barney, see to it that no big-eyed, broad-eared, loose-lipped whelp do hang about the room or doors. The gentlemen are here on business for the crown, and I would have no leaking of the affairs of state. Show the gentlemen in.   [*Exit Barney.*

I have the duke well won. If I can but get him to make avowal within the hearing of Pembroke and Smith, and if they but willingly listen, they will be so far committed that they cannot take even a backward step without showing their weakness; and then they, wanting better company, will seek to prop their slip by hoisting in my much-loved (?) friend, Sir William. Then, when that is done, I have no fears but what, to save themselves, they'll load the blame for this rank deal on the back of him who highest stands as statist, in favor of the queen. But they come.

Enter DUKE OF NORFOLK, EARL OF PEMBROKE, EARL OF SUSSEX *and* SIR THOMAS SMITH.

Duke of N. I trust, my Lord, you have not waited overlong for us.

Lei. I have stayed my impatient longing for your coming by the anticipated pleasure of your presence. My lords and gentlemen, I bid you all most hearty welcome. It doth speak well for the furtherance of our plans, that this meeting is graced by so goodly a company. It must be, gentlemen, that heaven will smile upon our cause, for the worthiness and nobility of these interested bespeaks, indeed, the blessing of God, on our undertaking.

Smith. Pardon me, my Lord, may we not, with due propriety, first acquaint one another with the full object of our meeting, before we seek to implore the blessing of God?

Lei. The object, my lords and gentlemen, doth afore so pave the way to God's approval that on the better understanding we may feel the full assurance of His blessing.

Duke of N. Thy devout salutation, my lord, doth vouch for thy munific nature. But, I pray you, gentlemen, let us to the consideration; and as to me may fall the burden of whatever reproach, if unhappily reproaches come, shall follow the fulfilling of our desires, let me state the object of this conference. There be present with us those who, with love of realm at heart, have bethought themselves how best to solve the grievous straits that do so sore oppress the queen our mistress. I hold that it be no treason, nor yet sedition, to speak the promptings of my heart, and say I believe the Scottish queen unlawfully held and detained.

Smith. By decree of commission, she doth stand adjudged a bedswerver and a murderess.

Duke of N. Those are heavy words, sir, heavy words. Haste rather than proof hath parented them.

Smith. My words, your Grace, are most fully sustained by evidence. With your own eyes you read the letters that the Scot wrote to the Earl of Bothwell, while yet her husband and lord was still alive.

Duke of N. True, sir; I did read the letters, and with more care, I trow, than hath another, even of the commission; and I am satisfied within my own soul, and I call upon God to witness the recording of my words, that the letters presented by the Earl of Murray and my Lord North, that were of the Queen of Scot's own writing, were such as she had written to her lord and husband, both before and after their marriage, and were found among the effects left by Lord Darnley at his death. This is more easily accounted for, as in addressing them no name was attached, but rather some term of endearment. And they could, my lords and gentlemen, have been ascribed as well to any gentleman present as to the Earl of Bothwell. There are other letters among them addressed by name. These, I am most sure, are but imitations, and are the issue of the Earl of Murray himself.

Smith. Why was not this matter more fully exhibited at the hearing?

Duke of N. Because of the impatience of the Scottish queen, who, smarting under an injustice that would have unmanned the best among you, sought to restrain the hotness of her indignation by withdrawing.

Smith. If we do admit that such letters as were exhibited could, under fuller light, have been explained, not to the Scot's harm, how, your Grace, will you weigh the amorous sonnets, which in themselves show such abandonment as to stamp their author a wanton?

Duke of N. Condemnation, however just, hath in it more weight when bestowed with mercy. These French songs, o'er which such loud prating hath been had, could not have been meant for the Earl of Bothwell, for he read not the French tongue. Of the seven sonnets produced, there are but two that might not have been read without offense by even Knox, should Cupid smite his heart. And these two exceptions have in them less of heat and suggestion than I have heard myself recited by sedate dames in French salons. It should be borne in mind, my lords and gentlemen, that this Scottish queen did imbibe in her early education more freedom in affairs of love than our English maids. What would rose the cheek of English matrons, would wreathe with smiles the French *madame's* face. But would you, my lords and gentlemen, hold in relentless captivity, and subject to merciless persecution this Scottish queen for a fancied slip in form of speech, or hot bespeak of love?

Pembroke. I fear, your Grace, thy close eyeing of the Scot's letters and songs hath kindled thy honest blood to rush.

Duke of N. That I do regard the queen of Scots with favor doth but herald my better instinct. I first, my Lords, measured out to this oppressed captive the fullness of my pity, and in such good soil were the seeds sown that they have grown to flowers of esteem, and fruits of admiration.

Smith. Why burden thy passion, your Grace, with so many titles? Write it down love, and then blush like an honest man, if you will; for color of cheek I hold to be no sign of weakness in one who breaks his lance to meet the approval of his own soul.

Lei. Well spoken, well spoken. And by thy speech thou hast won my ears, if not my heart.

Duke of N. My Lords and Gentlemen, now that I have displayed my reason, I crave your indulgence for the details of my thought. That I may make for the queen our mistress a lighter weight of cares, and thereby meet the wishes of my soul, I would, with your kind approval, seek to wed with the Scottish queen. And then, with approval of our queen, restore her to her rightful throne, with such guarantees as shall protect the religion of our realm, and hold at bay further interference by Scottish subjects with English affairs and laws.

Earl of Sus. Has the Scottish queen, your Grace, signified to you, or friend, that your approaches have in them a degree of gratification that would prompt her to approve your advances?

Duke of N. My lords and gentlemen, I have not moved blindly in this affair, but as one who, seeing his duty, and finding that it has in it the approval of his soul, moves by gift of wit.

Smith. If happily the Scottish queen could be removed, and then, by wifing with his grace the duke, the queen our mistress' sad unease be thereby stayed, I should, indeed, feel that it was a most happy ending of a most troublesome snarl; and our court and realm be the winners in the exchange. But how think you Sir William will let this matter rest upon his sensitive heart?

Lei. My lords and gentlemen, when most of numbers, as are here assembled, who sit in privy council, have agreed upon a measure, feeling that it is the best for all, may it not be carried as right doth dispose? But if there are those who from fear, or perchance motives yet thinner, do seek to withhold from queenly approval an act judged to be for the best good, both for realm and crown, may not those in the right use means to help the ends of fairness? It so happens that the justness of our measures do fully sanction resort to means more forcing than leading.

It be not a secret among us gentlemen, that good Sir William hath long withheld the payment of the dues to the Netherlands; and this, too, when the queen our mistress had supposed the debt well paid. Now, hark you! if he, Sir William, should withhold his approval from this righteous and goodly settlement, may we not, as loyal subjects, acquaint him with our purpose, that if his persistence be over-long, we will discover to the queen the fullness of his unlawful withholding of that whereof she did command should be met and paid? I hold that when this matter is presented to the queen our mistress, she will not hesitate to so hotly assail him, that he will be in danger of being discommissioned. And I have it within my heart, and I do betray it to you, my lords and gentlemen, that were this high secretary plucked, for the betterment of the realm, it would meet vulgar applause; for he doth so measure his favors that, except to his own clan, the plums of court are illy distributed.

Enter Queen Elizabeth.   [All rise.

Q. Eliz. God's death! My lords and gentlemen, I do, indeed, appear as an indignant sovereign. By the faithfulness of my agents, I have been warned of your hellish plot, and treasonable meeting.

Lei. Your Majesty——

Q. Eliz. Hold! my Lord, hold! I am not surprised now at this your presence. Your damned cunning will not save you from my most righteous displeasure. Look, my Lord, I have wished you well, but my favor is not locked up for you, that others shall not participate thereof; for I have many servants unto whom I have, and will at my pleasure, bequeath my favor, and likewise resume the same; and if you think you rule, I will take course to see you forthcoming. I will have but one mistress, and no master. So, look you well that no ill happens to my secretary, Sir William, least it be severally required at your hands. Ungrateful hound! Is this the return you would make for my kindness? How have I pampered you, and now when stress of realm did sore oppress, you turn and rend the very hand that has fed you.

If you would sleep to-night without the tower's walls, keep your words of excuses for those who care to hear them. No!

save your speech until you have forged it into more loyal words than your acts would companion.

And you, your Grace, have a care, have a care on what pillow you would lay your head. I have caught but a part of your drift, but enough to warrant me in branding you as more weak than crafty. Your silly sentiment for my wanton charge doth have in it so much of youth's sick gall that you are fitter to rove the fields by light of moon than even sit this assembly of fools. You seem here, my lords and gentlemen, without a head; I will supply the miss by the proffer of my will.

Earl of P. Your Majesty, we did but assemble that we might the better relieve your heart from a most grievous burden.

Q. Eliz. This were, indeed, a mark of your loyalty, to here in secret plot and plan to set aside my commands. And not only my commands, but the legal acts made and passed by my parliament in assembly. Look you, my lords and gentlemen, am I not an anointed and rightful queen? and are you not subjects? How then would you meet these two ends, I, as queen, you as subject. You would meet them, my lords and gentlemen, by crafty plot and seditious plans. You thought to overthrow my secretary, Sir William, by your devilish dip, and so weigh upon him by your hellish designs, as to force him to companion your own disloyal weakness. But, you have failed; for, by your acts, you have but strengthened my esteem for him. Look you, his loyalty is as far above yours as is Charles' wain above your empty pates. I shall counsel with him, and he shall adjudge your acts. Think you, my lords and gentlemen, that I am dead to tenderness of heart for this my weak sister? By her crimes she hath forfeited doubly her life; yet I have more regard for her and her distress than you, in your weak, silly illurement, can ever have. I would to God she were back upon her throne, with hands as free from blood as are her son's. My grief at her distress hath brought me more sorrow than your weak heads can know.

Did I love ease more, I might well let this sick matter take its own course, and she, the plotting ingrate, should be free tomorrow. God judge me, I would her stinking case were in other hands than mine. But no, lest my weakness do soften my resentment, I will save you further exhibit of your hurt, and so hold my sorrow that it shall stay my righteous resolve touching your miserable plotting.

Duke of N. May it please your Majesty, I feel not to brook this inviction of my honesty without offense to my conscience——

Q. Eliz. It is not well, your Grace, to further tempt me now. Such anger as I have in store I would hold in check. By that and grief I am so sore assailed that I may not drop to you the softest word. The full answering of this most grievous affront I leave for a more convenient season. It is my pleasure that you do attend me to-morrow and hear my command on this matter. And you, my lords and gentlemen, bear the reproach of my displeasure, and seek not to ease yourselves of its consequences until you have vouchsafed to me a fuller and more honest explanation for your base acts.

That you may not further try me, I command you to retire and await my pleasure.   [*Exeunt all but Leicester.*

Lei. Your Majesty, that there be not sad misfortune attend your but partial hearing of this conference, I pray you that those who had here assembled be allowed further explanations. These gentlemen, your Majesty, did visit me, upon my request 'tis true, but the full import of their designs I had not unfolded to me. I had no thought that the plans had in them the liberty of the Scottish charge.

Q. Eliz. I have no ear for excuses now, my Lord; they come poor from you. You have so conducted yourself as to throw upon me a full and perfect right to attribute such motives to this gathering as your indiscreet and pandering speeches do allow. But I have finished. Without counsel I would make no further accusations, and so hold my judgment in hand that I may not deliver a verdict born of my indignation.

My Lord, it is hard to be betrayed by those we have trusted; but it is harder still to be betrayed by those we have not only trusted, but have given our sweetest confidence to.

[*Exit Queen Elizabeth.*

Lei. This is a most unfortunate catch indeed. I must now lay on lush softness to overcome this bad slip.

But I trow the duke is so firmly hooked that he may not miss his deal. There must be other reaching to bring the wily William down.   [*Exit Leicester.*

SCENE II. *Room in the house of Dr. Dee, London.*

Enter QUEEN ELIZABETH *and* WORCESTER *disguised, with* Servant.

Servant. I pray you, gentles, tarry here. I will speak your presence to my master.   [*Exit Servant.*

Wor. This be indeed, your Majesty, a most strange adventure. That I am here doth testify to my loyalty to your person.

Q. Eliz. O Book, trouble yourself no more. If I have a fancy to humor this whim, you serve me best by staying your opposition.

Wor. I have no opposition, your Majesty. It be not your coming that doth lament me, but rather the manner of it.

Q. Eliz. Manner? What is there out of proper? Is not this gown trig? and there be nothing sluttish in these robes. Pray, Book, why tremble? Do you fear your father's ghost?

Wor. Nay, your Majesty! I beseech you save me from partnership in a jest with so dead a core.

Q. Eliz. Dead! Why, man, did you expect to meet the living in a place like this?

Wor. If disrespect to the dead, your Majesty, be a charm of discernment, I will keep my ignorance to meet the living, and let those at rest feel my respect through my silence.

Q. Eliz. Hush! Here comes the doctor.

Enter DR. DEE.

Dee. I salute your most gracious Majesty. The honor of your presence confers distinction on my humble abode.

Q. Eliz. I come not for claw, good doctor, that I may find thick enough at court. I came rather to consult your powers in dark and troublesome matters. The cares of realm do so oppress me that I fain would find through your magic a solution of the maze wherein I am bewildered.

Dee. Your Majesty, if you do come to consult the powers at my command, I pray you pardon me if I require the same of your Majesty as from a common.

Q. Eliz. Whatever your dark ways may ask, I do attest my willingness to follow your instructions by my presence.

Dee. Pardon me, then, your Majesty, if I do request you to robe yourself in your color, violet. To the better accomplish this, pray use this ante-room. A servant will robe you.

[Exit Queen.

[*To Worcester.*]   Are you, sir, a participant?

Wor. I am here by royal command. Whatever her majesty, the queen, may do I am ready to follow.

Dee. Then, sir, I request the same compliance from you as from her majesty. Please retire here; a servant will robe you in your color, blue.   [*Exeunt Worcester and Dee.*

Enter Servant.

[*Servant draws aside heavy red curtains and discovers the room of magic. Places three chairs in center of room, one draped in violet, one in blue and one in green. On stand, at right, burns red light, on left burns yellow light. On left wall hangs Egyptian sign of life, on right hangs a crescent and star. In the rear of the room hang black curtains, which conceal a large mirror-like surface, on which Dr. Dee commands pictures to appear. Servant rings bell.*]

Enter DR. DEE, *robed in green ;* QUEEN ELIZABETH, *robed in violet ;* WORCESTER, *in blue.*

Dee. I pray you, your Majesty, under no circumstance speak during the sitting, except in the propounding of proper questions. As your robes indicate, select your seats. Your Majesty, state the object of your coming.

Q. Eliz. The Duke of Norfolk, with other misthinking persons, do conspire not only against the state, but my own peace ; and the better to accomplish their wicked designs they do, against my express wish and command, seek to form an alliance between the Queen of Scots, my charge, and the Duke of Norfolk. I would learn how this devilish plan may be circumvented.

Dee. Make no outcry, your Majesty.

[*Draws aside black curtains, and discloses the Duke of Norfolk with head on block, executioner standing over him with axe.*]

Q. Eliz. But the duke is of noble blood. May not so harsh a remedy awake vulgar comment?

Dee. I pray, your Majesty, make no words; you do disturb the powers. [*Drops curtain.*

Q. Eliz. If I may not do this, but move less sterner, what shall follow?

Dee. This. [*Draws aside curtain and discloses Mary, Queen of Scots, and the Duke of Norfolk, crowned, sitting on a throne.*]

Q. Eliz. My God! this is my suspect. Do they reign as Scots or English? [*Drops curtain.*

Dee. Behold! [*Draws aside curtains, discloses the Scottish arms blended with the English.*]

Q. Eliz. God's death! How may this be prevented?
[*Drops curtain.*

Dee. Thus. [*Draws aside curtain, discloses Queen Mary with her head upon the block.*]

Q. Eliz. My duty is plain. God grant me strength that I falter not. I have accomplished the object of my visit. I pray you, good Dr. Dee, I would retire. [*Exit Queen.*

Wor. Ah, sir! This means more blood. Unhappy queen! Take your bloody fee. [*Gives him purse.*] [*Exit.*

Dee. This is a most loathy affair. I fear I have lent myself to a damned grievous hurt.

Enter EARL of LEICESTER.

Lei. Good Doctor, I saw your show; you are indeed a most cunning wizard. But for the price, you should have given her majesty yet more of creeps. But that man Worcester, he'll not sleep again for a month. But her majesty the queen is made of sterner stuff, and she so hates the Scot's winsome face that I hope her yellowness, and your shift, will work to rid the realm of this most ugly plague. If unhappily this moves not, I may have need to use your hire again; if should be, I pray you, good Dr. Dee, put more twist in this your next exhibit; and, if you do fetch blood on your further show, I will make my gift well worth your reach.

Dee. Your agent made to me, my Lord, the promise of further preferment at court.

Lei. This is a matter which may be arranged when success shall make the court good hunting ground for your magic. In the meanwhile move not in this business without my knowledge. Your oath to my agent is quite strong enough to make hush a virtue. [*Exit.*

Dee. I am now in this man's power. By so lending myself I have opened the doors of gain, but shut the gates of heaven. But this deception which I have palmed upon the queen, I do *tout de bon*, and it doth help to further the ends of right, thereby I ease my soul and help my poverty. I may serve this man, though he be a devil, if in serving him I help the state, and in helping the state increase my store.

Tout le monde, even dukes, earls and churchmen, further and foster wrong, propped by prayers for good, so I, while of less estate, lend the gift of my wit, to help the realm and myself a bit. [*Exit.*

SCENE III.   *Room in Tutbury Castle.*

Enter EARL OF SHREWSBURY *and* SIR RALPH SADLER.

Earl of Shrew. So thick and devilish does this thing grow that, without royal command, her ladyship shall exercise no more beyond the court. Look you, this French ambassador of hers, as well as my Lord Livingston, be not allowed further to speak to her, only in our presence.

Sad. Is there need for this harshness, my Lord? Will not so close confinement yet further mar her health?

Earl of Shrew. My eyes have not yet discovered evidence of failing health. And my good lady, with the sharp discernment of her kind, hath made no great find of uncommon weakness. But you will better see the need of this stricture, when you do acquaint yourself with the contents of these dispatches; for therein you will learn that our good friend, the Duke of Norfolk, hath been again committed to the tower, and with him the Scot's agent, Lesley, Bishop of Ross.

Sad. What new thing has come about, my Lord, that doth make such disquiet?

Earl of Shrew. I leave it to yourself to judge if I be wrong in making cut of the too easy freedom of this queen. By these dispatches we are informed that not only the duke's heart, but his gold and estates, are involved in the interests of this queen.

His agent, one Benton, hath confessed to secretly delivering
letters and dispatches to his grace the duke, and others to the
Bishop of Ross, to be forwarded to Philip of Spain, and the Pope
at Rome, and some that were to other foreign princes; these
dispatches were from our charge here. How she did forward
them, I wis not; but this I do know, her majesty the queen is
very hot over this slip, and will require a full answer to this untimely strew.

Sad. Did these look to this queen's liberty alone? or had
they in them yet deeper designs?

Earl of Shrew. My dispatches but inform me of the discovery
of the plot wherein the Duke of Norfolk sought to wed with this
queen, and thereby attempt her restoration. This, of truth
would be treason, if proven against the duke. He hath failed,
and now he doth nurse his failure within the Tower walls. By
these dispatches I am commanded to question the Scottish queen,
to the end that I may determine how far she be privy to this
most seditious plot, and for that end I have requested your presence, that happily we might the better discover, by some good
surprise, how far she hath involved herself and the weak duke
in this affair.

Sad. I'll able your lordship what I can, that I may thereby
offer devotion to her majesty the queen. [*Shrewsbury rings bell.*

Enter Page.

Earl of Shrew. [*To Page.*] Say to her ladyship, your mistress, that I do desire the presence of herself and charge
forthwith. [*Exit Page.*

That we may the better report, make good tax of your memory, to the end that no important word may escape noting.

Sad. How far is our charge to be discovered, my Lord? to
the involving of others? Shall we push our inquiries? or shall
our probing relate alone to this queen and the Duke of Norfolk?

Earl of Shrew. If forgetfulness attend not her speech, it may
be our good fortune to gather such hints as will make to her
majesty a fair suspect as to the designs, not alone of this queen,
but of others who may be at cross purposes with the state. I
trow her majesty well wishes this intriguer were safe enskyed,

so sore are her days with distress from this sad tax upon her time and patience.

Enter QUEEN MARY *and* COUNTESS OF SHREWSBURY.

Countess of S. My Lord, you did send for me, and in compliance with your request, I bethought me to suggest the kind attendance of our guest.

Q. Mary. My Lord, I will not attempt to disguise from you that I sense the approach of unhappy news. So thick are my days now set with pains, that I start at every *courrier*, fearing that the burden of new announcements may bring me yet further evil. So little is my world now, and so much of sorrow doth mark its slow dragging hours, that I rarely miss my anticipations when I assign a new grief as the salutation of incertain communications.

Earl of Shrew. Those who by their own acts curtain the light that would be a guide to their feet, lose time in complaining if they fall; and those who willfully shut their eyes, that they may not see the forthright, forfeit the sympathy of those who would otherwise pity, if they bruise themselves by sad misstep.

Q. Mary. My Lord, I came not hither to sue for pity, and if my weak words did betray but a single ache of mine heart, I pray you forgive the exhibit. I should have known, for I have been taught, that sympathy is not a flower grown in this part of the queen my cousin's realm.

Earl of Shrew. Madam, by royal command I am directed to acquaint you with the arrest of the Duke of Norfolk, and his committal to the Tower.

Q. Mary. Would the queen my cousin counsel with me? Elsewise she hath no need to inform me of the imprisonment of her subjects. Mine own imprisonment doth concern me most.

Earl of Shrew. When the Duke of Norfolk was apprehended, there were found on his person certain papers, letters and dispatches. Some were written plainly, and some in cipher. These papers, so I am informed, related in detail to the duke's purposes concerning yourself. I am also informed, madam, that some of these letters in secret cipher were written by yourself.

11

Q. Mary. The Duke of Norfolk, my Lord, hath such ableness that he may answer for himself. If he hath done an unlawful act, he may be held to answer to his queen. To me his imprisonment hath such interest only as one unfortunate should have toward another.

Earl of Shrew. Likewise, madam, your agent, the Bishop of Ross, hath been committed to the Tower; and one Benton, servant of the duke of Norfolk, hath also been made a prisoner. From these have been learned such contemplated violations of the law as will, indeed, work great sorrow for the Duke of Norfolk, and such as are concerned with him.

By command of her majesty the queen I am directed to demand of you how far you did incite, and do acknowledge the acts, committed and contemplated by the Duke of Norfolk and his agents.

Q. Mary. My Lord, that I am unlawfully detained, and in violation of the laws of hospitality, and the usages of nations, doth not give the queen my cousin the right to demand of me answers, if in answering I do thereby, as unhappily I might, without good counsel, involve myself and friends. That the queen my cousin hath imprisoned mine ambassador, the good Bishop of Ross, doth, indeed, forewarn me that mine own end be not far off.

That mine ambassador hath been imprisoned, and thus prevented from visiting me, doth embolden me to ask what disposal hath been made of the forty thousand pounds of my dowry from France? For myself, my Lord, I ask nothing, but for those who by their faithfulness and devotion have earned my gratitude, and the sweet plaudits of princes, I but crave such of mine own as will permit me to grant unto them a part of such reward as a Christian sovereign would give to the loyal, and an honest prince bestow upon the brave and good. I have no measure, my Lord, with which to speak of the full sense of mine own despair. Uncrowned, unwifed, broken in health, alone in the world. With my poor estate narrowed to four stone walls. With every hope dead, save that which touches heaven, I tremblingly call up the sad memories of mine once noble greatness. A queen of two mighty and powerful states, now the poor, weak, despised prisoner of a cruel rival. I stand before you, who stand between me and those who would help, and cry, strike! strike! If there be other depths to which your cruelty may yet descend, I pray you hold not back your fell invention, but rather lay on your relentless strokes of inhuman infliction. If the signs deceive me not, these lips may but for a little thus feebly protest against this most wanton wrong. But lest I be judged of overthoughtfulness for self, I would make plea alone for those, who, with my poor cause at heart, have brought upon themselves a sweep of that wrath that hath grown so strong in its bitterness against myself, that, finding me now crushed, it fain would spend itself on those whose love and fidelity is, alas, now mine only cheer.

But, my Lord, witness this for me: If, in my going out, I leave behind the remembrance of an unseemly word, make to my credit this one mark: as I have lived so shall I die, a Catholic, firm and true; counting the loss of all as small if, in the losing, I may make for my blessed religion a little gain, and the happy approval, that it were better to die for God than live for the world.

Earl of Shrew. There is no need, madam, for these dark allusions. The queen our mistress hath no designs, save such as are for your better condition. The imprisoning of the rebellious need not affect your comfort, if you be innocent of connection with the wicked.

But as you have so far cultivated distress as to make yourself unfit to heed my communication, I will delay a yet further avowal, stating only that which necessity doth demand; that it be now my command from her majesty the queen that you be prohibited from further interviews with your friends, except in the presence of myself, or some one named by me.

[*To Lady S.*] Pray you, my Lady, the condition of this, our guest, doth for the present, at least, require your watchful and kind attention, and that she may need nothing, see to it that your attendants do prevent all delays in the gratification of her every wish. You may retire now.

Q. Mary. My Lord, this be empty mockery. Why not be

honest, and command your lady to put a yet stricter watch upon me, for this be your cruel meaning.   [*Exit.*

Countess of S. My Lord, I pray you that you do speak with me when you have concluded your interview with Sir Ralph. [*Exit.*

Earl of Shrew. This mingling of melting softness and stirring fire in this queen doth forbode much mischief for us who must encompass her acts, and forstall her agents.

Sad. She hath, indeed, great force of speech, and doth so mouth her complaints that she would well gain pity. [*Exeunt.*

SCENE IV.   *Queen Elizabeth's Presence Chamber, Westminster Palace.*

Enter QUEEN ELIZABETH, LADY KNOLLYS *and* Page.

Q. Eliz. I am, indeed, sore of heart, and well nigh spent with grief. O, that I did consent to this which I do now see was so great a wrong. I have not slept, nor have I known a moment's rest since their great urging did drag me into this sea of troubled conscience.

Lady K. I pray, your Majesty, take not this past matter so to heart. There were need of this, elsewise there would not have been that fullness of accord in your Majesty's council that did so freely advise.

Q. Eliz. [*To Page.*] Say to my lords and gentlemen, that I await their presence.   [*Exit Page.*

That you may not witness the fullness and force of my address to the council, I pray you that you do retire and await my presence.

Lady K. I trust, your Majesty, that you will no longer allow this matter to prey upon your heart. The cares of state do so demand of you that your subjects pray for a continuance of your health. And you would wrong yourself and them by further lamenting a necessity that the welfare of your kingdom did but so surely require.   [*Exit.*

Enter LORD WALSINGHAM, LORD BURGHLEY, *and* SIR THOMAS SMITH.

Wal. Your Majesty, we salute you, and in the salutation signify our obedience to your commands.

Q. Eliz. O, my lords and gentlemen, I have this day taken

leave of my earthly peace. I do now regret me that I did consent to the untimely death of the Duke of Norfolk.

Burgh. Your Majesty, this regret doth indeed add charms to your goodness of heart; but your firmness and loyalty to duty have endeared you in the hearts of your good subjects.

Wal. Your Majesty, this, indeed, were a most unpleasant task. The duke unmisled was my friend; but I have no friends who are your enemies, or who are disloyal to the realm.

Q. Eliz. My lords and gentlemen, I speak but the words of my heart when I say that I do regret that I did permit this most harmful and unholy taking off of the noble Duke of Norfolk.

Look you, this man, whom you have forced me to block, was of noble blood, and more, was of our religion. O, that I did submit to your heartless importuning. Had I but waited, affairs might have shaped themselves so as to have spared the spilling of blood from such worthy veins. It was not my purpose that the sentence should have been fully carried out. I meant rather to have held the warrant, and my sign, as a stay to further plotting.

Wal. Your Majesty, there was, indeed, good and righteous need for this act, for so deep had the plot grown, and in such great danger was your royal person, that nothing but the watchful eyes of your trusted and faithful agents and friends saved you from dire hurt.

Q. Eliz. Gentlemen, I do await such communications as you have to make. I pray you that you do make but slight tax on my patience, for so painful is this regretting that I am illy fitted for matters of weight.

Burgh. Your Majesty. From letters received yesternight from the Earl of Shrewsbury, likewise from those arrived to-day from Sir Ralph Sadler, we are informed that it is impossible to longer house safely the Scot with the earl. To the end that there shall be no attempts at rescue, or wild schemes rising, as a result of the present disturbance, it has been suggested that twenty-six additional soldiers shall be furnished and forwarded for the better protection of the Scottish queen.

Wal. It has also been suggested, your Majesty, that there be need for better provision for the table of the Scot and her retainers. A part of the letters received were heavily burdened with loud lamentings as to the poor napery and other furnishings allowed.

Q. Eliz. My lady hath indeed grown mighty proud. Did she transmit her bill signifying fully her dainty needs? Gentlemen, we shall have need for a new levy if this, my fine lady, doth swing herself yet more freely. Last month the stink was of the wine and beer, the month before the meat and bread were not to her liking. Now, with little of modesty, and less of grace, she doth clamor for finer linen. Fig on the tossy! Such as she should say her prayers, and be thankful for crumbs; but no, she doth demand the best, and even when the best is served, she doth exhibit such greenness that her demands are more uncomfortable than the winds of March.

Burgh. Shall the same order, your Majesty, be made as was last forwarded?

Q. Eliz. The same, save the wording of it need not be so couched as will act as sop for further unjust demands.

Burgh. And the troops, your Majesty?

Q. Eliz. If they be necessary to hold this ungrateful churl, let them be forwarded. The expense of quartering must be limited. Make to me the order when I will sign. If you have done, gentlemen, you may retire.   [*Exeunt Council.*

O, what sad demands do forge my heartless words. I would give the half my realm were this grievous prick removed. How long! O, how long shall this thing ride upon my tired heart?

Exit.

ACT V.

SCENE I. *Room in Leicester's House.*

Enter LEICESTER *and* LORD WALSINGHAM.

Lei. My Lord, it were better that this thing were done. If we do wait for more lengthy trial, or slower creep of nature we shall have willed the sowing of seeds for yet deeper plots and more hellish cabal.

Wal. How, my Lord, may this thing be done? If I speak its right name, and to it add our consent, we are murderers.

Lei. Nay, my Lord, necessities are the end of law, and removal by compliance with the necessities, would meet the full approval of all legalities, and add such justification as would gain the favorable decision of the courts.

Wal. There be not justice, at least so the larger tribunal of the world would decide, in two taking unto themselves the full pre-rogatives of law. That the ends would satisfy the extraordinary means would not, I fear, my Lord, meet the deep inquiries of those who feel not the full burden of the case.

Lei. I am informed that already the Scot is so much weak-ened, and so racked by infirmities, that those able to judge, for-swear her recovery. And be there not then sweet mercy to quickly end that which in prolonging doth but grant still greater pang? And I fear this pain of body doth increase her wit; for in all the years of her confinement, plots have not ripened and thickened so fast as they have in the days when most distress hath smitten her. I remember, my Lord, an ancient saying, that, if not of the gospel, hath in it still the spirit of mercy. In the down country they say that when age killeth opportunities, and disease eateth out desires, there be no longer fitness for one so smitten to live, save a hope in such restoration as the grave shall bring.

Wal. But how, my Lord, shall this thing be done?

Lei. I have in my employ a good and trusted agent, one acquainted with drugs, and cunning in their administration: he hath such foreign lore in the way of quick dispatch, that those who have enjoyed his lopping have in the quitting of life, so easy and quiet was the taking off, only regretted that the speed of departure cut short the opportunity for the return of thanks to the skillful dispatcher. Not in my service, but from truthful report, which I am the more willing to believe because of skill displayed in other delicate affairs, I learn that he hath in his possession a subtle drug, that one might take without suspect, and fall asleep, and sleeping, dream he died, and, failing to wake, learn in another world the dream was true.

Wal. O, my Lord, you are cunning and persuading; and your anxiety to serve our queen hath made you to harbor that which in less trying straits would awake your honest horror. No, my Lord, it is better, with the proof we have, to wait the slower end of law. She cannot escape us, and now that her secretaries have made so good a puke, we have already enough to damn, even if the object of our anxiety were twice the strength she be.

Lei. I, my Lord, I know the law will still this wench, and have no fear but that the honorable judges will find naked guilt with little looking, and right quick pass condemnation; but here the lameness of the case will make its sorry halt, to drag and tire the patience of those who would hide this stink that hath so long vexed the queen, and this our land. For look you, if righteous judgment be found in a day, and sentence given as the justice of God would not oppose, yet we might fail to meet fully the find of law through the over-softness in heart of this our queen; for it is not so long, that we have forgot what sorry work we had in measuring justice to the deluded Duke of Norfolk; and I do believe the queen would have saved his silly head, had not we, by devices that the stress of the times did approve, hasted his dispatch.

Wal. No, my Lord, I am determined, and, while I commend your zeal, I will yet obey my own judgment. I pray you dismiss this thing, and leave to lawful ends the dealing out of justice.

Lei. My Lord, I did make dependence upon your friendship in revealing my scheme. Let me set a higher merit still upon it by asking that, if you do not join me by you approval, you will continue to meet my confidence by letting this matter remain as between us two; and as a token of your judgment, and as an earnest of my appreciation of your better thought, I will dismiss this matter, and offer you my hand; and in the offering signify my willingness to join you heartily in furthering the ends of the commission appointed to try the Scottish queen.

Wal. Right! my Lord, right! I am glad to see this evidence of your better nature, and I do account it an honor, if my words have surfaced this which you did have in your heart.

Lei. Thanks, my Lord, thanks. I shall join you in every thing that shall tend to confound the adversaries of our queen.

Wal. Meet me then, my Lord, at the house of the treasurer. It is well that we make note of the matter to be heard before we have betrayed it in the presence of the Scot. *Au revoir.*

[*Exit Walshingham.*

Lei. My lord is lab but sly. I think he will not, howso, missay me. That I had his ear doth stay him.

[*Claps hands thrice.*

Enter FELANGO.

Piano! piano! How now, what word? Did you succeed with your devilish *aqua tofana?* You should report to me that her belly is in knots, or that her body is boarded for cooling. Is it so, or have you failed?

Fel. That I have failed, Maëstro, doth speak well for Sir Amias Paulet, who so closely keeps his prisoner that even a friend who would lull her to sleep may not play his kind office. Why, so close does he keep this fair lady, that even death may find it hard to enter in, and woo her. I showed this valiant keeper your pass, and, as broadly as circumstance would permit, hinted the sweetness of my intent; but he would none of me, and said: "Without royal seal, even my lords of the 'privy council' could not enter the chamber of his prisoner."

Lei. I fear you are losing your cunning, but as the reward I offered was great, I will stay my judgment; for, as you make no return that should claim the offer I made, I fain would think you assayed a trial.

Fel. So I did, Maëstro, but I cannot contend against so cunning a keeper; so, lest I might be discovered, and unhappily bring you embarrassment, I made a grace of my retiring.

Lei. Go you now, but meet me at Radoes to-night, at eleven o'clock. See to it that none notice our converse.

[*Exit Leicester right, Felango left.*

SCENE II.   *Great Hall, Fotheringay Castle.*

High Commission discovered. (Fourteen earls, thirteen barons and the knights of the Privy Council.) Chancellor Bromley at head.

Lord Chief Justice at table in center of hall, with the Queen's attorney-general, three solicitors, two sergeants and two notaries, with the high sheriff.

At head of the table sets a chair of state, draped with purple. Common chair at left, undraped, for the Queen of Scots.

Enter MARY, QUEEN OF SCOTS, *in deep mourning, two pages bearing train. All rise. Master of Ceremonies conducts her to her seat.*

Q. Mary. I see many learned in the law here, but I see none who appear for me.

Brom. The Sheriff will proclaim silence.

Sheriff. Oyez! Oyez! By grace of God, Elizabeth, the high and mighty Queen of England, France and Ireland, hath appointed this honorable High Commission to rightfully hear all matters that may be lawfully brought before it. Therefore let all keep silence! Silence!

Brom. The high and mighty and most gracious sovereign, Elizabeth, Queen of England, Ireland and France, having with great grief of mind been informed that Mary, commonly called the Queen of Scots, heir of James V. of Scotland, hath conspired the destruction of her, and of England, and the subversion of religion, hath, out of her office and duty, and lest she might seem to neglect God, herself, and her people, and out of no malice whatsoever, appointed this honorable commission to hear the charges objected against the said Mary, and how she can clear herself of them, and make known her innocency.

Q. Mary. I came into England, my lords and gentlemen, to crave aid from your queen, my cousin. She had promised it to me. But not only has she not kept her promise, but here have I been unjustly retained as a prisoner, above eighteen years. I solemnly protest that I am no subject of the Queen of England. I have been, and am an independent and absolute queen, not constrained to appear before commissioners, nor any other judge whatever, save before God alone, the judge of all. Were I to admit the right and jurisdiction claimed over me, I should derogate from the majesty of my rank and station, and prejudice the King of Scots, my son his successors, and the honor of princes in general. Be it, therefore, fully understood that the whole and sole object of my appearing personally before you, is with a view to refute the calumnies and crimes invented and objected against me. Deprived of any friend, supporter, or legal adviser, I have no resource other than to pray that mine own attendants do bear witness in my behalf.

It grieves me, my lords and gentlemen, that the queen my sister is misinformed in my regard; and that I, having been so many years straightly kept in prison, and become disabled in my limbs, and having been suffered to lie neglected, after offering so many reasonable conditions for my liberty, and though I have forewarned her of many dangers, yet has not credit been given me; I have already been contemned, though most nearly allied to her by blood. When the Association was entered into, I foresaw that whatever danger might threaten the queen my cousin, either from foreign princes, or at home, or for religion's sake, I must bear the whole blame. So I did, therefore, subscribe in all good faith and honesty to the articles of the Association; but what, my lords, hath it credited me? Mine honesty was suspected, and my purposes questioned.

Brom. Madam, you do but delay the hearing which shall the more easily establish your innocency, if, happily, you may establish it as you claim.

Q. Mary. I do object, my lords, to the legality of this proceeding. You say that I am under the protection of the laws of
England. That there are laws I have no doubt, for honorable
gentlemen have so informed me, but what manner of laws they
be I know not, for I am ignorant of all form, and have no knowledge vouchsafed to me of what special or general law I am
charged with violating, by being held all these weary years.

There be nothing left for me, my lords, in justice to myself,
mine ancestry, or my son, the King of Scotland, but to adhere to
my resolve, and declare that I am no subject; and that the
Queen of England, my cousin, hath not the right to command me
to appear before a tribunal that be not of my peers, or that if they
do try me, as by the warrant you do seem determined, I, being
an independent queen, ought not to be held by your verdict.
Examine your consciences, my lords; look to your honor; God
will reward you and yours for your judgment against me.

Hatton. You are accused, madam, of conspiring against our
lady and queen anointed; you are accused, but remember that
you are not condemned. You say you are a queen; be it so.
But, in a case like this, royal dignity is not exempted from answering, either by civil or common law, nor by the law of nations, nor
by nature. If you be innocent, you wrong your reputation in
avoiding a trial. You protest yourself innocent, but Queen
Elizabeth thinks otherwise, and that not without grief and sorrow for the same. To examine, therefore, your innocency, she
has appointed commissioners, most honorable, prudent, and up-
right men, who are ready to hear you according to equity, with
favor, and will rejoice with all their hearts if you shall clear
yourself from this crime. Believe me, the queen herself will be
touched with the greatest joy. She affirmed to me on my leaving her, that never had anything more grievous befallen her,
than that you were charged with such a crime. Wherefore, lay
aside the bootless privilege of royal dignity, which can now be
of no use to you; appear in judgment and show your innocency,
lest, by avoiding a trial, you draw upon yourself suspicion, and
lay upon your reputation an eternal blot and aspersion.

Q. Mary. My lords, if I shall consent to appear before this
commission, it is not as one who would consent to a trial, but

rather that I may, if happily I be allowed the opportunity, show mine innocency of the foul slanders objected against my good name. I will, therefore, consent to this much of your proceedings as will afford me the opportunity of denial.

Brom. That we may proceed regularly, as by due form of law provided, I would request that the statement of the charges against the accused be read.

Atty-Genl. [*Reads.*] " *Greeting. Know all men by these presents, that Mary, commonly known as the Queen of Scots, heir of James V. of Scotland, now lawfully and legally detained and held, and heretofore properly and legally summoned to appear as defendant, is now by these presents charged, to wit :*

" *That said Mary, commonly called Queen of Scots, did, by her knowledge and by her consent and encouragement, aid and abet one Anthony Babington, rebel, in a most unholy and rebellious plot, and attempted uprising against the peace of the realm and the life of her Majesty Queen Elizabeth ; and also with aiding and abetting one Nicodemus Hislop, rebel, and one Leopold Savage, rebel, and one George Freefair, and other persons, subjects and foreigners, who did combine, devise and plan against the peace of the realm and the safety and life of her Majesty Queen Elizabeth. And the said Mary did, by her encouragement and knowledge of the acts and purposes of the aforenamed Babington, Hislop, Savage, Freefair and others, rebels, became a party to and a participant in their rebellious plots and seditious plans.*

" *And it is further charged that the said Mary, commonly called Queen of Scots, did receive certain letters written by the said Anthony Babington, rebel, and that she did return answers thereto. And further, that the said letters written by Anthony Babington, rebel, and the answers which Mary, commonly called Queen of Scots, did return thereto, contained rebellious plots against the peace and safety of her Majesty Queen Elizabeth, and seditious plans for the overthrow of the realm and against the peace and quiet of all loyal subjects.*

" *And it is further charged that the said Mary, commonly called Queen of Scots, did seek to entice foreign princes to land their arms and forces within the domain of her majesty the queen,*

*against the peace and quiet of the realm.   Therefore, it is hereby
commanded that the said Mary, commonly called Queen of
Scots, shall appear before a high commission, herein by these
presents named and forthwith appointed, to answer the charges
herewith by this warrant made and attested.*

*" Given under my seal and by my hand this ninth day of Sep-
tember, in the year of our Lord Jesus Christ one thousand five
hundred and eighty-six, and of our reign the twenty-sixth.*

" ELIZABETH, R."

Brom. By this authority, and in obedience to this invest-
ment, it becomes my office to proceed as by royal commands we
are directed.

Q. Mary. My Lord, these are, indeed, serious charges. If I
be but guilty of the least of them, I am by right held, and by
justice contemned. True, my lords and gentlemen, I did seek
aid from foreign princes, making their proffered offers of assistance the grounds of my hope of liberty. So long had I been
straightly kept that I did seek, as any creature might, to gain
my freedom. I did not hold for the queen my cousin any bitterness, save that she did unlawfully detain me. And that I
might the better seek to remove myself beyond the queen my
cousin's power, I did intercede with friends and allies for the
forcible breaking of my prison walls.

As to my connection either by word or thought with the man
Babington, which you have named, and his wicked plans against
the life of the queen my cousin, I do deny that I was a party
thereto, or that I did encourage him in any way or manner.

Brom. Madam, the charges you have heard. To meet them
it will be necessary to dispute by the introduction of proofs the
truthfulness of the accuse.

Q. Mary. My Lord, it is a right easy thing to charge that a
lone, weak woman did plan and conspire to overthrow a mighty
kingdom, and seek the life of its powerful queen. This might
be charged against a babe. You do miss the ends of justice, my
lords and gentlemen, and fall far short of exact honesty, if these
charges which are objected against me be not stayed by attempts at proof, and I be not allowed to meet and answer my

accusers, and examine written testimony, if such you possess,
that you do intend to introduce, and use against me.

Burgh. My Lord, may we not meet the ends of justice, and
answer the full letter of our instructions, if we do proceed without impatient interruptions from the accused.

Q. Mary. My Lord, this whole matter has in it so much to
stir the blood of innocence, and is without such due forms of
legality, that interruptions that are spurred by indignation have
in them as much grace as do the appearances of righteousness
with which you seek to awe me.

Brom. If the defendant will restrain her impatience, we may
proceed more orderly, and waste less time. I would lay before
you for your consideration, my lords and gentlemen, and also
for such answer thereto as the defendant may make, certain correspondence, consisting of notes, letters, messages and dispatches,
which have passed between the defendant, Mary, commonly
called Queen of Scots, and the late Anthony Babington, rebel.
A portion of these letters were used in the trial of the late Anthony Babington, rebel, and through them largely was his guilt
established. Many of these writings were written in a secret cipher, but by the assistance of the secretaries of the defendant,
these letters have been carefully and truthfully deciphered, and
copies have been made. By these letters, and other corroborat-
ing testimony, we are fully justified in assuming the guilt of the
defendant as alleged in the charges heretofore submitted.

The guilt of the late Anthony Babington, rebel, and those associated with him in his most unholy and rebellious plot, and
who so justly met their deserts by forfeiture of their lives, was,
after a fair and most careful trial, fully established. If these
were deemed worthy of death, who played but secondary parts,
should not the instigator and master spirit in this most wicked
and murderous plot against the peace and life of the queen, her
majesty, be held answerable ? And, if found guilty, be adjudged
worthy of the same punishment as was meted to her blind and
fanatic dupes ?

Q. Mary. These extravagant assertions, my Lord, do, when
unsupported by your noisy eloquence, lose entirely their force
and significance, and are only entitled to respectful attention

when you have stayed them with a promise of proffered proof, which shall meet honest scrutiny and command respectful attention.

Burgh. Less boastful straining, madam, for words to assist your bold brag, would meet better the seriousness of your situation.

Q. Mary. If it be brag, my Lord, to attempt to stay this flood of vile slander against my good name, I pray God that I be more fully endowed with *vanter courage,* and so employ defiance that I may shame your wicked designs.

Brom. This exhibition of unseemly ranting, if allowed to continue, would make a mockery of our high office, and set at naught the commands of her majesty the queen.

Q. Mary. The mockery, my Lord, hath with sore travail pains been brought forth. All this show of gaudy pomp, and all this array of learned, legal talent, which would assist in its sham christening, may not make legitimate that which was foul in its conception and a bastard by birth.

Hatton. Madam, such flippant familiarity with things *grossier* illy becomes a lady, much less one claiming to be a queen. You do but make more difficult your task of establishing your innocency, if you indulge in your attempts to traduce your judges in the language of criminals and the low trickery of a dissimuler. Bethink yourself, madam, rather how you shall meet these most serious objections that have risen up against you.

Q. Mary. If I am but to meet hearsay, I do, indeed, well offset it by replying in such terms as would meet your own groundless allusions.

Chief Just. My lords, this is, indeed, a hearing, but it requires much charity of thoughts to dignify it with other appellation than that of brawl. If we are to consume the time by listening to vain denials and boastful tongue-antics, we would do well to employ a merry Andrew to sustain with credit our part of the drollery.

Q. Mary. If the froth of speech constituted a verdict, my lords, you might well return to the queen my cousin, and say me guilty after the gustful speech of yon legal dignitary.

Brom. To make good the accusations, or to support them by

testimony as yet undisputed, I would here introduce portions of the correspondence heretofore alluded to. I would, therefore, call upon the queen's counsel to read exhibit marked " A." This is a letter written by Anthony Babington, rebel, and is dated May 16, 1586. The counsel will read.

Atty.-Genl. [*Reads.*]   " *To her Most Gracious Majesty, Mary, Queen of Scotland, England and Ireland :*

" *Afflicted and distressed Sovereign: With the full consent of your trusted friends, and by the advice of those wise in counsel, we have, through the grace of God, enlisted such sympathy and gained such willing hands, that we may now safely regard our scheme as fully matured. By recent advices from the King of France, and, through him, from the Holy Father at Rome, we have received full assurance of the hearty sympathy of the noble and generous Philip of Spain, in this our most righteous and holy cause. After due deliberation and most careful planning, we have the train so carefully laid and friends so judiciously stationed, that we make no thought of failure. As for her who has risen as your unjust keeper, we have most carefully planned a speedy removal. It but remains for the signifying of your pleasure in the counseling of your friends to attempt with us your liberation and restoration. With feelings of the approval of God and our own conscience, we trust we may soon offer you the fruits of our exertion, your personal liberty and full vindication.*

" *Yours for Christ and Crown,*

" *A. B.*"

Q. Mary. My lords and gentlemen, if this you have read be true or false I know not, but this I do know, I never received such a missive. If a subject may so far forget himself as to rise up against his rightful sovereign, he should be punished. If he should write letters to innocent persons, who sympathize not in his dark deeds, and these letters are discovered, is it just to hold the person to whom they are wrongfully addressed as *particeps criminis?* But I claim, my lords and gentlemen, that the letter just read by the queen's counsel may not be true, either as an original, or as a copy. My Lord Bromley, has admitted that this which you have heard is but a copy. To hurt my

12

reputation, and befoul my good name, and to ensnare me, perhaps to my death, might not one evilly disposed add to or take
from that which was written, whether good or ill?

My lords and gentlemen, not of knowledge, but of mine own
opinion, I would hold the poor late Anthony Babington not a
silly; and yet, if he did write such bilk as this letter you have
heard read, and so broadly hint the taking off of my cousin the
queen, he could well spare his empty pate, for he would have
proven it was a useless noddle, and far too big to house his little thought. Men with great plans do not thus blab, either by
mouth or by writing, when they would reach and overthrow a
kingdom or set aside a queen. I fear me that in this hatching and
strain of effort to make seeming good proof to deepen my sorry
plight, some over careless hands, with little love for truth, have
made attempt to unwind this so-called secret cipher, which my
Lord Bromley has so loudly commented upon. I have it within
me to discover mine own suspect, and speak my mind, and say,
that I do feel that the letter just read hath about it a most
striking exhibit of rank *fausseté* and wicked *malignité.* So
strong is this feeling and such acute suspicions doth it awake
that I cannot forbear to openly declare that my Lord Walsingham was not only privy to this most wicked deceit, but that he
did counsel and assist in the preparing and presenting of this
most shameful and false letter.

Brom. Madam, this is a most bold and wicked accuse.

Wal. Pardon me, my Lord, permit me to speak the force of
my indignation, and make denial of this wanton draff. My
lords and gentlemen, you will not lay to my door that I do lack
patience, or that I am a stranger to forbearance; but the loud
mouthings of this shame-faced ingrate have quickened my denial of her foul slur. If we are, my lords and gentlemen, to
listen alone to the vain stomaching of this brazen plotter, we
might with better prudence have lent our ears to fish-wives'
scandal, or saved this tax upon our good natures to meet the
ends of justice. I do hurl back in my own behalf this empty
charge against me laid. There were no need, my lords and
gentlemen, to alter or amend this accursed letter, for, without
this, there be such damning proofs of her full consent, and quick

desire to break the peace of the realm, and take the life of her majesty the queen, that I had it in my thought to save the prick of this sharp instrument from inflicting a heart by guilt made sore; but now my lords and gentlemen, I counsel that nothing be kept back; for, not content with plotting against the realm and crown, this hardened, ungrateful and brazen woman, doth fling in our very faces her bold affront, and hopes by loud denials, and windy accuse to turn aside the sword of justice.

Q. Mary. Softly, my Lord, softly; I did but speak that which was repeated to me. Powder doth not explode without the touch of fire. Innocence would be amazed, but may not guilt seek to hide beneath anger's fiery speech its blushes of self accusing? You, my Lord, stand surrounded by your friends and sympathizers; the sharpness of your words meets their approval. If I do turn your blows by arguments that circumstance doth suggest, you flash upon me the anger of your spite. I would not seek to awake your sympathies, my lords and gentlemen, by much speaking. If you have already agreed upon your verdict, you might well command my silence. My interest ceases when I may not answer your foul calumnies, and so for me this farce might end, and I seek within my prison chapel the consolation of prayer.

Brom. My lords and gentlemen, yet another letter from the same person, and addressed, as was the first, to the accused; this is dated June 15, 1586, and is from Northumberland, that breeding-place of rebellion and nest of sedition. The Counsel will read.

Atty.-Genl. [*Reads.*] " *Gracious and mighty Queen, ruler of Scotland and England, the grace of God salute you, peace of Christ be with you. By the time that your eyes have met this writing I shall be on my way, with good Father Ballard, and D——, and P——, and other chosen spirits whose hearts are filled with the right- eousness of your cause, toward Richmond House. If, by grace of God, we pass all obstacles, and find ourselves within striking distance, take to yourself the full assurance that what God has directed, courage will accomplish. And before your morning prayers, we trust, by grace of God, that she who holds, and by the holding curses, shall be dispatched, and that the first dawn-*

*ing of the coming of the true religion and your own sweet
liberty shall break.*

" Faithfully for God and right,

" B——."

Still another, my lords and gentlemen, dated 9th of July,
1586, and upon this hangs the connection with those just read,
for it proves, not only that the accused had full knowledge of
the awful plot, but that some of the details were suggested by
herself. The Counsel will read.

*Atty.-Genl. [Reads.] " Beloved and gracious Queen, by grace of
God, peace.   Yours of the 3d, sanctified by your wishes and blessed
by your prayers, reached me two days after its dispatch.   We
had fully agreed upon accepting the proffered aid of Broadbent,
but upon the receipt of your letter, which disclosed to us your
suspicion of his faithlessness, I at once dispatched D—— with
instructions to play upon his mind, and, by making pretense of
necessity, dispatched him foreign, and so haply he is out of the
way.   As to your suggestion as to the best means of surprising
your guards, I will say that it shall be acted upon as you direct.*

*" I am pleased to receive your sanction for the point of our
scheme.   Other matters to your interest are prospered of God,
and for your comfort and safety we offer daily prayers.*

" Yours faithfully,

" B——."

Brom. My lords and gentlemen, I have little need to continue,
A mind without prejudice, that is able to comprehend, must see
that the contents of these letters more than prove all we have
objected against the accused.

Q. Mary. My Lord, you have but read the letters which you
claim this man Babington forwarded to me. I do deny that I
ever received them, and, while I admit, without prejudice to my
case, that this man did write letters intended for me, yet I most
earnestly deny that any that had the fortune to reach me contained any word or sentence in which the life or peace of my
cousin the queen was threatened.

Burgh. My lords and gentlemen, is it not more proper that
we proceed, and avoid these frequent interruptions? Thus far
we have missed the form intended.

Q. Mary.   Form?   My lords and gentlemen, you have missed all form in the conception of your ideas of justice.

Brom.   In the great mass of written testimony in possession of the crown, we possess a number of letters, notes, dispatches and messages.   After what has been already read, the counsel for the crown doth not deem it necessary to submit other samples of this most conclusive proof of the guilt of the accused, except one letter written by the accused herself, and addressed to the aforesaid Anthony Babington, rebel.   As this letter is long, the counsel will read only that portion in which the defendant clearly and unmistakably gives her consent to the rebellious plans and aims of the aforesaid Babington.   This letter is dated June 17, 1586, and was sent to Dethick House, Derbyshire. The Counsel will read extract marked " 1," in the margin of exhibit " D."

Atty.-Genl.   [*Reads.*]   " *I do give, most trusted friend, my full consent to your suggestion of the second.   I would counsel the greatest care, not only in adhering to the time agreed upon, but also to the choice of assistants.   You know my abhorrency for blood-shedding.   I am aware that so great a move may not be accomplished without some disquiet.   It must follow that there shall be those who may receive from your hands some dis-ease, but I pray you, as you are a Christian, that there be no unnecessary taking of human life.*

" *See to it that those whose duty shall be to strike for my rescue, shall temper boldness with mercy, and that those who seek to prevent the queen my cousin's interference with my restoration, be instructed to accomplish their purpose with as little force and harshness as may be.   To the rest of your plan I most heartily agree.*

" *Yours with trusting, and hope, and faith in God's eternal justice.*   " MARIE, R."

Q. Mary.   My lords and gentlemen, have I not already sustained from your hands indignities enough?   Lest in my towering indignation I forget my denial, I would say once and for all, that that which you have just heard read is not, nor ever was, either my letter, my composition, or my thought.   My Lord Bromley says the original was in secret cipher; if so, this alleged

copy is baser, more false, more devilish than those you have
heard read as the productions of poor Babington. Shame! Shame!
dignitaries of the law! Shame! Shame! Honorable Knights
of the Privy Council! Shame! Honorables of high and low
degree! Shame on all who have lent themselves to this accursed
invention! Not content with holding me, unlawfully, a prisoner
for years, and robbing me of my dowry, you now seek, by bare-
faced forgery and low, designing cunning, to so ensnare me that
I may be entrapped to my death, and be to all posterity damned
of reputation. But look you, the world shall, even as God doth,
judge me, and your dark and devilish inventions shall avail you
nothing. If I am drawing near to my end, and you, my lords,
are to be the promoters of my death, my going out shall credit
me more than your cruel and unjust verdict shall you.

As in the beginning I did earnestly and plainly state, I am no
subject of the Queen of England, nor am I bound to respect her
laws. I came as one craving an asylum of rest. I came upon
the urging of the queen my cousin, and I do wear to this very
hour upon my finger the ring which she did send me as an earnest of her regard, and a pledge of her sincerity. How has this
pledge of friendship been kept? How have I been treated? Of
what doth this ring, the pledge of a queen, profit me?

I ask you, my lords and gentlemen, if you have within you,
yet not wholly dead, a spark of sympathy or a grain of justice,
to consider my case as one in which rank injustice, cold and un-
feeling heartlessness have been, from the first day of my landing
upon your shores, my constant companions.

I have been dragged from one stronghold to another, deprived
of my people, and mine attendants driven from me. I have been
forced to submit to every form of indignation and insult. And
what, I pray you, is my crime? Urged by the wickedness and
weakness of those who should have been friends, I, who am a
rightful queen, and a royal mother, am deprived of my throne
and forcibly kept from my child. Is this a crime? No, my
lords; I am persecuted because I am not of the religion as is
the queen my cousin. This is my only crime; for this I suffer
and am held a prisoner. Now that your queen my cousin may
finish her exquisite tortures, I am summoned before this high

tribunal, composed of gentlemen, learned in the law, and with favorites who seek to earn the smile of their queen by urging my tears.

I see before me men of law, who are armed and capped with subtle intent to probe me to the quick. That I may be the better ensnared, your queen has sent her most cunning and crafty sergeants to entangle my speech, and suggest befogging questions. That I may be humiliated, and my rank and majesty latched by slander and blackened by falsehood, the most unscrupulous and designing of the untruthful have been retained to appear against me. And those bent alone on malicho are invited to spew their filthy slanders upon my defenseless head.

I am alone, deprived of an advocate, stript of my papers, and even mine own words and statements are uncredited. Every attempt I make to answer your foul calumnies is met with scorn and contempt.

I stand before you a maligned, neglected, unfriended woman; confronted by paid legal talent, and bribed and dishonest witnesses. In this position, and under these circumstances, I am on trial for my life. I ask not for pity, not for mercy; I only ask for that justice that you would give the most vulgar criminal. As an earnest of mine innocency, I demand through you of the queen my cousin, that, if I am to be tried, I be tried before my peers. If this may not be, then I crave and demand that my hearing shall be in your open parliament. This, indeed, have I a right to demand, being an independent queen. Go on with your mockery; this I may not prevent, but spare me further participation in your wanton inflictions.

Brom. It is not of election, my lords and gentlemen, that we read further of these letters; their striking similitude unnecessitates the waste of time by their repetition. They may be considered in council, and, as the accused has denied the truth of their contents, and even their originality, I will not detain you by a more lengthy reading.

Q. Mary. Had you, my Lord, as much solicitude for my bruised heart as you have for the tender ears of my would-be-judges, I might be spared a part of the cruel punishment inflicted upon me.

Burgh. My lords and gentlemen, the overspeaking of the accused is not proof. I am tired, as you must be, of this noisy and undignified mouthing. The accused has made statements which I cannot, in justice to her majesty the queen, let pass at this time unnoticed, for there may be those who would think that her majesty has been unmindful in her care of the accused, and neglected her comfort, if there should be no positive denial of her unwarranted accusations.

It is the testimony of those who have been with the accused since her coming hither, that she has been well treated. That she hath been detained, as was lawful, I make no denial. How far she has been a prisoner you may judge, my lords and gentlemen, when I state, as a truth, that when I went, in company with the proper officers, to summons her to appear before this legal and rightfully constituted commission, I found the accused fully robed, and elegantly mounted, about starting on a day's sport with her protector, Sir Amias Paulet, and attendants, in a romping hunt over the hills and vales. The annals of the Tower, or the records of our county gaols, do not mention that prisoners within their keeping were permitted to join frolicsome out-door sports.

When first this person came to our shores, a fugitive from justice, pursued by indignant and wronged subjects, she brought in her train upward of seventy people. They came without means, and most of them with but a single shift to their backs. In such sad straits was the accused herself, that she did importune her majesty the queen for a change of gown; and with that liberality and sweet goodness of heart that hath so gladdened her reign, the queen her majesty sent to her the honorable and most noble Lady Scrope, with full and abundant orders to supply the every need of the pursued, and quondam queen. She complains, my lords and gentlemen, that she was dragged from one stronghold to another. How much truth there is in this, judge. She was lodged at first with the good and honorable Lord and Lady Scrope, and her army of attendants was permitted to remain in her company. She had not been housed in the comfortable and elegant castle of my Lord Scrope for a quarter year before she began her quarrelsome complainings, that the situation was unhealthy, and churlishly demanded that she be removed. With great patience and goodness of heart her majesty the queen did consent to her removal; but as the tax was over-great for the maintenance of so hungry a crowd as sought, by clinging to the fortunes of their fallen mistress, to be nursed by the bounty of her gracious provider, it was deemed right and proper, as prudence will acknowledge, that a part of this mob should be returned to Scotland. And so this now-grown-fat and impudent herd was reduced to the number of thirty. This included the Scot's private chaplain and his assistant, her own surgeon and his apothecary, four maids, her own cook and two scullions, three pages, two private secretaries, and fourteen ladies and gentlemen in waiting. These have been with her constantly, with only such restraint as her own unlawful acts have forced those to use who have acted as her protectors.

She has had daily exercise as her own wishes would suggest. She has also had full indulgence in all pastimes, including tennis and the chase. Horses have been at her disposal, and she has freely accepted their proffer.

As from year to year she persisted in her unlawful acts and seditious intrigues, such watch has been kept upon her as the peace of the realm and the safety of her majesty the queen demanded. I leave it to you, my lords and gentlemen, from the testimony already submitted, whether or not it has been conducive to public good to restrain the accused, and whether, from the undisputed evidence of her guilt, and her intentions as to the destruction of her majesty the queen she may not be rightfully condemned and righteously executed.

Q. Mary. O justice! O law! What shame and wrong may not be enacted in thy name. Power and might are thy weapons, and cruelty and oppression thine allies.

My lords and gentlemen, I have never thought to harm the life of the queen my cousin. I have sought my liberty, as in nature any creature might; there is naught in this that by rights should deprive me of my life or make it needful to accuse me of attempted murder. I have been watched day and night. By night a sentinel has lodged at my chamber door; by day a paid shadow has dogged my steps; my very breathings have been counted, and my troubled dreams regarded.

Burgh. Such watching only, my lords and gentlemen, as was necessary to circumvent the plottings of the accused was exercised.

But enough; I will not tire longer your good sense by denying her loud stomachings. Let us consider the proofs offered in further testimony of the support of the truthfulness of the letters already read in our hearing. As a means to this end, I would ask my Lord Bromley to call for the reading of the confessions of the two secretaries of the accused.

Q. Mary. Are the statements of my late secretaries made under oath?

Brom. Under oath, madam. My lords and gentlemen, these men, though foreign, and with no interest save that they should make their own acts blameless, have made a full and free confession of the part taken in the wicked plots and plans of the late Anthony Babington, rebel, by their mistress. This, or these confessions, are made under solemn oath.

Q. Mary. My Lord, of what worth is this oath? When these, my late secretaries, did seek employment in my service, the usages of court and the requirements of circumstance did exact from them a solemn oath of secrecy in all matters pertaining to affairs of state, as well as mine own private correspondence. If they have, by threat, or even torture, been urged to violate their most solemn obligation to me, they are no longer worthy to be believed under any circumstances, for it is shown by your own statement, my Lord, that they regard not the binding force of an oath, and in all courts wherewith I am acquainted, a person who is known to violate his oath in one instance is held incompetent to give further testimony.

And further, my lords and gentlemen, I am told that your parliament has lately enacted a law, with the full approval of the queen, my cousin, that no person shall be condemned as conspiring against the person or life of a prince, except he be so condemned on the testimony of two good, competent witnesses; and the law plainly reads that the accused shall be brought face to face with the accusing witnesses.

If, my Lord, these my late loose secretaries, have accused me, their benefactor, why do you not, as by law directed, bring them into my presence, that I may question them, and thereby confound them ?

Atty.-Genl. It is not meet, my lords and gentlemen, that an accused of such known and unscrupulous dissimulation, and outrageous duplicity, and one who, through the debasing superstitions of her enslaving creed, has so worked upon her retainers, that they do her bidding without questioning or sense, should be allowed to interrogate her accusers, who may not have wholly overcome their blind infatuation, or weak enchantment. The spirit of the wise law, so flippantly referred to by the accused, would, undoubtedly, sanction broad discretion in its administration.

Q. Mary. When a sworn advocate of the laws not only sanctions, but urges, the open violation of statutes, the innocent may well despair of justice, and the accused unthink of mercy.

My lords and gentlemen, with me this unseemly and cruel farce should end. As you, apparently by a forefixed determination, have shaped your conclusions, you may continue without serious interruption to your deliberations, without my presence.

As a witness I am deprived of the opportunity of testifying. As mine own advocate, I may not speak without invoking slurring and insulting comments. By your heartless and unmercied decrees I am without friendly defense. Why should I for longer, by my participation in your wanton inflictions, intensify my sufferings ?

Brom. By command and direction of her majesty, the queen, we are instructed to conclude our deliberations of this most trying matter in counsel with herself.

Q. Mary. My lords and gentlemen, if you are to conclude this *faux epreuve* and render your already determined verdict in secret council, I may, without disturbing your deliberations, now retire. If you so easily halt at your own legal enactment, the forms of common law may be wholly disregarded, and you not only find your verdict, but pass your sentence without the presence of the accused.

But I have done. Appeals to the heart, petitions to legality, are alike useless.   Do with me as you will; but forget not this: God will hold you accountable for your judgment of me, and posterity render to my reputation that justice you so shamelessly withhold.

Brom. Does the defendant refuse to continue to answer to the charges?

Q. Mary. My Lord, I have answered the charges as read. As there are no witnesses present for me to meet and question, my further attendance would but afford you opportunity to inflict yet deeper and more painful hurts. In respect, therefore, to my rank and station, and that I may preserve my dignity, I would now decline to further lend myself to your proceedings. For, if I do continue my presence, I may seem to sanction this unnatural assuetude.

Brom. The necessity, my lords and gentlemen, for further continuance of the present hearing need not be pressed.   The churlish refusal of the accused to answer the lawful questions of the counsel for the crown, and her determination to retire before the full testimony is presented, leaves the commission only the alternative of proceeding without her, or adjourning for council deliberations, as directed by her majesty the queen.

Atty.-Gen. We may continue the hearing, my Lord, and by exhibition of lawful force compel the attendance of the accused.

Burgh. Not without unseemly and harsh means, and the use of such force as would provoke comment, and invite a question as to the legality of our proceedings.

Chief Jus. If undisputed testimony can convict, the accused is, of truth, condemned. But, were the testimony made of non-effect, the shame-faced confession of the wretched plotter would, indeed, adjudge her an ungeld.

Q. Mary. Reach no further, my Lord, for terms to wound; the heart your blows would crush may not feel an added pain. See! The woman within my poor nature shrinks at your merciless stabs, but the queen resents your foul slanders.

[*Queen Mary speaks aside with Lord Burghley and Hatton, then exit.*]

Brom. My lords and gentlemen, the retirement of the defendant should signal the closing of this assembly.   The further consideration of the matter may be left to the full council. Therefore, by authority in me invested by her most gracious majesty the queen, I do hereby declare and announce that this sitting is now closed. All who have been commanded to appear at this hearing will hold themselves to answer the summons of the proper officers of her majesty's court.

Master of Cer. O Yes! O Yes! By grace of God, Elizabeth, the high and mighty queen of England, Ireland and France, does by her rightfully appointed officer, hereby declare this assembly closed. Let all retire in order; and may God preserve her gracious majesty, and confound all enemies.

[Curtain.

SCENE III. *Audience room, Westminster Palace.*

Enter WALSINGHAM, BURGHLEY, LEICESTER *and* HATTON.

Hatton. My lords, if this matter must be urged, I pray you that you do sanction my silence. I dare perform any mission that hath in it the approval of my heart, but this which you would now press upon the queen her majesty hath not the full approve of my soul; therefore, my lords, I pray you to grant me my asking.

Lei. My lords and gentlemen, whatever of censure there be in this it will not rest upon us. Parliament has already voted measures urging this most righteous execution. They will at this hour so inform the queen her majesty.

Enter Keeper.

Keeper. Her gracious majesty the Queen! my lords and gentlemen, the Queen!

Enter QUEEN ELIZABETH.

Q. Eliz. My lords and gentlemen, I do attend for such communication as you have to make. I pray you be seated. If you have come to urge upon me the necessity of action that shall cut short the life of the Scot, I pray that you withhold further urging. Already am I broken in sleep and disturbed by day. Food hath lost its savor, and so sore is my heart with this most awful and dire distress that I have within me no ease.

Burgh. Most gracious Majesty, I did but yesterday receive from your honorable ambassador at the court of France, message which doth pertain to the very matter wherewith we would address you.

Q. Eliz. That I may not lack in my duty, I would listen to such as are prompted by sense of right. Read to me the letter of the ambassador.

Burgh. Such portions, your Majesty, of the honorable ambassador's letter as relates to the business in hand only need be read. [*Reads.*] " *Say to her majesty the queen that I am persuaded, both from the knowledge I have gained at this court and from such as reach me from the court of Spain, as well as from Rome, that for her majesty to longer delay the righteous execution of the condemned Scottish queen doth endanger her peace, and thereby the safety of her realm. Too long already hath she nursed this she-wolf. The bigotry of her religion, and the blindness of her followers, would sanction the darkest means, and urge the foulest ends to restore her to liberty, and to re-establish her vile religion. Say to her majesty the queen that not only her own realm, but the friends of liberty in foreign lands, look to her that she shall fearlessly perform her just duty.*"

Q. Eliz. My lords and gentlemen, this might have been more softly put. It hath in it a tone of curstness little less than unrespect. Have I grown so weak that I do need this loud proclaiming to teach me my duty? I will say to my honorable ambassador, that he hath good need to soften his manners and polish his expressions.

Lei. Your Majesty has missed the disturb among the people. The necessity of this righteous move is strongly felt by the commons, and by them the decollation hotly demanded.

Q. Eliz. Do my people demand of me this thing?

Lei. That they do, your Majesty, may be the more fully answered by their representatives. In outer room doth wait the committee from Parliament, who would inform your Majesty of their recent and most righteous act.

Q. Eliz. If these gentlemen be in attendance bid them enter.

Keeper. Gentlemen, enter by her Majesty's command.

Enter Committee of Parliament.

Q. Eliz. Gentlemen, I am informed that you would make a communication to me as expressing the will of Parliament.

Snow. [*Reads.*] " *Most gracious Majesty. By vote of Parliament in assembly convened, we are directed to communicate to your gracious Majesty the vote whereby the assembled body did pass, and do urge for your early action, first, their approval of the sentence as righteously found by your royal high commission against the person and forfeited life of Mary Stuart, heir of James of Scotland; and your Parliament would ask that you do issue your royal seal that the sentence already found be duly and speedily carried out upon the person of said Mary Stuart, who hath so well demerited it.*"

Q. Eliz. Gentlemen, as you have in writing expressed your desires, I can but request that you leave with me for consideration the expressions of your vote. Say to Parliament that I shall give this matter my most earnest and prayerful attention, and that only such delay shall precede my resolve as prudence and mercy shall dictate. Gentlemen, you may retire.

[*Exeunt Com.*

Lei. This answers, your Majesty, your query as to the demands of the commons. Not alone they, but those who hold the sacredness of your royal person as in danger, and who tremble for the peace and safety of your realm. How long, your Majesty, how long will the tenderness of your heart plead against your better judgment. The years agone bear full testimony to your mercy; and but the graciousness of your forbearance hath permitted this most grievous and hurtful wrong to disturb your own quiet, and threaten the stability of the whole realm.

Burgh. Your Majesty, not alone have you to think of the well-forfeited life of this treacherous Scot, but regard your own personal safety, and the welfare of your subjects.

Q. Eliz. My Lords, I pray you leave me, I would no longer have you goad me with this matter. I will confer further when I have more thought touching this most awful business.

You may retire. My Lord Leicester I would a word with you.

[*Exit Burghley, Walsingham and Hatton.*

My Lord, see to it that the doors are securely closed. I would speak with you upon this matter as we have before conferred, in trust and confidence.

Lei. Your Majesty, it doth pain my heart that stress of the times doth demand the settling of this foul and unhealthy matter. I would, your Majesty, that I might take from your heart this, the burden of your necessities. I have wept for you, and my own heart aches as only yours must have ached in this sad and most trying position. I know how much, your Majesty, you dread the shedding of human blood, and how you would gladly withhold your royal seal from the consent of this execution, if you but obeyed the promptings of your soul.

Q. Eliz. Oh my Lord! How much my heart aches none may know save God. Is there not some way to turn this blow aside? Cannot this decree be changed? May not the Scot be yet longer held in some secure castle, where, by faithful guards she may be prevented from working further harm?

Lei. It is not, your Majesty, so much a question of securely holding the rightfully condemned Scot, as it is to prevent the meddlesome interference of the over zealous and designing. We may, indeed, securely detain her, but while she doth remain alive, she is still a spark around which her hot and unscrupulous friends and co-religionists may fling their embers of dire attempts, and so fan and keep alive within your realm a spirit of discontent, that shall prevent the sway of peace and the approach of quiet. Mary dead is peace assured. Mary alive is the nursing of broils. Such sweet prosperity hath followed your gracious reign that you have gained the love of your subjects and the praise of sympathizing princes ——

Q. Eliz. O, that this deed were done, and that I might turn and by loud denouncing disclaim my sanction of the act.

Lei. So may you, your Majesty. Leave to me, I pray you, the righteous ending of this sorry affair. I will not only bring you quiet, but so silently despatch this business as to satisfy the people, and in so doing bring to you the full approval of all good subjects.

Q. Eliz. Let the secretary bring to me to-morrow the warrant, I will sign it, but it shall not have my seal for its execution. I would hold it until this softness doth congeal. I would that I might fall asleep, and on awakening find that the will of the people had been met.

Lei. No longer, I pray you, your Majesty, keep this sad pressure on your heart. The secretary shall attend, and when you have signed the warrant, it shall be held for your further pleasure.

Q. Eliz. Oh crown! Oh throne! Oh royal birth! so few the joys thou bringest, that he who hath the most of these hath most of pain and least of ease. God, thou King of kings, Thou Ruler of princes, search Thou my heart. Support me with Thy strength, O, God, that my fainting soul may not shrink from duty.   [*Exeunt.*

SCENE IV.   *Room in Earl of Leicester's House, London.*
Enter FELANGO.

Fel. [*Extinguishes light.*] Now is this my opportunity. Those papers are in this drawer; once in my possession, his churchy lordship must dance to my harping. [*Unlocks drawer, removes papers, conceals them.*] Fortune is kind; I have waited long for this, but it is all the better for waiting. These papers, like wine, have improved with age. I have safe now within my keeping the compact made between the good earl my master and the pious Bishop of Ross. These show how the good earl trapped the weak Duke of Norfolk to his death, and they also show that the good, loyal earl had his finger in other treasonable plots. With these for threats, I may well serve myself, and humble the proud earl a bit. With these I may smooth the way to an easy end.   [*Falls over chair.*

Enter BARNEY.

Barney. Sure! By me soul, I heard a din. If there be within this room one with less right than I, sure I'll work a stay in his hide. By the powers, there's a head behind the case! Holy mother! teach this dag its duty.

[*Barney fires; Felango falls.*

By me skill, but I've scored him, sure.

Enter LEICESTER.

Lei. Ho! what's this? Who fires?

13

Barney. I, me Lord; and by me firing proved me skill. Sure, I discovered the breaker as he was about your lordship's table, and from his move I knew he was thieving; so, with small ado, I clouted him.

Lei. Know you the man? Is he dead, or have you but winged him?

Barney. Who he is, my Lord, I know not, save he's as still— My God, me Lord, it is Signor Felango, and dead, me Lord, dead!

Lei. [*Aside.*] Thank heaven, now am I well delivered. Man, you have slain a fellow creature, you have spilled human blood; God shall require of you full answer for this foul deed.

Barney. If there be foulness, me Lord, in defending your property, then I am dirty, indade; and, if answer be axed of me, sure, I am ready to make it. Sure, this man hath, by his unholy thieving act, brought the judgment of God upon himself; and if he hath a sore head, it be his own fault, for honest men prowl not in the dark, where dags go off.

Enter Servants *with lights.*

Lei. There hath been a robbery here, and my man Barney hath, as was his good duty, defended my house, and in so doing the robber hath been shot. Go you, Wellson, and inform the proper officers that they may view the corse and take it away, and restore quiet to my house. Bear you the body into another room.   [*Exeunt Servants with Felango's body.*

Barney, remain in the house. Did the wicked devil open any of the cases, or drawers?

Barney. No, me Lord, they be securely locked.

Lei. You may retire now. See to it that you make little mouth of this affair, until you are questioned by the officers. Tell but one tale, and lay to that like the skin on your heel. Mind you, this man was trying to break open my coffers, and in the dark. I have heretofore missed property, now I know this man was the thief. I trow the officers will find some of my gilt on his person even now.   [*Exit Barney.*

How strange the ways of God, how divinely move his plans. To think that this villain should be thus removed, just as I had done with him, and he had so many of my sweet secrets that he was beginning to be dangerous. Ah, well! God prospers the deserving, and defeats the ends of wrong. With this man well out of the way, I may breathe easy.

Enter BARNEY.

Barney. Me Lord, a gentleman from me Lord Burghley be without, and would speak with you.

Lei. Admit him. Barney, see to it that you tell but one tale as to the killing, and cleave to that, my man, as you would escape pesterous entanglement with the officers of the law.

[*Exit Barney.*

Enter DAVISON.

Lei. What word friend Davison? Have you the seal?

Dav. Nay, my Lord, I may not bear it from the office, but, as was directed, I have affixed it.

Lei. You have, then, her majesty's sign? How wrote she, bold? or did the creeps make the sign tremble ?

Dav. I have lost much sleep in this business, my Lord, but not without some return. Her majesty's sign was without significance, being not properly made to the warrant. To make this good I have, by direction of my Lord Burghley, and under the eye of my Lord Walsingham, made so good a copy of her majesty's sign, that I have no fear that the gentlemen in charge will delay to act, when they have this warrant which is so duly signed and sealed.

Lei. Ah, signed and sealed. Now that we have moved thus far in this skittish business there must be no halting.

Dav. No halting, my Lord, and less delay. Will your lordship inspect the warrant?

Lei. This be a most cunning shift. Not only is it like her majesty's sign, but does her fist proud. Think you not, friend Davison, that you have over-tailed the " E " a bit? And have you not been a little free with the blot at the end ?

Dav. I did, my Lord, assay at this business nigh unto thirty attempts, some light, some heavy, and this which at last seemed worthy of the warrant, I did append as most like to that which should have more rightly graced it.

Lei. I make no lurch at the manner, and would, were the business other than it is, praise your skill. Howbeit, this affair be so fraught with danger of discovery, that I am near to losing my admiration for your good draft in the dread of expose.

Dav. Not you, my Lord, so much as I, have to fear the dangers of expose. By this sly forgery I do fix the hour for another's death, with no excuse, save I do the bidding of my betters. I have your promise, my Lord, that if this deal do miscarry, or bring displeasure from her majesty the queen, you will stand between me and royal anger.

Lei. One so easily shaken should not have undertaken so stiff a business. If you feel within you this sick weakness, even before the warrant hath left your hands, how think you, you will hold and control your slim belly when this good paper shall have worked the full measure wherefor it was drawn?

Dav. Think not, my Lord, I am weak. I do but use such expressions as flow from caution.

Lei. You, nor I, nor any whose hands are in this reach, may now turn and plead excuse, lest we clothe ourselves with shame. Her majesty will privately rejoice when this deed shall be well over. Publicly she will rave and damn a bit, but we who bow to her majesty in public, and coddle her in private, know full well that these queenly storms do lash but for a little; and so, with our knowledge of how sharp and stiff the brunt shall be, we may not shrink from our duties. Has my lord arranged for the forwarding of this goodly quit?

Dav. He has, my Lord. If the messenger miss not his way, and there be no interferences, the Earl of Kent will receive the warrant safe.

Lei. Go then, while this stiffness hold you to your part. See to it, as you value your head, that you make no word of this to living soul. Let not any indulgences loose your tongue, nor let confidence trap you into blabbing. Say to my Lord Burghley that I may not meet him to-night. A robbery has taken place in my house this hour, and my trusted agent has been detected and slain as the robber.

Dav. It shall be as you wish, my Lord. I have my own hand too fast in this matter to now turn back. I will deliver your message to my Lord Burghley. I heard of the sad killing of your agent, and do regret it, as he was a most valuable man to you.

Lei. Accept my thanks for your kind sympathy. Make no further allusions to the distressing affair. I wish you God's speed in the safe delivery of this important paper.

[Exit Davison.

So shall end at last this checkered life. She did but have faint gleams of grandeur; even these did quit her company ere she had basked in the light o'er much. Vain, O vain, was all thy pride, O queen. Ere the sun shall make another day's march, thou, O crushed beauty, shall be suing at heaven's gates for forgiveness. Ah! this waiting hath been long, but the sweet satisfaction shall be sweeter for all this long delay.

To-morrow shall see England's enemy, and my proud disdainer meet a quick and sure despatch. My prayers have not been in vain, and what my prayers have lacked, my wit has supplied. The hour of my revenge shall date when Mary died.

[Exit.

SCENE V. *Queen Elizabeth's audience chamber, Westminster Palace.*

Enter BURGHLEY, SMITH *and* HATTON, *and others of the privy council.*

Burgh. Gentlemen, this, indeed, is a most grievous affair. This Italian has been long in the employ of the Earl of Leicester, and possessed far too much knowledge for the earl's good comfort. I do not accuse that the earl was privy to his murder, but this I do know, that violent deaths have so frequently occurred in the household of the Earl of Leicester, that it be but prudent now to make deep inquiry touching this affair. The papers that we found on the body of the Italian, and which he had secured, evidently from the earl's safe keeping, and to possess which he was prowling in the library in the dark when killed, are such as my Lord Leicester would not freely expose to all eyes.

Hatton. These papers, my Lord, relate to agreements and transactions made during the lifetime of the late Duke of Norfolk; may not the earl have good excuse for a thing so long past?

Burgh. What matter; these papers clearly show the designs and attempts of the Earl of Leicester. If circumstances did prevent the maturing of his plans, it was the good fortune of the realm, and not the loyalty of the earl that let this thing pass from us.

Smith. Is it your purpose, my Lord, to acquaint her majesty the queen with the drift of this affair?

Burgh. By oath, we are compelled to lay this matter before her majesty. If the Earl of Leicester hath a good and proper excuse, it were but lawful that he should make his explanations to the queen her majesty. If these letters and despatches be read aright, the person implicated by the contents is guilty in the eyes of the law of treason. That they do relate to past acts doth not change the case a whit.

Enter LEICESTER.

Lei. My lords and gentlemen, sweet morning to you all. The absence of clouds from your faces, and the light of heaven within your eyes, bear good witness that the peace of God hath attended you in your slumbers. As for me, if I do bring gloom in my face and sadness in my voice, I can but crave your forbearance, and offer as excuse, my lords and gentlemen, my sore affliction, and the dire calamity that overtook my agent last night. Did not the consolation of heaven attend me, I might well excuse myself from your assembly.

Burgh. It were grace, my Lord, to hold in check your excuses; if you are not well supplied, the poverty of your explanations may confound you.

Lei. How so, my Lord, what mean you?

Burgh. Turn your impatience, my Lord, to forbearance, and save your inquiries, that you may forge them into good answers. Though ready of speech and soft of word, you may find that all your long schooling and successful ambling will stand you in good need.

Lei. You do accuse, my Lord, accuse! I demand ——

Burgh. I trust, my Lord, that all demands shall be met.

Enter Page.

Page. Her Majesty the Queen! my lords and gentlemen, the Queen!

Enter ELIZABETH.

Lei. [*To Burghley.*] My Lord, no more of this matter before her majesty. I will further with you at a more opportune hour.

Burgh. I have my duty to perform, my Lord, and from it I may not be thrown aside.

Q. Eliz. My lords and gentlemen, I await the presenting of such matter as may be properly considered. If there be such as require action, let us despatch it at once, for I would not make this sitting over long.

Burgh. Your Majesty, as in duty bound, I would acquaint you with a recent discovery. It is not unknown to your Majesty that last night the agent of the Earl of Leicester was slain ——

Q. Eliz. This be not a matter for council, my Lord; the proper officers may, as directed by law, attend to this unfortunate affair.

Burgh. To the killing, your Majesty, yes; but this act did uncover a most strange and darksome exhibit.

Q. Eliz. How so, my Lord, how so?

[*Leicester turns to leave the room.*

Burgh. Your Majesty, stay my lord the Earl of Leicester; this matter doth concern him.

Q. Eliz. The Earl of Leicester may not retire.

Lei. Your Majesty, it be necessary that ——

Q. Eliz. My Lord Burghley had not finished. It were more orderly that we do hear what communication he would make.

Burgh. The officers, your Majesty, who took possession of the body of the late agent of my lord the Earl of Leicester, upon making search, as was proper, found concealed these papers. As was right, by virtue of my office, I did make careful reading of them, and, to my sorrowful amazement, discovered that they are the private papers of my lord the Earl of Leicester; and that they do show that the Earl of Leicester, the late Duke of Norfolk, the Bishop of Ross, with sundry other persons known to be confidential advisers of the Scottish queen, had entered into a solemn compact, not only to further the marriage of the Scottish queen to the Duke of Norfolk, but also to secure the liberation and restoration of the justly confined Scot. Nor is this all, your Majesty, for here are letters, despatches and messages from the King of France, Philip of Spain, and even the papal court.

Lei. Your Majesty, these papers, that my Lord Burghley doth so loudly proclaim, are indeed my private papers, and as such are not fit subjects for council discussion.

Q. Eliz. If true, they are indeed, alas, not only fit but unfit for council discussion.

Lei. Your Majesty, by your gracious leave, what appears so monstrous may, when reviewed in calmness, prove the stale results, and records of loyal attempts, in years agone, to serve faithfully your Majesty's best interests. The letters and despatches from foreign courts are such as my agent, now dead, had secured surreptitiously from the Duke of Norfolk. I did but retain them as matters of reference, and they only came into the possession of my agent through my having carelessly left them within easy reach after I had used them during the trial of the Queen of Scots.

Burgh. Granting, my Lord, that this excuse be true, and I pray God that it is, there still remains this dark and treasonable compact to which your signature is boldly affixed, in most glaring and imprudent array, with known and condemned enemies of her majesty the queen.

Q. Eliz. Oh, my Lord, turn this from me; already is my burden greater than I can bear. Make to me some answer that shall draw this cruel iron from out my soul. Thou art fickle, but O God! O God! make not to me the fearful accusation that the trusted Earl of Leicester is dishonest of heart, and proditorious to his country.

Lei. Most gracious Majesty, you yourself, by your own fair hand, did sign and warrant to me *carte blanche* in the matter touching the detect of the late Duke of Norfolk. That I might the better encompass him, and fathom his treasonable acts, I did assume an interest that I might better thus gain his confidence. And to make the seeming yet more blind I did enter into an implied compact, of which the paper held by my Lord •Burghley is a copy thereof. This I may not only fully explain, but, your Majesty, abundantly prove, if happily I may stay judgment and restrain envy.

Q. Eliz.   God grant me strength that I may take up this new burden.

Burgh.   That be not all, your Majesty.

Enter Keeper.

Keeper.   Your Majesty, my Lord Walsingham tarries without, and would a word with you.

Q. Eliz.   Admit him.

Enter WALSINGHAM.

Wal.   Most gracious Queen, I salute you as one who brings most welcome tidings.   The shifting scenes of life's earnest dream have brought at last your quiet.

Q. Eliz.   Quiet, my Lord; so long, alas, have I been a stranger to the fullness of this sweet word, that I have need to ask your Lordship that you shall make a better explanation of your meaning.

Wal.   By grace of God, who in his mercy and sweet providence hath vouchsafed your Majesty's eternal peace and welfare, I break to your Majesty the full knowledge that the burden of your distress hath been removed.

Q. Eliz.   Removed?   My Lord, what mean you?

Wal.   Peace, your Majesty, peace.   Thine enemy, Mary, Queen of Scotland, is dead.   Executed this morning. as was just.

Q. Eliz.   Dead! no! no! my Lord, no! not dead! Make to me no lies.   Take back these awful words — not dead!   Mary dead? My God, my God!   Who hath done this cruel deed?   Who hath wrongfully sealed the warrant?   My Lord [*to Leicester*], this be a devilish trick of yours.   By your glib, oily words you did blind me to sign, and then, with low fubbery and damned mockery, you did make to me a promise that it should be withheld.   Liar! Villain!   Murderer!   Get you hence, accursed of men.   You have put upon my soul this blighting blotch of blood.   Go! your face sickens my very soul.   Go! and on your knees pray God's forgiveness — mine shall eternally be withheld.   Murderer!   Liar! My God!   Mary dead! dead! and by my warrant.   Farewell peace, farewell!   No more shall quiet rest within my soul.   Fare-

well innocence; farewell joys of earth. I am now undone. Out,
murderers; out all of you; remind me no longer of my companionship in your foul crime. Out! Out! and let me not watch
your going, for your very footsteps have in them the marks of
blood. [*Exeunt Burghley, Smith, Walsingham, Hatton and
Leicester.*] [*Enter* LADY KNOLLYS.] Leave me! leave me! At
this hour let me intercede with God alone. I would have no
human eyes witness this my weakness. Leave me alone; leave
me. [*Exit Lady Knollys.*] Oh! my God! dead! Mary dead!
My own blood spilled upon the block. Dead! Awake, asleep,
her poor body shall stalk before me — her bleeding, torn body.
O, I cannot shut out this foul murder! God blind my soul, dull
my eyes. Oh, God! Have I consented to this murder? Ha, ha.
See, all is red, red blood! Everything is blood. O, tear away
these draperies; they have blood on them; my clothes, my robes,
even my hands are drenched in blood. God! shall I live through
this? Life, O, what will life be when all sense of peace and innocence be gone? Farewell, farewell, joys of earth. I am a
queen, but my heart is dead. O, Jesu, pray for me! O, Holy
Mother, pray for me!

Enter LEICESTER.

Lei. Your Majesty, may I not offer ——

Q. Eliz. No! no! back! Let me not see your awful face; you
do make all about me blood. Offer me nothing but your absence.
You are all murderers, damned, cruel murderers. Out, I say,
out. Let not your accursed face add to my misery. Out, dog!
out! My God! I, too, am a murderer. [*Exit Leicester.*] Why,
there is blood here — there — why, it is blood running down
everywhere. My hands, my face, these tears are bloody. I walk
in blood. My God! My God! I am accursed of thee.   [*Falls.*

END.

GLOSSARY.

S., SCOTCH ; O. E., OLD ENGLISH.

Atuck, O. E., tucked in bed.
Acknown, S., acknowledged.
Albins, S., perhaps.
Amaist, S., almost.
Awsome, S., frightful, terrible.
Ae', S., one.
An', S., and.
Aboon, S., above.

Becomes, O. E., fine clothes.
Bashy, O. E., fat, swollen.
Ban, S., bone.
Bishops, O. E., bustles.
Bat-fowling, O. E., catching birds at night ; any sly, after-dark work.
Breed-bate, O. E., breeder of quarrels.
Beit, S., to help.
Barns, S., babes.
Brands, S., legs.
Busk, S., dress or gown.
Brats, S., rags.
Blether, S., foolish talk.
Blaw, S., blow.
Bars, S. and O. E., lacings worn by ladies in the front of the dress.
Billy, S., brother.
Braw, S , fine in dress.
Bauld, S., bold.
Baith, S., both.
Blin, S., never.
Buff, S., nonsense.
Bush, O. E., an inn or ale-house.
Bedswerver, O. E., an adultress.
Balder, O. E., coarse, rough words.

Clinty, S., hard, difficult.
Chat-tow, S., chat, gallows; tow, rope, gallows-rope.
Cob, O. E., a rich person.
Culzie, S., to quiz, to pump.
Clurs, S., swelling from a blow.
Canty, S., cheerful and merry.

'Currents, O. E., occurrents.
Claver, S., to talk silly.
Cosie, S., warm, sheltered place.
Ca', S., call.
Chucky, S., a hen.
Clepe, O. E., to call or name.

Dag, O. E., a pistol.
Dight, S., to clean or cleanse.
Dirle, S., a smarting pain.
Dree, S., suffer, to suffer.
Dunt, S., a stroke or blow.

Ear, O. E., to dig up or plow.
Explate, S., explantion.
Eard, S , the earth.

Farthingale, O. E., a hooped skirt or petticoat.
Flirt-gill, O. E., a wanton, loose girl, a common.
Falsing, O. E., deceptive.
Fail, S., many, great number.
Fause, false.
Fosy, S., soft,
Forleet, S. forget.
Forbears, O. E., forefathers.
Fother, S., fodder, food.
Forleeting, S., forgetting.
Forfairn, S., abused, bespattered.
Fou', S., full.
Flewitt, S., a hard blow with the hand.
Frae, S., from.
Fawn, S., fallen.

Geed, S., went.
Gesse, S., guess, to guess.
Gambit, O. E., opening, beginning.
Gan, S., gone.
Groff, S., course.
'Gree, S., agree.

Gin, S., if.
Gilt, O. E., gold.
Gurly, S., rough, cold (weather).
Gowling, S., howling, crying.
Greet, S., weep.
Gar, S., to make, to force, to cause.
Gossie, S., gossip.
Guid, S., good.

Hempy, S., a rogue born to be hung.
Havins, S., breeding, good bringing up.
Het, S., hot.
He'ven, S., heaven.
Hooly, S., slow.
Ho's, S., single stocking.
Harns, S., brains.
Haly, S., holy.
Haviour, O. E., behavior.
Haffet, S., cheek, side of the face.
Hae, S., have.
Hald, S., hold.
Hack, S. and O. E., common.

In, O. E., thieves' slang; to get a person *in* another's power.
Ingliss, S., English.
Impeach, O. E., hinder, to stop.

Jo, S., sweet-heart.

Knacky, S., witty, funny.
Knoost, S., a large lump from a blow.
Keek, S., to peep, to pry into.

Laits, S., manners.
Lane, S., alone.
Lugs, S., ears.
Link-men, O. E., men with lights.
Laithful', S., loathful.
Leal, S., true, faithful.
Low, S., law.
Lud, S., lad.
Looe, S., love.
Lure, S., rather.
Lown, S., calm, to keep calm.
Lounder, S., a smart stroke with the fist.
Liggs, S., lies, falsehoods.

Mowsing, S., jesting, joking.
Mou', S., mouth.
Mools, S., earth over a grave, a grave.
Mends, S., satisfaction, revenge.

Nist, S., next.
Nevel, S., a sound blow with the fist.
Nive, S., the fist.
Nae', S., not.
Norsed, S., nursed.

Naught, O. E., bad, naughty.

Out, O. E., thieves' slang; to put a person *out* of the way, to kill.
Orp, S., to weep with sobs.
Owk, S., a week.

Pu'ed, S., pulled.
Prets, S., tricks.
Pit, S., put.
Parish-lantern, O. E., popular name for the moon.
Puggy, O. E., nasty, thick, big-headed.

Rap, O. E., to trade, to exchange.
Rackless, S., reckless.
Rift, S., to belch, the breath.
Raught, S., sought.
Runyon, O. E., a term of contempt applied to a strong masculine woman.
Ri't, S., right.

Stroot, S., stuffed full, drunk.
Scuds, S., small ale.
Seid, S., cunning, foxy.
Sair, S., sore.
Slabber, O. E., to drivel, to slobber.
Steek, S., to shut tight, to close, to stop.
Slidery, S., slippery.
Swatch, S., a mark, a scratch.
Stang, S., a smart pain soon over.
Sae, S., so.
Sib, S., a kin, a relative.
Sunkets, S., something.
Speer, S., to ask, to beg.
Swelt, S., to choke.
Sin, S., sun.
Spelder, S., to stretch, to spread out.
Sta', S., a stall or booth.
Sta'k, S., stock.
Speel, S., to climb.
Spanging, S., to jump, leaping.
Sain'd, S., sainted.
Sell, S., self.
Sic, S., such.
Sma', S., small.
Skyt, S., to move quickly.
Sturtsome, S., trouble, disturbance.
Spae, S., to guess, to foretell.
Steut, S., to stretch, to strain.

Taz, S., scourge, hard task.
Tensome, S., by tens.
Taikens, S., tokens.
Toom, S., empty.
Twa, S., two.
Thrane, S., throne.
Taps, S., heads.
Thig, S., beg.

Tauld, S., told.
Tooly, S., to fight, a fight.
Thir, S., these.
Tarre, O. E., to urge, to set on.
Taller, O. E., braver, better.

Unco, S., strange.
Ungeared, O. E., undressed.

Wyte, S., blame.
Weers, S., to oppose, to stop.
Whilk, S., which.
Wha, S., who.
Wow, O. E., wonderful, strange
War, S., worse.

Wad, S., would.
Wud, S., mad.
Wi', S., with.
Weel, S., well.
Wangrace, S., wickedness.
Wat, S., wisdom.
Woody, S., gallows.
Wyson, S., throat.

Yeding, S., contending, quarreling.
Yellowness, O. E., jealousy.
Youdith, S., youthfulness.
Ye, S., you, or your.
Yuke, S., the itch.

www.ingramcontent.com/pod-product-compliance
Lightning Source LLC
Chambersburg PA
CBHW032008060726
47497CB00017B/2387